Had she finally found someone who could tell her who she was—*what* she was?

Mark Allars lived a block away from the retirement home in a single fronted Victorian-style house that was probably worth a fortune, despite its rundown appearance. She studied the building as she climbed out of the car. The small front yard was filled with gate high weeds, and the window to the right of the door was boarded up with wood. It looked abandoned—until you looked up and saw the state-of-the-art satellite dishes sitting on the roof.

The gate creaked when Gabriel opened it. She limped through and knocked on the door.

"Who the hell is it?" a rough voice demanded.

She raised her eyebrows and glanced at Gabriel.

"He's your average, cranky old recluse," he said, then raised his voice slightly. "It's Gabriel Stern. Charles's son."

Footsteps shuffled towards the door. Seconds later it was flung open. An old man stood before them, wearing blue pajama bottoms and a battered, smoke-stained sweatshirt. His feet were bare, toenails yellow and a good inch longer than his toes.

He leaned forward, peering at Gabriel with red ringed, weepy eyes. "So it is. Fancy that."

His gaze turned to her and recognition flicked through the rheumy eyes. He stiffened, his knuckles white as he clenched the door.

"You," he breathed softly. "You're dead. They said you were dead."

S0-AQM-497

With thanks to the LuLus—
great writers, great friends.

Other Books
by Keri Arthur

Nikki & Michael Series
Dancing with the Devil
Hearts in Darkness
Chasing the Shadows
Kiss the Night Good-bye

Damask Circle Series
Circle of Fire
Circle of Death
Circle of Desire

Werewolf Series
Beneath a Rising Moon
Beneath a Darkening Moon
(Coming in 2005)

Urban Fantasy Series
Memory Zero (Book One)
Penumbra (Book Three)
(Coming in 2005)

Generation 18

***

Keri Arthur

The sale of this book without its cover is unauthorized. If you purchased this book without a cover, you should be aware that it was reported to the publisher as "unsold and destroyed." Neither the author nor the publisher has received payment for the sale of this "stripped book."

Generation 18
Published by ImaJinn Books, a division of ImaJinn

Copyright ©2004 by Keri Arthur
Printed and bound in the United States of America. All rights reserved. No part of this book may be reproduced in any form or by any means (electronic, mechanical, photocopying, recording, or otherwise) without prior written permission of both the copyright holder and the above publisher of this book, except by a reviewer, who may quote brief passages in a review. For information, address: ImaJinn Books, a division of ImaJinn, P.O. Box 545, Canon City, CO 81215-0545; or call toll free 1-877-625-3592.

ISBN: 1-893896-49-8

10 9 8 7 6 5 4 3 2 1

PUBLISHER'S NOTE:
This book is a work of fiction. Names, characters, places and incidents are products of the author's imagination or are used fictitiously. Any resemblance to actual events or locales or persons, living or dead, is entirely coincidental.

Books are available at quantity discounts when used to promote products or services. For information please write to: Marketing Division, ImaJinn Books, P.O. Box 545, Canon City, CO 81215-0545, or call toll free 1-877-625-3592.

Cover design by Patricia Lazarus

ImaJinn Books, a division of ImaJinn
P.O. Box 545, Canon City, CO 81215-0545
Toll Free: 1-877-625-3592
http://www.imajinnbooks.com

One

Being a spook wasn't what Samantha Ryan had expected. Long nights, sleepless days, yes. She'd faced that, and worse, during her ten years as a State Police Officer. In that time, the agents of the Special Investigations Unit had breezed in and out of situations, always on edge, always on the move. Always looking like they loved what they were doing. So the sheer and utter boredom that filled ninety percent of a spook's job had come as something of a shock.

She sighed and shifted slightly, trying to find a comfortable position on the icy metal step. Watch the back door, Gabriel had said. Make sure the vamps don't hit the blood bank from the alley. This, despite the fact that in the five previous robberies, the vampires had always gone in through the front door.

Why the hell would they change a successful routine now?

They wouldn't. He knew that. She knew that.

She rubbed her eyes wearily. She could hardly argue, though, as he was her senior and in charge of the investigation. And with intel stating that this blood bank would be the next one hit, she couldn't argue with orders that were little more than covering all the bases.

What the intel wasn't saying was whether it was actually vampires doing these robberies. Hell, with recent estimates saying that at least thirty percent of newly-turned vampires were unable to control their blood desire, *human* blood had become a hot commodity on the streets. Combine that with the recent spate of deaths through infected blood products in all the major hospitals—leading to the situation where private blood banks were inundated with people wanting to stockpile their own blood—and you had the perfect opportunity for those wanting to make a quick buck on the streets.

So here she sat, in the cold night, on a cold step, waiting for robbers who weren't likely to come by the back entrance, while her goddamn partner watched the front door from the warmth of the car.

Bitter? Her? *Oh yeah.*

He was certainly making good on his statement that he would never work with a partner. Whenever possible, he left her in her box of an office doing paperwork, or he sent her on inane errands. This was her first "real" duty in the three months since her transfer, and she suspected she was here only because Byrne had given him a direct order to take her.

The wind picked up, running chill fingers through her hair. She shivered and flicked up the collar on her coat. Overhead, the starlit sky was beginning to cloud over. The rain they'd been predicting for days was finally on the way. She could smell the moisture in the breeze. Could feel the tingle of electricity running through the night air, charging her body with an odd sense of power.

Why she could feel these things was another point of concern, though it was one she kept to herself. There were only two people she trusted enough to sit down and talk to, anyway. Finley was still on leave, recovering from the injuries he'd received in the bomb blast three months ago, and her goddamn partner was harder to nail down than a snowflake in a storm.

And it wasn't just on a professional level that he was keeping his distance, but a personal one, as well. Given how well they'd gotten on during their investigations of her former partner's disappearance, she'd thought that they could at least be friends. Obviously, she'd been very wrong.

God, how bad was it when he wouldn't even go for a cup of coffee with her?

"Sam, you there?"

His warm voice whispered into her ear, so close she could almost feel the caress of his breath across her cheek. Except that he was tucked nice and warm in the car half a block away.

She was tempted, very tempted, to ignore him. But she'd spent ten long years as a cop doing the right thing, following all the rules—like keeping in constant contact when on watch duty. Even when her partner was being a bastard and deserved to suffer, it was a habit hard to break.

"What?" Her tone left no doubt of her mood. He'd left her sitting here so long her butt was almost frozen to the step. If he expected civility, he needed a brain transplant.

"Just checking you're still awake."

Yeah, right. Like *she* was the one sitting in the nice warm car. "The cold's doing a fine job of that, thank you very much."

He paused. "Do you want to swap for a while?"

She raised her eyebrows. Just for an instant, the compassion in his voice reminded her of the man she'd known before she'd become his partner. "You got coffee on board?"

"Freshly brewed."

And he hadn't offered her any until now. It was lucky he'd only equipped the two of them with stun rifles, because she was tempted, very tempted, to march right over there and shoot him. "Sure you can spare a cup?" she said tightly. "I mean, you older types need some sort of stimulant to keep you awake at this hour of the night, don't you?"

"Do I take that as a yes or a no?" His warm tones held an undertone of annoyance.

But she was way past caring at this particular moment. "That depends."

"On what?"

"On whether you intend to freeze me out, figuratively or literally."

He made no immediate reply. She waited, wondering what he'd do now that she'd finally called him out. Down the Main Street end of the alley, she heard a soft thump, as if someone had jumped off a rooftop. A dog yelped somewhere to the left of that thump, a short sharp sound that spoke of fear. She frowned and stared into the darkness. The electricity filling the night stirred, running over her skin, standing the small hairs at the back of her neck on end. Heat followed quickly. Then her senses exploded outwards, and she was tasting the secrets of the night.

A kite creature walked towards her.

"Sam—"

She jumped and quickly pressed the earphone, cutting him off. He'd once told her the kites hunted by sound and movement. She wasn't about to chance the creature hearing his voice, no matter how unlikely that might be.

The kite came into view. It almost looked like a large white sheet, except that it had feet and talon-like hands. The creature hesitated as it neared the steps, sniffing the night like a dog. It turned milky white eyes in her direction. She controlled the urge to reach for the stun rifle and remained still.

After a moment, it lumbered past, moving to the other end of the alley. Avoiding the yellow wash of the street light, it slunk round the corner and disappeared. She rose and picked up her rifle before switching the earpiece back on.

"A kite just made an appearance in the alley. I'm about to follow."

"Negative. You're not equipped—"

She snorted softly. "Neither are you, partner. You continue

to keep watch on the blood bank, and I'll see what the creature is up to."

"Stun guns won't—"

"Gabriel, remember imperative one?" The SIU had only become aware of the Kites two months ago, but since then, the creatures had reached the top of the SIU's extermination list. With an edge in her voice that imitated his own, she continued, "Find and stop all kites, regardless of the cost."

"That doesn't mean you have to do a suicide run after them when you're not properly equipped to deal with them."

"Please credit me with a little bit of brain power. I'm merely going to see what the thing is up to. Besides, they just may be using the creature to pull us away from the blood bank."

"I don't particularly care about the damn blood bank."

Meaning he cared more about her? Given his recent behavior, she found it a little hard to believe. She stopped at the end of the alley and carefully peered around the corner. The kite lumbered across the road.

"But Byrne does. If the vamps follow the pattern, this one *will* be hit sometime tonight."

The kite disappeared round the corner of the opposite street. She ran across the road and then edged forward, keeping to the shadows of the three-story apartment building.

"I'm calling for backup," he said, voice terse.

"Fine." It only made sense to do so. "I'll keep in contact."

"You'd better," he growled.

She grinned. She might well pay for it later, but damn, it felt good to annoy him.

She reached the corner. The kite was nowhere to be seen. Wondering how the creature could have moved so fast, she frowned and glanced up—and found it. The loose skin around its arms flapped lightly as it climbed crab-like up the wall.

The wind tugged at her hair, throwing it across her eyes. She brushed it back and listened to the sounds beneath the soft cry of the wind. Two men were talking, their voices harsh and grating. A radio near the top of the building played classics. Between the two, the squeak of a bed and a whispered good night. Sounds she wouldn't normally have heard except for the odd sense of power flowing through the night and into her soul.

The creature seemed to be headed for the apartment in which the radio played. She watched it as long as she dared. When it stopped and pressed a taloned hand against a window, she turned and ran for the apartment building's front door.

"Gabriel, the kite's about to break into a top floor apartment on the corner of Gibb and Macelan Streets."

"Help's on the way. Stay where you are."

The words had barely whispered into her ear when she heard the sound of glass shattering. A heartbeat later the screaming began. Sickening visions swam through her mind—bloodied images of the street bum she'd found three months ago, his body a mass of raw and weeping muscle stripped of skin.

She swallowed heavily and pounded up the stairs. "Negative. It's attacking. I'm in pursuit."

"Damn it, you're not equipped to deal—"

"Just get backup here quickly." She pressed the earphone, cutting him off again. She didn't need to hear what she could and couldn't do. Not when a man's life was at stake.

Two flights...three. She leapt over the banister and up the remaining stairs. People milled in their doorways, their eyes wide and fearful. Not one of them appeared willing to investigate what was happening to their neighbor. City living, she thought, sucked. But then, would neighbors in suburban areas be any more willing to risk investigating screams as fierce as the ones currently shattering the silence? She suspected not.

She slithered to a stop outside the apartment door and glanced back at the pajama-clad crowd. "SIU, folks. Go back inside and lock your doors."

The crowd melted away. With her laser held at the ready, she stepped back and kicked the door. Wood shuddered, splintering. She booted it a second time. The door flung open, crashing back on its hinges.

The kite was in the middle of the living room, its sheetlike form covering all but the stranger's slippers. His screams suddenly choked off, and all she heard was an odd sucking sort of noise. Blood seeped past the flaccid, winglike sections of the creature's arms, forming pools that seemed to glisten black in the darkness.

She raised the stun laser and fired at the creature. The blue-white light bit through the darkness, flaring against the kite's leather-like skin. If it had any effect, she certainly couldn't see it.

She switched her aim to the creature's odd shaped head and fired again. The kite snarled and looked up. It had no mouth, she saw suddenly. Or rather, its whole body was a mouth. It was sucking the stranger's flesh and blood in through pores on its skin.

She shuddered and fired again, this time at its eyes. The creature snarled a second time, the sound high pitched, almost bat-like. It shook its head and jerked upright. Bloodied strips of half consumed flesh slid down its body and puddled at its feet. Her stomach churned, but she held her ground and kept on firing the stun gun at the creature's eyes. It obviously wasn't stunning it, but it *was* doing something, because the kite's movements were becoming increasingly agitated.

It screamed again, then turned and stumbled for the window. She edged into the apartment. The kite smacked into the wall, then flung out an arm, feeling for the window frame. It was almost as if it had lost all sonar capabilities. Maybe there was something in the blue-white beam that addled its keen senses.

It grasped the window frame, felt for the other side to position itself, and then dived through the shattered glass. She ran over to the window and leaned out. The kite was floating back to the street, its arms out wide, loose skin stretched taut to catch the light breeze. She pressed the earphone again.

"Gabriel, the kite is now in Macelan Street, heading west."

"Do not go after it. I repeat, do not go after it. Stay in the apartment."

Her smile was grim. If the tone of his voice was anything to go by, he was madder than hell. He had a right to be, she supposed, but what else could she have done? Let the kite devour the stranger?

Not that her intervention had saved him. She turned away from the window and dug out her viaphone, the latest in gadgets from the SIU labs. It was similar to the wristcom the State Police used, only it had a cell phone and camera attached as well. And all in one palm-sized package. She hit the record button and panned the camera from the doorway she'd kicked open to the window and then down to the body.

"The kite smashed through the living room window and attacked victim at 3.15 a.m. SIU Officer Ryan intervened and drove kite back through window." She hesitated, walking across to squat beside the body. "Victim is male, probably mid-sixties."

She panned the camera down the length of his body and captured the bloody detail of the murder. What remained of his flesh hung in strips, almost indistinguishable from the remnants of his red and white striped pajamas. His eyes were wide, mouth locked into a scream—a look of astonished horror that was now permanently etched into his features.

Why this man? Why not the two men talking in the flat below? Or the woman who'd only just joined her partner in bed? She glanced up and studied the room.

The kite had come straight to this apartment—had obviously wanted this man, and no other. What they had to find out now was why.

She rose and walked across to the shelving unit. After sitting the camera on the shelf, she dug a set of gloves out of her pocket and put them on. Then she turned off the radio, picked up the camera and panned it across the photos lining the shelf.

Each photo contained the same four men, either fishing, drinking, or standing around a barbecue. All of them looked to be at least fifty or sixty. She glanced at the body. The only hair the victim had was scraggly wisps of white near either ear. He wasn't in any of these photos, then. Maybe he'd been taking them.

She picked up one framed photograph and then turned at the sound of footsteps. Gabriel entered, his gaze sweeping the room until he found her.

"I could put you on report for your behavior here tonight," he said, stopping just inside the doorway.

Though his face was impassive, his hazel eyes were stormy with anger and, surprisingly, a touch of fear. She fingered the viaphone's off button, then shrugged and left it on record. Procedures stated any and all activity at a crime scene had to be recorded. If that had to include her being told off, then so be it.

"Do it. Maybe then you'll get your wish and be rid of me." She hesitated. What was the point of arguing about it here? There were far more important matters to be worried about—like why the kite attacked this man. "Do you know who our victim is?"

For an instant, it looked as if he might say something more. Then he shoved his hands in his pockets and walked across to the body. "Male, in his mid-sixties, obviously." He glanced around the apartment. "And fairly well off. Those paintings are by Kyle Parker."

She glanced across to the stylized landscapes. To her admittedly untrained eye, a three-year-old could have done a better job. And yet Parker's paintings sold for millions.

"If he could afford those, you'd have thought he'd have installed better security."

"Security doesn't usually stop the kites."

"No, only decapitation or the sun can do that." She frowned down at the body. According to the SIU labs, the kites were some sort of offshoot from the vampire family tree. The SIU researchers were desperate to get their hands on a live specimen to do some tests, but as yet, no one had figured out a way to capture one and stay alive. "This wasn't a random attack. The kite came straight to this apartment."

"Maybe the victim was the only one moving around."

She shook her head. "There was movement in several apartments. The creature ignored them all and came straight here."

He frowned. "There's been no evidence that the kites can be programmed to kill certain individuals."

"But there's been no evidence that they can't, either."

"True." He studied her for a moment, hazel eyes intense. "How did you drive the creature away? Stun rifles don't work on kites."

"No, but they definitely don't like it when you fire at their head. It seemed to lose its sense of place."

He raised his eyebrows in surprise, but any comment he was about to make was cut off as a viaphone beeped. His, not hers.

He reached into his pocket and dragged it out. "Stern," he said, a hint of impatience in his voice.

Given the tightening of his already annoyed expression, the news obviously wasn't good.

"What?" she said, the minute he'd hung up.

"Looks like our serial killer has struck again. Byrne wants me to investigate."

Me, not we, she noted, and wondered if, in fact, Stephan had said that, or if Gabriel was locking her out again. "Where this time?"

"Elwood."

She raised her eyebrows. If it was the same killer, then he was certainly showing no preference for a particular area. So far, he'd killed in Toorak, Broadmeadows, and now Elwood. And it was more than just miles that separated the three suburbs—each one held a different step on the social ladder.

"What about the blood bank watch?"

"Briggs and Francis have taken over."

Lucky them. Though she'd seen the two working together

before, and she had no doubt that Briggs would be considerate enough to offer her partner a hot coffee long before his butt froze to the step. "So let's go investigate."

His gaze narrowed, as if he'd sensed the hint of sarcasm underlying her words. "You disobeyed orders and came after the kite. Now you're stuck with the case, I'm afraid."

And if the kite hadn't attacked, he would have found some other reason to keep her away from the murder investigation. Had it been anyone else, she would have sworn it stemmed from distrust—both of her and her ability to cope with the job. With Gabriel, it was something deeper. And if it *was* distrust, then it was more distrust of himself.

Not that *that* thought made any sense at all.

"Well, at least its better than filling in endless rounds of paperwork."

His brief smile held a grim edge. "You've been with the SIU for just on three months. You've yet to go through full training. Do not expect to be treated as anything more than a trainee."

She snorted softly. "Don't worry. Any expectations I might have had have *long* since died."

Anger flared briefly in his eyes. Then he glanced at the cell unit in her hand, and his face became impassive once more. "Keep in contact. I'll see you back at the office."

He turned and walked away, his movements sharp and somehow aggravated.

She stared at the door for several minutes after he'd disappeared, and then she turned and walked across to the bedroom to see what she could find.

***

Gabriel showed his ID to the black-clad police officer keeping watch and then ducked under the yellow crime scene tapes. The rotating red and blue lights of the nearby police vehicles washed across the night, splashing the otherwise somber, glass-walled building with color.

Like so many other buildings built in the area recently, this one had no real character. Its only purpose in life was to provide a decent view for those wealthy enough to afford an apartment so close to the city and the beach. He glanced up—ten floors in all. Surely, this time, they'd find a witness.

His brother walked down the steps as Gabriel approached. Stephan was a multishifter capable of taking the form of any human male he touched, but the shape he mostly wore these days was that of Jonathon Byrne, the head of the SIU. Gabriel raised his eyebrows in surprise. It was unusual for the head of SIU to become involved in routine investigations such as this. Something had to be up.

Byrne stopped in front of him, blue eyes narrowed. "Where's Ryan?"

Gabriel shrugged, even though he knew his nonchalance would only irritate his brother more. Right now, he didn't really care. "Handling the kite murder."

Stephan shot an aggravated look at the two police officers standing nearby. Gabriel smiled grimly. Their presence restrained Stephan from saying too much. It was a well-known fact that Byrne had very little to do with his six assistant directors. Being too familiar now might just blow Stephan's new identity out of the water.

"Damn it, Stern, you're supposed to be partners."

"I don't want or need a partner." And his brother, more than anyone, should have understood why.

"Andrea was a long time ago," Stephan said softly, an edge of compassion in his voice.

"Mike wasn't." He tried to control the almost instinctive rush of anger, but the desire to hit someone, anyone, was so fierce his fists clenched. "Death comes in threes, Byrne. I'm due one more."

And come hell or high water, that death was *not* going to be Sam.

Stephan studied him for a long moment, then shook his head and headed back to the apartment building. Gabriel fell into step beside him. The matter of a partner might have been dropped, but it was definitely not forgotten. But this was one battle of wills his brother was *not* going to win.

"Why are you here?" he asked, as they entered the building.

"It's a personal favor for Frank Maxwell."

Maxwell was the Federal Minister for Education, and one of the few friends the real Byrne had actually had. As such, he'd posed a very real threat to Stephan securing his new identity. Luckily, the two men had seen little of each other in the last year. Any differences Maxwell might see in Byrne now he'd surely put down to time. "Why?"

"It's his son who's been murdered."

Gabriel glanced at his brother in surprise. "A male? You

sure it's the same killer, not a copycat?"

Stephan's smile was grim. "You'll see when we get there."

Which could only mean the clinical brutality of the previous attacks was evident here also. He eyed the police officer guarding the express elevator and frowned. The same young officer had been guarding the doorway after Jack had bombed Sam's apartment. Odd that he was here now, too.

"Is Marsden on scene?" he asked softly.

Stephan met his gaze and gave a minute shake his head. The young officer stepped aside as they approached the elevator. Gabriel glanced at his nametag. Sanders.

"Tenth floor, sir?"

Gabriel nodded, noting Sander's eyes were a deep, unfathomable green, and somehow seemed older than his years. It was almost as if the soul behind the eyes had seen more than one lifetime.

The officer pressed the button, then stepped clear as the elevator doors slid shut. Stephan raised an eyebrow at Gabriel. "Why the question about Marsden? He's a beat cop, not homicide."

He shrugged. "That kid was working with Marsden when Sam's apartment was bombed."

"He might have been transferred."

"Maybe." Maybe he was just getting suspicious in his old age. Still, it wouldn't hurt to check why the kid was here, when he had the time. "How old was Maxwell's son?"

"Twenty-five, same as the others."

The lift came to a stop, and the doors opened. The hallway beyond was pale blue, offset by gold carpet. Four doors led off the hall, and a police officer stood guard at the far end. Gabriel glanced up at the ceiling. Monitors were stationed at regular intervals, tracking them silently.

"You requested the security tapes?"

Stephan nodded. "Copies have already been sent back to your office."

"Good." He stepped into the apartment. The place was huge, and the wall to ceiling glass flanking two sides of the apartment only added to the feeling of space. What few inner walls the apartment had were pale blue, but the carpet and the furniture were white. A spherical-shaped crimecorder hovered in the middle of the room, red light flashing to indicate it was recording.

"He obviously didn't have any youngsters visiting, not with all this white furniture," he commented. "What's the victim's name?"

"Harry. And there're no kids, no wife, and as far as Frank knew, no girlfriend."

He raised an eyebrow. "What about a boyfriend?"

"A possibility. Frank was rather brusque when I asked if there was any particular woman his son might have been seeing."

The body lay on one of the white sofas. He walked to it. As long as you didn't look below the waist, it would be easy to think Harry had merely died in his sleep. His arms were crossed, his face peaceful. There was no terror, no hint that he'd known he was about to die so brutally.

"Cause of death?" he asked, despite the fact it was obvious. No man could loose his penis and scrotum, and survive the resulting shock and blood loss unless he had medical help *real* fast.

"Same as the others—blood loss. There's an ashtray full of cigarette butts on the dining table, too."

"Same brand as before?" He squatted to inspect the gaping wound. The blood staining the leather no longer smelled fresh, and the wound itself was beginning to blacken.

"Yes. We've scanned for prints, but he was wearing gloves again. All we got was a latex smudge."

"There's one difference, at least. There's no real effort to be precise in his knife work here. He's basically just hacked it all away."

Stephan snorted softly. "Hell of a lot easier to part a man from his penis than it is a woman from her womb."

"True. But all three victims were obviously unconscious before the murderer operated, so why the care with the women and not young Harry here? There are several deep nicks on his right inner thigh."

"Maybe our murderer gets perverted pleasure from gutting women and wants it to last longer."

He frowned. Something in that statement didn't sit right. The murderer had been meticulous in every detail so far—why would he change anything just because this victim was a male? The fact that the murderer had sat back and watched the blood pour from their bodies suggested it was the death, rather than the cutting, that he enjoyed more.

He rose and then hesitated. On the back of the sofa, near

Harry's right hip, a hair glinted softly in the light. It wasn't one of Harry's. His hair was red, the same as the other two victims. This was blond and long, with dark roots.

Gabriel dug a glove out of his pocket and carefully picked up the hair. "Got a bag?" he asked.

Stephan dug one from the crime kit sitting on the table. "Maybe he did have a girlfriend."

"Could still be male. Long hair is fashionable in the rave scene at the moment. I'll run a check on Harry's acquaintances and see what I can find."

Gabriel secured the bag in the crime kit and turned back to the sofa. He had an itchy feeling that there was something else to be found. In the previous two murders, the killer had been careful not to leave anything behind. No hair, no prints, nothing that might give him away.

This time he'd been less than precise with his cutting. Maybe, just maybe, he'd been less than precise with his clean up. He studied the position of the body for a long moment, and then walked around to the back of the sofa. Blood had stained through, contrasting starkly against the white, embroidered material. Oddly enough, the thick carpet showed signs of a recent vacuuming.

He frowned and studied the crisscrossed suction patterns across the carpet. Only the small section between the sofa and what looked to be the bathroom had been touched. Near the bathroom door, a faint footprint marred the lush white lawn.

"How many people have been in the apartment since the body was discovered?" he asked, squatting near the print.

"The usual—the two state officers who attended the original call, the building super who let them in, and us. Forensics is still on the way. Why? What have you found?"

"A print." He glanced up at the crimecorder. "Record image and location of print."

The black sphere responded immediately, zipping across the room to hover inches from his head. "Image recorded," a metallic voice stated.

"Resume original position." He knelt to study the print. As he did, he noticed a slight stain near the door. Liquid of some sort had been spilled near the doorframe. He touched it lightly— the carpet was dry and stiff, almost as if had been glued together. He sniffed his fingers. The faint but unpleasant mix of urine and rotten eggs had him screwing up his nose in distaste.

"Jadrone," he muttered, coughing to ease the sudden stinging in the back of his throat.

"What the hell is Harry doing with something like Jadrone? Frank's family is human, not shifter."

"Which means maybe our killer is shifter." It would certainly explain why no one had noticed any strangers hanging about in the two previous murders, particularly if their killer was a multishifter.

Though Gabriel doubted if the killer would actually be taking the stuff himself. Jadrone was designed to ease the inevitable bone and muscle problems that afflicted most shifters late in life, but it also had an unpleasant side effect. After several months of continual use, the ability to tell truth from fantasy blurred. Life became one big dream for the user. Their killer was too practical, too careful, to be on some Jadrone-inspired trip.

So why in hell was there Jadrone on the floor?

"The government took Jadrone off general prescription a year ago," Stephan said. "It shouldn't be too hard to track through records and find out who's still taking it."

He smiled grimly. It might not be too hard, but it was a task he had no intention of doing. Sam could. It would keep her out of his way a bit longer. Her anger and frustration had been all too evident in her smoke-shrouded blue eyes tonight. A few more pushes, a few more inane tasks, and she'd be asking for a transfer. All he had to do then was convince Stephan it was for the best.

He rose and continued on into the bathroom. The stark whiteness was practically blinding—it had to be hell on the eyes when the sun hit it. A slight breeze stirred the hairs at the back of his neck. He glanced at the ceiling to make sure it wasn't the air conditioning and then turned. A hole had been cut into the thick glass wall.

"Crimecorder, record bathroom evidence," he stated. As had been the case in the two previous murders, this hole was barely big enough to fit his fist through. And the edges were razor sharp, indicating laser cutting.

"Any thoughts on these holes?" Stephan asked from the doorway.

Gabriel shrugged and stepped out of the crimecorder's way. "Escape route, maybe."

"If the killer's using Jadrone, he can't be a shapechanger."

"No." Jadrone was as deadly to shapechangers as it was helpful to shapeshifters. No one knew why, though Karl, a good friend of Gabriel's and one of Australia's top herbal scientists, thought it might have something to do with body chemistry. "Nothing's making much sense in this case."

"Well, it had better. If the killer keeps to his current schedule, you have precisely twelve hours before he strikes again."

Twelve hours to find someone as illusive as a ghost. What could be simpler? "It would be a damn sight easier if we could find some sort of pattern. Other than being the same age and having red hair, the victims have nothing in common."

"The answers are there. All you have to do is find them." Stephan hesitated and then smiled grimly. "And I want Agent Ryan brought in on this case."

Gabriel stared at his brother, wondering why he was so determined to see him and Sam as a team. "No."

"That's a direct order, Stern."

And it was one he had no intention of ever obeying—if only because Sam had red-gold hair, the same as the three victims. She might not be twenty-five, but he wasn't about to chance her safety. Not with his track record.

"Are you listening, Stern?"

"I'm all ears, sir."

Anger flared briefly in Stephan's blue eyes. "Good. Report to me hourly."

He turned and walked away. Gabriel stared after him for a long moment, and then he glanced up at the crimecorder. "Position of autopsy team?"

"Entering building now."

"Good. Resume original monitoring position." Gabriel followed the crimecorder back out to the living room. The clue was here somewhere. He could feel its presence, like an itch he couldn't quite scratch. He stared blankly at the corpse for a long moment and then turned.

Why had the killer vacuumed? Why just the section behind the sofa?

Frowning, he crouched down, studying the vacuum marks intently. Something had to have been spilled or dropped here— why else vacuum? He shifted slightly, and caught sight of something glittering deep in the white pile. He carefully plucked it out—a shard of glass. He ran his fingers through the carpet. A plate size section near his feet felt damp. He sniffed his fingers again. Ginger and lemon, mixed with something spicy he couldn't define. Its touch burned across his skin.

He knew the scent. *Heat*, the latest rage in female perfumes and one designed solely for female use. The manufacturers claimed it made the wearer irresistible to the male gender—a claim that had proven so true the government was considering putting the perfume on the dangerous drugs list. Oddly enough, when used by a male, *Heat* lived up to its name in an entirely different way, burning where it touched.

Harry had no wife, no girlfriend. No reason to buy *Heat*.

The killer was female, not male.

Two

Sam leaned back in her chair and rubbed her forehead wearily. She'd had an almost constant headache for the last two days, and sitting for hours in front a com-screen certainly didn't help. Nor did lack of sleep. In fact, that was probably the cause of it.

But if she slept, she dreamed. Though she couldn't remember what those dreams were about, she always woke drenched in sweat, her heart pounding at the walls of her chest, as if trying to escape. And always, *always*, there was a name dying on her lips.

Joshua.

Why, she had no idea. She had no friends by that name. She'd never even met a Joshua, so why dream of him? And why were those dreams always so full of fear?

Sighing, she opened her eyes and stared blankly at the com-screen for several seconds. It was seven thirty in the damn morning. She should go home and get some rest. Shower, at the very least. But the apartment just didn't seem right any more. It was too sterile, too neat. The builders and painters had restored the living area after the bomb left by her ex-partner had basically destroyed the place three months ago, but no one could ever replace all the knickknacks and books she'd collected over the years. The apartment just wasn't the same without them.

Maybe she should sell it and start anew. Hell, she'd done it before. She'd left the orphanage with nothing more than the clothes on her back and a hand drawn picture of her mother. At least she now had a job and a decent amount in credits to fall back on.

The com-screen blinked to life. Dizzy Izzy, a hot pink fur-ball that was the current rage in adult cartoons, stared at her while slowly swinging the end of a purple boa. "Search completed, sweetie."

"Split screen, and show results."

"Can do."

The screen split in two. One side held the images of the four men she'd downloaded from the viaphone, and on the other, their names and addresses, courtesy of the Motor Registration Board. Fortunately, they insisted motorists update their license photos every two years. As a State Police Officer, there'd been countless forms to fill out before she could access the MRB's information. The SIU, it seemed, was all-powerful. She'd yet to find a system she *couldn't* get into.

"Do a complete background on those four men, as well as our murder victim, Frank Lyle. Concentrate on current work details and banking activities."

Izzy frowned, and the boa went into overdrive. "That'll take time, sweetie."

"I know. Proceed."

"You're the boss."

"Only in this shoebox," she muttered, and then turned as the door opened. Gabriel walked in and dumped a file on her desk.

She eyed it wearily. "What's that? More of the newly turned to be catalogued?"

"No. I want you to do a search and find out who's still being prescribed Jadrone."

She raised her eyebrows in surprise. "Why?"

"Because we found it in Harry Maxwell's apartment."

"Harry Maxwell? Frank Maxwell's kid?"

He frowned and sat down on the edge of her desk. Given her office was little more than a glorified broom closet, he practically loomed over her. "Yes. Do you know him?"

She snorted softly. "Sort of. Jack and I often ran across him during our shifts."

"Doing what?"

"He was a regular at Maximum. *"*

Gabriel raised a dark eyebrow. "Never heard of it."

Like *that* was a surprise. From what she'd gathered in the last month, Gabriel and Stephan lived and breathed work—whether it was SIU or for the Federation. Life beyond that just didn't happen. Not that she was much better, but hell, they had friends, a family. A choice.

Though in Gabriel's case, that choice certainly didn't extend to her.

"It's an underground rave house. Popular with the gay scene, and for those after prescribed or illegal drugs."

"So Harry was a user?"

"He's what I term a prescribed druggie. Used to hit up on Jadrone."

"Jadrone has no effect on humans." He hesitated. "Even when used by a shifter, it has to be taken daily for several months before it has any effect."

"So says the government, but take a large enough dose and you're floating. Old Harry couldn't have been entirely human, because he regularly got blasted."

He studied her for a minute, his hazel eyes intense and unreadable. "Why was he never pulled in?"

"He was. Several times. But Frank Maxwell knows all the right people. The department kept dropping the charges."

"Do you know his supplier?"

"No." She hesitated. Truth was, she did, but if she told Gabriel, she'd remain stuck in this shoebox for yet another day. "But I can find out, if you want."

"I want. I've got nine hours before the killer strikes again."

I've got, not *we've* got. He still wasn't letting her in. "Anything else?"

His sudden smile was almost predatory. Here it comes, she thought. The inane task to end all inane tasks.

"I want you to get a list of everyone who's bought *Heat* in the last month."

She stared at him. "But that could take days! *Heat* is the perfume world's flavor of the month."

"Then you'd better get started, hadn't you?"

He rose and left, but not before she'd caught the amused glint in his eyes. "Damn you to hell," she muttered, and kicked the door. Easy to do when she was so damn close to it. It slammed shut with wall-shaking force.

"Hey, careful!" yelled the guy in the neighboring shoebox.

She snorted softly. She'd probably woken the old bastard up. Her office was in an area the SIU called the vaults, and more commonly known as the black hole. Once in, never out, so the saying went. It was a cataloguing area and generally reserved for those close to retirement or no longer able to cope with the pressures of SIU investigations. Gabriel's excuse for putting her here was lack of office space elsewhere.

His office was large enough for four desks.

He was obviously trying to piss her off, and he was certainly succeeding. But she wouldn't quit, and she wouldn't ask for a transfer, if that was what he was after. She'd ride it out, if only because being his partner gave her access to a whole new range of computer systems. And in one of them there surely had to be some clue to her past.

She leaned forward and picked up the folder. Inside she

found photos and the crime scene report. She thumbed past the photos, barely bothering to look at them, and then scanned the autopsy results.

Interestingly enough, no traces of Jadrone had been found in Harry's system. Which meant he couldn't have had a fix for at least a week. Harry was a junkie—if he'd been off Jadrone for any longer than three days, he would have been a mess. Frowning, she sorted through the papers and found the follow-up report. He'd shown up for work, on time, every single day.

She'd seen Jadrone junkies being weaned off the drug. Harry shouldn't have been able to piss on his own, let alone get up and go to work.

Maybe she should head down to Maximum and find old Max, the owner and chief supplier. "Izzy, I need two more searches done."

The pink fuzz ball reappeared on the screen. "I'm stressing out here, darlin'."

"You'll live. I want a complete list of everyone who's bought *Heat* in the last month."

The purple boa became a blur. "Why don't you ask for the moon to turn blue? Hell of a lot easier."

"Tell me about it," she muttered. "The other search I want done is for eight names." She hesitated and dug the birth certificate out of her drawer. After unfolding it, she read out the eight names. "That's a priority one search. All channels."

The purple boa stilled. "By what authority?"

"Gabriel Stern, Assistant Director, badge number 5019."

"The director has a note on-line to be informed if you request information on these eight names."

The only way Gabriel could have known about the birth certificate was if he'd been snooping through her desk. She certainly hadn't mentioned it. "Then inform him and get on with the search."

"Search underway. It may take the whole day, sweetie."

And she wasn't about to hang around waiting. "Save all results to my personal folder and scan a copy onto disk." Working with Jack for so many years had taught her to be careful. Computers could be hacked into, data erased or changed. But if you made a hard copy of everything, you at least had a backup.

"Consider it done. Have a nice day."

"Yeah, right." She rose and stretched. A shower and a few

hours sleep were a first priority. Then she'd head to Maximum, and have a cozy little chat with Max. Harry had been a rich source of regular cash for at least three years. If Max didn't know how Harry had come off the drug with no side effects, no one would.

She grabbed her bag, and headed out the door.

***

Gabriel entered his office, yanked off his tie, and tossed it across the arm of the nearest chair. Then he loosened the top two buttons on his shirt and walked across to the auto-cook. "Coffee, black, two sugars."

He whistled tunelessly until the coffee was ready, then walked across to the desk and sat down.

"Computer on."

The com-unit hummed softly. "Good afternoon, Assistant Director."

"I want a complete background check on Harry Maxwell. Priority one."

"Proceeding. Search results for Anna King and Raylea Burns completed."

"Split screen and show results."

"Proceeding."

He leaned back in his chair and sipped the steaming coffee. They'd begun using decent beans in the A.D.'s machines of late, and the coffee actually tasted like coffee, rather than a bitter metallic substitute. It was a nice change.

The com-screen came to life, displaying the bloody images of the first two women killed. Underneath the photos were their histories.

He scanned through them both quickly and frowned. They'd been born on the same day, in the same military hospital.

"Display the birth certificates for both women."

"Displaying."

The two documents came onscreen. He raised his eyebrows. A birthday wasn't the only thing they'd shared. They also had the same mother. So why hadn't Emma Pierce raised her daughters? And how could both girls be listed as being born at 10.15 p.m. if they had the same mother?

"Who was attending gynecologist on the births?"

"Doctor Frank Lloyd."

"Where can I find him?"

"Doctor Lloyd is the resident physician at the Hopeworth

Military Base."

Hopeworth was something of a black hole when it came to military bases. Little was known about its activities, and it was one of the few areas the SIU computers could not hack into. Officially, Hopeworth was a weapons development area. Unofficially, who knew?

But why would they want a full time gynecologist? Were the staff so bored the base was experiencing a population explosion?

"Dig up Harry Maxwell's birth certificate. And see what you can find on Emma Pierce." If Emma worked at Hopeworth, there wouldn't be much to find. The base guarded the identity of its personal almost as fiercely as its activities. It was surprising they'd let the birth certificates slip into the general information pool, although, perhaps, because both children had ended up being adopted, they'd been forced to.

"Agent Samantha Ryan has just requested a priority one access all search."

"Indeed?" He smiled. So she'd finally done it. He had begun to wonder if she'd ever take the risk. "The search is approved. Post a copy of results to me but otherwise continue."

The key to who—or perhaps that should be, what—she was lie not in the present, but in a past she couldn't remember. He was certain of that much. But it wouldn't do him any good to do the research, because he had no idea what might or might not pull a memory from her mind. She *had* to be the one to look, which was why he'd allowed her full computer access in the first place—something that went against all SIU rules.

The computer blinked to life again. "No current information available on Emma Pierce."

He frowned. "What do you mean?"

"No purchases made with credit cards in the last month. No transactions within bank accounts. Utilities to home have been cut due to nonpayment."

"No death certificate issued?"

"Death records scanned. No match."

If she wasn't dead, then what the hell was she up to? "Last known address?"

"14 Errol Street, Melton."

His frown deepened. Why would someone like Emma Pierce, who'd obviously been military employed and should have retired with a nice fat pension, be doing in a place like

Melton? The Government had bought out a good sixty percent of the suburb some ten years back, with the aim of providing both the homeless and low income earners dependant on government housing with somewhere cheap to live. Or, as the critics of the move had observed, basically dumped them. Out of sight, out of mind.

"Was she in government or private housing?"

"Government funded."

"Is there a husband or living relative listed on file?"

"No marriage certificate on record. No listing of immediate family available."

"No record of parents?"

"Parents were killed in an automobile crash sixty-two years ago. Emma Pierce was listed as their only child."

"Do a complete background check on Emma Pierce, as well as the two men listed as the fathers of her children—James Brooks and Reg Norris. Post a copy of all results to viaphone 5019."

He finished the rest of his coffee and rose. Time to go to Melton, and pay a visit to Emma Pierce.

***

Sam climbed out of the car and glanced skyward. Gray clouds stormed across the sky, so low it felt as if she could reach out and touch them. Electricity burned through the air, tingling across her skin, through her soul.

She took a deep breath and, for a moment, imagined the power of the storm filling her body, strengthening her. Changing her.

She frowned and wished Finley would hurry up and get back from sick leave. She really needed to talk to him. Needed to understand the changes she sensed were happening.

Thunder rumbled. It was a sound she felt rather than heard. A sound that seemed to vibrate through every cell in her body. Fear stepped into her heart, but she thrust it away. For now, there was nothing else she could do, because there was simply no one she could talk to.

She reached back and grabbed her jacket off the back seat, then climbed out. The car locked automatically when she slammed the door shut. She turned and studied the concrete, slab-sided building. It didn't look like much, not in daylight, anyway. But at night, the blue painted concrete became the perfect foil for all sorts of computer animation. And it attracted creatures as weird and as wild as its graphics.

Slinging her jacket over her shoulder, she walked up the half dozen steps and opened the front door. In her ten years as a cop, she'd never known this place to be closed—even though it only had a license to operate at night.

Smoke drifted past her body, thick and somehow cloying. With it came the smell of hopelessness. Jack, her now-dead ex-partner, had often asked her to define what she meant, but it was something she found hard to explain. Even at night, when the place was full of people and noise and life, it was there. It was a sense of desperation, perhaps. Or maybe it was the smell of death hovering close. So many of the people who came to Maximum's were on a downward spiral to oblivion.

She closed the door but didn't move further inside, allowing her eyes time to adjust to the darkness. The place was quieter than usual. There were only a half dozen people in the front bar, either wearily nursing drinks or hiding in the darkness of the booths to her right. Josie, the gum chewing, red-haired bartender, stood at one end, looking as disinterested as the rest of the patrons.

She walked across. "Hey Josie, Max around?"

Josie's golden brown eyes jumped into focus. "Officer Ryan. It's been a while."

Her pupils were large, speech somewhat slurred. She wondered what Josie was taking these days. "That it has. I need to see Max."

"You here to haul his ass downtown?"

She smiled thinly. "If I was, would I be here talking to you, giving Max time to run?"

Josie sniffed. "That's okay, then. He's upstairs."

"Thanks. I remember the way."

Josie nodded vaguely and went back to polishing, a somewhat erotic smile touching her lips. *Minds Eye*, Sam thought, catching the candy-sweet scent as Josie moved. It was, in many ways, an aphrodisiac for the brain. Wondering which patron Josie was having mind-sex with, she headed through the door into the main rave area.

The huge dance hall lay in darkness. Her footsteps echoed against the wooden floor, the beat a tattoo that set her nerves on edge. Wishing she'd bought something more than a stun gun, she frowned, made for the rear stairs and ran up to the next floor.

Max's office lay at the end of the long corridor. She stopped and eyed the shadows warily. With the approaching storm running liquid fire through her veins, and seeming to expand her senses to new heights, she knew that no one lay in wait. And yet something felt *wrong*.

She reached into her pocket for the viaphone but stopped. Calling Gabriel for help wasn't the answer. He'd only tell her off for coming here in the first place.

Besides, there was probably nothing more dangerous here than a case of nerves. This was the first time she'd come to Maximum's without Jack by her side.

She took a deep breath and released it slowly. Jack might be dead, but her life was no less complicated. And in truth, she missed him. Missed having someone to talk to, to laugh with. In the darkest hours of the night, she couldn't help thinking that even a friendship based on a lie was better than no friendship at all.

If only she could find out *why* Gabriel was so determined to get rid of her.

Frowning, she pressed the viaphone's locator button, giving the SIU her immediate position. Then, stun gun in hand, she walked toward the door.

It opened before she got there. Max's grotesque figure loomed large in the doorway, his smile flashing in the gloom.

"Officer Ryan. Pleased to see you again."

His tent-sized Hawaiian shirt was buttoned up wrong, and he wore no shoes or socks. She held back a slight grin. Maybe she'd interrupted something. "Yeah, right. Back up, Max."

He held up his hands and backed away from the door. She checked left and right before entering. Max was the only human in the room.

But he wasn't alone.

She glanced up. The office ceiling was a good fifteen feet high and made entirely of glass. Vines twisted their way across a network of wires, and flowers hung in chains, dripping pink and red petals to the floor. Budgerigars flittered through the greenery, bright splashes of yellow and blue. One of them was a shapechanger, but the birds moved too fast to define which one.

"They have to be hell on the furniture," she commented. "Why the sudden fixation on budgies?"

Max shrugged. It sent ripples running across his flesh, like waves in an ocean. "They amuse me. Besides, I have plenty of money to spend."

She kicked the door shut and leaned back against it. "Then why not try weight reduction surgery? You might live longer."

His answering smile was gentle. "They will not operate. They say I am too large."

"Sue them."

"Oh, I am." He moved around the desk and squeezed his frame into a chair the size of a two-seater sofa. "Now, I'm presuming you did not come here to discuss my weight."

"No. But first, where's Morris?" Max's ape-sized bodyguard was rarely more than two feet from his side.

"I sent him for a walk."

Wanted a little privacy with his budgie friend, no doubt. Though from what she'd heard, he normally didn't mind having an audience. "Tell me about Harry Maxwell."

Max returned her gaze evenly. No surprise there, though. When he wanted to he could act right up there with the best of them.

"I haven't seen him in over a week."

"When was the last time you *did* see him then."

"Last Thursday."

"And did you sell him any Jadrone?"

"No." A bead of sweat formed on his forehead.

"If you didn't sell him Jadrone, what did you sell him?"

The bead rolled down his cheek. Max swatted at it heavily. "I don't—"

"Do drugs, illegal or otherwise," she finished for him. "Yeah, I've heard the song before. Just give me the truth."

He shifted in his chair. Metal groaned into the brief silence. "I didn't sell him anything. Honest."

"His absence must be putting a strain on your finances. He was one of your best customers, wasn't he?"

He made no comment, just stared at her somewhat sullenly.

"Have you tried to find out where he is?"

Fingernails, almost lost in the envelope of flesh hanging over them, began to beat a rhythm against the desk. Nerves rather than anger.

"Yes."

"And?"

His hand edged toward the left side of the desk. "He said he didn't need me no more."

She raised an eyebrow. "He had a new supplier?"

"No. Said he didn't need the drug no more." His hand moved again.

"We both know he was a junkie. We both know he could never have given up cold turkey." She hesitated, saw a budgie dive bombing her head, and ducked. Bird shit splattered across the door just near her ear. "I don't think your bird likes me, Max."

He made no comment, but the look in his brown eyes suggested she wasn't on his list of favorite people, either. It wasn't exactly a surprise. She'd hauled his ass downtown more than a dozen times over the years.

It was more than that, though. She crossed her arms and regarded him steadily. There was something going on here, something she couldn't quite define. But it had something to do with the shapechanger whose presence fairly itched at her skin.

"You know Harry's dead, don't you?" she said, keeping her voice conversational. "He was victim number three of our serial killer."

Max jumped. For the first time she saw fear, true fear, leap into his eyes. He hadn't known about Harry.

And the murder scared the shit out of him.

He knew the killer, she thought, watching the glittering beads of sweat roll down his cheeks. Or at the very least, knew who Harry was with the night he was murdered.

Dodging the dive-bombing budgie, she walked across to the desk. Placing her palms on the table, she leaned across until her nose was only inches from his.

This close, he smelled of sweat and fear and sex.

"Tell me who Harry was with the night he died, Max."

He licked his lips, tongue lizard-like in his agitation. "I don't know what you're talking about. I told you, I haven't seen Harry in over a week."

God, this close his breath literally reeked. He'd obviously been overdoing the garlic and onions again. "But you know someone who has seen him since then, don't you?"

He didn't deny it. Merely sat and sweated some more.

"I want to know what you know, Max."

"I can't." The denial came out a strangled whisper.

She leaned back a little, more to get a dose of fresh air than anything else. "I'm not beat police any more, you know. I'm

SIU. I don't have to follow the rules. I can beat your fat ass to a pulp and no-one would ever question me."

He moved his hand again. She unclipped her laser and shoved it under his nose. "I'd really love for you to go for the weapon under your desk."

He raised his hands and leaned back in his chair. She frowned. Something about this felt wrong. Despite the fact that he dealt in death for a living, there was no way in hell Max would get mixed up in something like the serial killings. It just wasn't his style.

So why wouldn't he talk? The budgie, maybe?

"That your girlfriend up there, Max? Why don't you invite her down for a chat?"

His gaze jumped to the ceiling. His growing look of horror was one she didn't understand.

"What do you mean?" he whispered.

"I mean that mean-looking blue chit who keeps trying to shit all over me. She the jealous type, perhaps? Or doesn't she know about the business sidelines you have going?"

"Yes. I mean, no." Max hesitated, licking his lips. "She's not my girlfriend."

But they were involved at a basic level, at least. Why else would he smell of sex?

"The sooner you tell me what you know, the sooner you and your girlfriend can get back to business."

His cheeks reddened slightly. He looked like a kid caught lying to a teacher. "I can't tell you anything, officer."

"Then maybe I'll have to interview your girlfriend." She clicked the safety off and aimed the laser at the ceiling. "I'll shoot every one of them if that's what it takes."

She wouldn't, but Max didn't know that. He'd seen Jack in action often enough to think she meant what she said.

Max sighed and rubbed his eyes. He suddenly looked like a man in defeat. A man despairing. "She means it."

Something blue fluttered to her left—a budgie, gliding to the carpeted floor. Power ran across her skin, a faint tingle that burned a warning into her soul.

The shapechanger was on her right, not her left.

She turned, stun gun rising. She wasn't fast enough by half.

Something smashed into the side of her head and the lights went out.

Three

Errol Street sat in the heart of the Government-owned housing. Gabriel slowed the car, searching for numbers on the shabby looking brick and concrete residences.

Twelve . . . Fourteen. He stopped and climbed out. The wind swirled around him, thick with the scent of rain. He glanced skyward. The clouds were black and looked ready to burst. He reached for his coat, shrugging it on as he walked across the road.

Number fourteen was different from its neighbors in that no one had tended the garden for at least a month. Weeds twined their way through the imitation picket fence, crowding the sad looking roses. What there was of the lawn had died some time ago.

The house itself was little better. The porch drooped at one end, as if the foundations had given way. Several of the front windows were smashed and had been roughly boarded up. The second story looked thrown on, and sections of the tin roofing rattled noisily in the wind.

He walked up to the front door and rang the bell. He waited for several minutes for someone to answer. When there was no response, he knocked loudly. Still no one came to the door. He stepped back and studied the second story. No lights; no sound.

The house looked and felt deserted.

He walked around to the back. Several sweaters and skirts hung on the line, flapping almost forlornly in the wind. If the bird shit caking the side of one navy skirt was any indication, they'd been there for a while.

The back door was locked. He stepped back and kicked it open. The handle took out a large chunk of plasterboard from the wall behind the door. Dust flew high, itching his nose and making him sneeze.

Clothes lay scattered on the laundry floor—whites separated from colors, but both piles gathering dust. He stepped past them and into the hallway.

The air smelled stale, as if it had been locked up for a long time. He turned right and found himself in the kitchen. A loaf of bread sat on a board near the sink, so green it was almost unrecognizable. A carton of milk sat nearby—even from where he stood he could smell its pungent sourness. Someone had prepared breakfast and not come back to clean up.

Both the dining room and the living room were empty of life. The stairs were at the back of the house, but on the first step, he stopped. No light filtered down from above. Darkness hunched over the top of the stairs like some demon waiting to pounce. But it wasn't the lack of light that stopped him. It was the smell. Meat, long gone rancid.

Death waited above.

He slowly climbed the stairs. Darkness wrapped around him, as heavy as a cloak. On the top step, he hesitated, waiting for his eyes to adjust. Shapes loomed out of the blackness—several bookcases lined the walls on either side of the doors.

The odor came from the room on his left. He walked through the doorway.

Emma Pierce sat up in bed, her body supported by several cushions, watching a TV that no longer worked. Her eyes were still open, jaw hanging loose. Her skin had a waxy look to it, pale cream in color tending to green near her neck. A tray, containing a half eaten slice of molding toast and a cup of what looked to have been coffee, sat by her side.

Her death obviously wasn't recent. And given how cold it had been lately, she could easily have been dead for over a month. Bodies tended to deteriorate far slower in lower temperatures.

And while her death appeared to be natural, he couldn't take any chances. Not when Emma Pierce was related to at least two murder victims.

He called in a SIU cleanup team, then put on some gloves and walked over to the window, opening the blind. Light flooded into the room, highlighting the decay—human and otherwise. Several envelopes sat on top of the drawers next to the bed. He picked them up. Bills, mostly. One envelope caught his eye— the return address was Hopeworth.

He tore it open. It was a letter from Doctor Frank Lloyd, asking Emma to contact him immediately. The request was dated August seventeenth—the day after the first murder.

If Emma Pierce had been dead by then, who had cleared her mail and brought it up here? He put the letter in his pocket and opened the first of the drawers. Neither the drawers, nor the room itself, gave up any further secrets.

In the second bedroom, he discovered a wardrobe full of clothes—modern stuff, not the type worn by most sixty-year-old women. Someone else had stayed in the house with Emma, and for some time, if the range of apparel was anything to go by.

So where was that person now? And why hadn't they reported Emma's death to the authorities?

He searched the remaining bedroom, but he didn't find anything else and went back downstairs.

He was in the kitchen when the pain hit. Fire flashed through his brain and sent him stumbling forward. He grabbed the bench, holding on as the kitchen danced around him. Sweat rolled into his eyes, stinging, blurring his vision. For an instant, everything went black.

Then it was gone, as swiftly as it had come. Leaving him with the certainty that Sam was in trouble.

"Assistant Director, you okay?"

He swung around. Michaels stood in the doorway, regarding him with concern.

"No. I think the smell finally got to me." He took a deep breath, fighting the urgency beating through his veins. "The body's upstairs."

"Foul play evident?"

"No. But look for it. I want cell analyses included."

Michaels frowned. "That'll take time."

"Emma Pierce has nothing but time. Get the sweepers into the second bedroom, too. Someone else has been staying here— see if you can pick up DNA traces."

Someone had cared enough to stay here and look after Emma as death approached. Why hadn't they cared enough to report the death and bury her?

Michaels nodded. "You want us to contact you if we find anything?"

"Yes. Send results through as soon as you have them."

"Right." Michaels headed for the stairs.

Gabriel dug out the viaphone. SIU's digital secretary answered almost immediately.

"Christine, we got a location signal on Agent Ryan?"

"Sector Five. One-five-six George Street, Fitzroy."

He raised his eyebrows. Right in the heart of the dance rave area. What the hell was she doing there? "Any reports of trouble in that area?"

"None, sir."

No reports of trouble, no indication that Sam herself was in trouble. So why was he so certain that she was? "Christine, send someone to collect my car. I'm heading out to join Agent Ryan."

"Yes sir."

He put the viaphone away, walked outside and called to his alternate shape. Power surged, burning through his body, snatching away sensation and pain as every nerve ending shuddered, twisted, to find new form. Then sensation died, and an odd sense of emptiness followed. A heartbeat later, he was a hawk soaring skyward, heading towards the city.

***

Smoke tickled Sam's throat, making her cough. She tried to swallow, but her mouth was dry, empty of saliva. Her throat felt raw, parched, as if she'd been sucking in heat and had scalded it. Even her lungs burned.

She groaned and rolled onto her back. Moisture ran past her ear, tickling her scalp. She swatted at it, and her fingers came away damp. It was a sticky dampness, like blood.

Why was she bleeding? Had someone hit her over the head? Maybe the budgie had been armed with a big brown club. The image made her smile, but only for a second. Smoke swirled, thicker than before, catching the air in her throat and sucking it away.

Urgency began to beat through her, but it was distant, muted, as if fighting its way through a veil.

She opened her eyes. The budgies flew above her, their movements frantic, panicked. High-pitched cries of terror itched at her ears, but it wasn't only the birds. One of them was human.

Frowning, she turned her head. Across the room a fire danced, all gold and red. It flung bloody fingers toward the ceiling, and sashayed across the floor towards the desk and the fat man. A fat man whose shoes burned.

"Please," he said, his voice a mix of hysteria and urgency. "Help me."

The flames were beginning to dance toward his trousers. His legs jumped and twitched, as if in time to the silent music of the fire.

"Officer Ryan! You must get up! You must help me!"

The desperation in his voice bit through the fog enveloping her mind. She groaned, and rolled onto her hands and knees. Her stomach heaved, jumping into her throat, and sweat beaded her forehead. Heat flashed across her skin, followed quickly by an icy chill.

Swallowing heavily, she inched forward. The flames raced up Max's trousers. Too fast, some dim part of her mind protested. Max only wore natural fibers—wool usually. Only some form of accelerative would make his clothes burn so quickly.

She reached the wall and inched upwards. It was like moving through glue, as if her mind and her limbs were on separate planes. Snagging the extinguisher from the wall, she pulled out the safety catch, then pressed the lever and turned. Foam gushed from the nozzle, a blue-white cloud that arced across the room like canon-blasted snow.

Max screamed when it hit him—or maybe he'd always been screaming and it just hadn't registered until now. The flames hissed as they died, and the smoke in the room became thicker. She coughed, her vision blurring with the tears streaming down her face. When she could no longer see flames eating Max, she turned the extinguisher to the rest of the fire.

The door behind her flew open. Men dressed in black and gold ran in, hauling silver snakes that reared up and spewed water at the flames. Her vision wavered. She dropped the extinguisher and reached out for the wall. It danced away, laughing.

Then the floor rushed up to greet her.

***

Outside the darkened ambulance in which Sam sat, someone slammed a car door. The noise vibrated right through her, then reached into her brain and squeezed tight. She groaned, and held her head in her hands. Any minute now, it was going to explode. A head could only take so much pain, and hers had surely reached saturation point.

She wouldn't mind so much if it were only her head, but her whole damn body ached just as fiercely, and her stomach felt as steady as an umbrella in a windstorm. If she moved, she'd puke, no doubt about it.

Footsteps approached the ambulance. They rebounded through her brain like a freight train. Then the rear door opened and light flooded in.

She hissed and squeezed her eyes shut. "Shut the door, damn you."

The door closed softly. She took a deep breath, waiting for the pain behind her eyes to subside a little. The ambulance creaked as someone sat on the seat opposite. The earthy scent

of exotic spices, mixed with the warm freshness of the sun and
the wind, invaded the room. Gabriel, she thought, and bit back
another groan. That's all she needed right now. Her damn partner,
here to witness the mess she'd made of a simple questioning.

She leaned back against the ambulance's cool metal wall,
not opening her eyes, not wanting to see the anger in his eyes.

"You okay?" His voice was little more than a whisper and
devoid of emotion.

"No," she muttered. "I feel like shit."

He was silent for a second, but she could feel his gaze on
her. Assessing. Watchful.

"The doctor said he wants you in the hospital."

"The doctor can go to hell." And she'd told him as much,
several times. She needed rest, not endless prods and pokes
from curious medical staff.

"He says you're lucky to be alive."

She didn't feel lucky. She wiped the sweat from her forehead
and opened her eyes. He leaned forward, chin resting on his
interlocked fingers, regarding her with an odd expression in his
warm hazel eyes. Had it been anyone else, she might have
thought it was concern.

"I asked them not to call the SIU."

One dark eyebrow arched upwards. "They didn't."

Then why was he here? Checking up on her? She regarded
him for a moment, then closed her eyes again. The rolling in
her stomach was getting worse. The last thing she felt like right
now was any sort of confrontation with her so-called partner.
She just wanted to go home, to hide in the darkness. To forget
the image of the blackened mess that was Max's legs. "Any
word from the hospital about Max?"

She could almost feel Gabriel's frown. "If Max is the
proprietor of this dump, then yes. Third degree burns, but
nothing unsalvageable."

"Is he conscious?"

"No."

Damn. She needed to talk to him, needed to know why his
girlfriend had tried to kill them both.

"Do you remember what happened?" he said.

She snorted. Like she could forget. "Yeah, I was attacked
by an angry budgie."

His surprise rippled around her. "A shapechanger?"

"And probably a hooker, if I know Max. She was the one

who clubbed me. When I woke, the office was on fire, and so was Max."

He was silent for a moment, yet his gaze swept over her, a touch that seemed both calculating and troubled. "Do you think she administered the Jadrone?"

She opened her eyes. "Max was given Jadrone? Why on earth would she do that? He was human."

"Not Max. You."

She blinked. "Me?"

He nodded. "Enough to kill, apparently. The doctor can't understand why you're still sitting here."

She stared at him. Not so long ago, her late partner Jack had said she wasn't human. She hadn't wanted to believe him. Had hoped it was yet another of his lies.

Jadrone didn't affect humans. It certainly couldn't kill them. But it killed shapechangers outright, and it could certainly kill shifters, if enough was given in one dose. Her stomach rolled, and sweat broke out across her brow. She put a hand to her mouth, battling to hold back the rising tide.

Damn it, she *was* human. The Jadrone *shouldn't* be affecting her.

"I'm going to be sick," she muttered.

He grabbed a nearby container and shoved it under her mouth. Just in time. When she'd finished, he silently offered her a towel. She wiped her mouth and closed her eyes, leaning back again. "I need to sleep."

"No." There was a hint of alarm in his voice. "Not for the next twelve hours."

Not sleep for the next twelve hours? What drug was *he* on? "Just take me home, Gabriel. I'll answer all your damn questions after I've gotten some rest."

"You rest, you die." His voice was tight, hinting at anger, barely suppressed.

She met his gaze. "What do you mean?"

"I mean that there's enough Jadrone in your system to kill several shifters. The doc wants you in the hospital. He doesn't know why you're still breathing, let alone conscious, but he's certain if you do slip into sleep, you may never wake up."

"No hospital. And he's already told me I'm not going to die. He only wants to run tests on me." And she had no intention of being anyone's lab rat. Not for the sake of the doctor satisfying his curiosity, anyway.

She rubbed her arms. Damn it, if she wasn't human, then what the hell was she? A changer who couldn't shape change?

Even if that *were* true, how would the budgie have known? For all intents and purposes, she presented as a human. It was only that unknown chromosome, and Jack's mysterious words, that suggested anything else. So why had the budgie tried to kill them? What had the fat man known—what had *she* seen— that had forced the budgie's hand?

"What did you do or see in that office?" Gabriel's question mirrored her thoughts.

"I don't know." She rubbed her forehead wearily. "We were discussing Harry. Max knew something, something he was afraid of."

"Max was Harry's supplier?"

She nodded. "Jack and I used to bust his butt regularly. It didn't seem to make a great deal of difference to his business."

"Small time supplier?"

"Medium. Max liked his freedom too much to ever get involved with the big syndicates."

He was silent for a moment, and then he reached out, gently wiping the sweaty strands of hair away from her forehead. His touch felt so wonderfully cool against her fevered skin. It was all she could do to resist the temptation to lean further into his caress. "You'd better come back to my place. It's safer, at least until the Jadrone has run from your system."

One minute he couldn't wait to get rid of her, and the next he was acting like he cared. What was going on with him?

"Haven't you got a murderer to catch?"

"Yes. But I can access the reports from home. Can you walk?"

Just thinking about it made her stomach turn. "I'd keep the bucket real handy."

"What about the sunlight? How bad is it affecting your eyes at the moment?"

"At the moment, it's not. Mainly because there's no light here in the ambulance."

A smile tugged the corners of his full lips. "But if you were outside, you'd be screaming, right?"

"Just a little."

"We'd better use the ambulance as transport, then." He dug out his viaphone and quickly dialed.

She closed her eyes, listening to the rhythm of his speech

rather than his actual words. There was something very soothing in the resonance of his voice. Something that made her just want to drift—

"Sam!"

The word leapt through her brain and jarred every nerve ending. She jumped, and then she opened her eyes and glared at him.

"What?"

"You were going to sleep."

"I was just resting my eyes, for God's sake."

"Yeah, right." He hesitated. Someone climbed into the front of the ambulance and the engine roared to life. "Tell me what happened in the office just before you were knocked unconscious."

"Nothing happened. Max wouldn't tell me anything, so I suggested his bird come down so I could talk to her."

"Did he tell you she was up there?"

She frowned. "No. I sensed her presence the minute I walked in."

"So she wanted her presence kept a secret."

"Looks like it. Setting a fire to kill the two of us was going a trifle overboard, though."

"Not if she was involved with Harry as well as Max."

Her frown deepened. "I got the impression Max knew who Harry was with the night he died, but I got knocked out before he could say anything."

He leaned back and regarded her thoughtfully. "What makes you think Harry was with someone? There's no mention of it in initial reports."

"I asked Max the question. He said he didn't know, but he was lying. He was so scared I could almost taste it."

"Then maybe Max was involved."

She shook her head. "Not Max's style. He'll push death in the form of drugs, but he'd never get involved in something like these murders. Max has standards, lines he won't step over."

"What did he say about supplying Harry with Jadrone?"

"Harry told him he didn't need the drug any more."

Gabriel arched an eyebrow in surprise. "That's not possible—not if Harry was as addicted as you say."

"I know. He must have found some other form of drug to sate his need."

"Supplied, perhaps, by the mysterious shapechanger.

Anything else you remember about her?"

"Yeah, she tried to shit all over me."

He smiled. "Birds shit when they're scared. Fact of life."

"And do you suffer this problem, Assistant Director?"

His smile widened, lending warmth to his angular features. "Hawks don't scare as easily as budgies."

Didn't scare at all, from what she'd seen. In the brief time they'd known each other, they'd been shot at, bombed, even gassed. The only time she'd seen the slightest hint of fear in Gabriel's eyes was when his brother Stephan had gone missing in the SIU explosion. Family mattered more than personal safety, it seemed.

His viaphone buzzed into the brief silence. He gave her an apologetic look, though why she wasn't entirely sure, then quickly answered it. The warmth lingering on his face quickly disappeared.

"What?" she said, the minute he hung up.

His expression was grim as he glanced at her. "It would seem our serial killer has just thrown out her schedule."

Four

Gabriel leaned sideways and banged on the communications hatch. The small door opened, and light flooded in. Sam hissed.

"Change of direction. Head for Two-Eighty Elizabeth Street."

The ambulance driver nodded, and the hatch closed, encasing them in darkness again.

"Who are you dumping me on?"

Though her voice was even, her underlying anger was something he could almost taste. She was so pale she looked like death, and the thought chilled him. He didn't want to lose another partner, but he almost had, yet again. "What makes you think I'm dumping you?"

"Well, gee, maybe because you've used any and all excuses to keep me away from everything except paperwork."

"I've done it for your own safety."

"Yeah, right. Tell that to someone who hasn't spent ten years with the State Police."

"And the mess you made interviewing Max proved just how capable you are, didn't it?"

It wasn't a fair statement—had their positions been reversed, he doubted if he'd have coped any better. And the Jadrone would definitely have killed *him*.

Her hands clenched briefly by her sides. It was the only sign of the fury he could almost touch. "One of these days you're going to have to trust me."

"I do." With both his and his brother's lives. He just didn't trust fate.

Not that he had much choice in the matter at this particular moment. As much as he *did* want to loose her, he actually couldn't. There were only two people he'd trust with her safety—Karl was still on vacation with the family, and Stephan had a series of high-level meetings to attend.

"Then start acting like you do. Stop giving me inane tasks, and start giving me some real work." She raised a hand, as if to stop his answer, then closed her eyes and leaned back against the ambulance wall. "You know, it doesn't matter. Forget about it."

He watched a trickle of sweat roll down her pale cheek.

"Sam, Two-Eighty Elizabeth Street is where the murder happened."

She opened her eyes, and her smoky-blue gaze swept him from head to foot. Then a slightly bitter smile touched her lips. "You can't dump me. You haven't got anyone you trust to watch over me."

She was altogether *too* perceptive. "Are you sure you're up to this?"

"I think the question should be are *you* sure I'm up to this."

"Well, it wouldn't be a good idea to puke all over the evidence," he said, half in jest.

Her gaze narrowed. "I won't puke. I won't even comment, if that's what you prefer."

He grimaced. It was times like these, when all the laughter, all the warmth, had died from her face that he really regretted what he had to do. Stephan was right—they did work well together. But two people had died simply because they'd had the ill fortune to be his partner. She would not be the third.

The ambulance jolted to a stop. She winced.

"Watch your eyes," he said, then opened the door.

The light flooded in, and though she made no sound, her eyes were little more than slits through which he could see the glimmer of tears. He climbed out and then held out a hand. After a slight hesitation, she accepted it and got out.

Above, the sky was leaden, the clouds so heavy they looked ready to burst. Thunder rumbled, an ominous sound that vibrated through his body.

She stopped and breathed deeply. Electricity tingled across his fingers where they touched her arm, a sensation that was warm rather than threatening. It was almost as if she were sucking in the power of the storm itself.

"You okay?" he asked.

Though she was still unsteady on her feet, she definitely looked better than she had five minutes ago. But that didn't really surprise him. When her feet had been cut to the bone by laser fire, she'd still managed to walk when most people would have been unconscious.

"Yes." She took another deep breath, and color began to warm her cheeks. "Let's go."

She shook off his hand and walked unaided into the building. But despite the show of strength, her hand trembled when she punched the elevator button.

"Maybe you should sit down here and wait," he suggested, indicating the nearby bench.

She gave him a wry smile. "You're not getting rid of me that easily."

He was beginning to see that. He followed her into the elevator and pressed the button for the twenty-third floor. The doors closed and the elevator zoomed upwards.

She gulped at the sudden movement, and sweat began to redarken the red-gold strands of hair near her temple. She leaned back against the wall and closed her eyes, full lips pursed. Fighting her stomach, he thought.

She had guts; there was no doubt about it. If he *had* been in the market for a partner, he certainly wouldn't have found a better one.

The elevator came to smooth stop. Once the door had opened, he led the way through the foyer. Two State police officers guarded the door at the end of the corridor. He dug out his ID, and showed it to them. The two men stepped aside, allowing them access into another corridor.

The metallic odor hit almost immediately. The bloodshed had to be bad if he could smell it this far away from the body.

A third officer glanced up from a com-unit. "A.D. Stern?"

Gabriel nodded. "And Agent Ryan."

The detective glanced at Sam and almost instantly dismissed her. Either he wasn't very perceptive when it came to people, or he didn't care a great deal for female law officers. Or maybe he was just plain stupid, Gabriel thought, and looked at the man's ID. "What have we got, O'Neal?"

"A woman, mid-twenties, in the reception area. Multiple knife wounds to the throat and stomach regions. Apparently she's the resident doc here."

"Time of death?"

"Estimated to be around twelve-thirty."

During lunchtime. They probably wouldn't find many witnesses. "No sign of forced entry?"

The detective shook his head. "No witnesses so far, either."

"What about the security cameras?"

"Several. We're investigating them now."

"I want copies sent to my office."

The detective nodded. Gabriel continued to the small reception area.

It was worse than any of the previous murders. Blood had

sprayed across the white walls, splashed over the cheerful flowery patterns on the carpet and across the pristine whiteness of the reception desk. The body lay between the desk and the sofa, one hand outstretched, reaching for the nearby phone.

He glanced at Sam. She was sheet-white. "Why don't you sit, while I check out the body?"

"Why? Afraid I'll fall over and contaminate the crime-scene?" She crossed her arms and glared at him mutinously.

Anger surged, and it was made worse by the fact that he only had himself to blame for her reaction. If he didn't treat her like shit, she wouldn't be flinging it back at him. "Check the damn desk, then. See if there's anything there."

She nodded. He squatted beside the body. Overhead, the crimecorder buzzed. "ID please."

"Assistant Director Gabriel Stern and Agent Sam Ryan, SIU," he replied absently.

There was nothing patient, or gentle, in this woman's death. The murderer had slit her throat before gutting her—and had probably done so while she was still alive. There was tape stretched across her mouth, and a look of terror was permanently etched on her face. If it was the work of the same killer, something must have gone terribly wrong. Either that, or the madness that had set the killer on this path of destruction in the first place was getting progressively worse.

"It's not madness; it's anger," Sam said softly.

He looked up. She wasn't even looking at him, but somehow, she seemed to know his thoughts. It was almost as if there was some kind of connection between them—yet that was impossible, given he'd learned to raise shields so strong that not even his twin could share his thoughts. "What do you mean?"

She motioned almost absently towards the victim as she continued to leaf through the paperwork on the desk. "The murderer was angry with this woman. There's no care taken here, no time. Look at the way the victim's throat has been slashed. Another eighth of an inch, and she wouldn't have even hit the carotid."

He swept his gaze around the room. No ashtray full of cigarettes sitting on any of the tables. No immediate evidence that the killer had even stayed to watch this victim die. In fact, the only thing linking this victim with the other murders was the hole in her gut and the color of her hair.

"Why the anger here, though?" He glanced back at Sam,

interested in hearing her observations—or was it something else? Not the training of a cop, but a perception coming from developing psychic talents? The clouded look to her eyes certainly suggested it was the latter. "Why not with the previous three victims?"

"That's presuming it's the same killer."

He nodded. She pursed her lips, her gaze finally rising from the desk and sweeping the room.

"Maybe in this case, it's something as simple as the white coat the victim is wearing." She hesitated, frowning. "I don't think the killer was expecting a doctor."

He frowned. "Yet the precision of the wounds on the first two victims indicate the killer has some sort of medical background. Our killer might even be a doctor. Why react so strongly against a fellow practitioner?"

Her gaze came to rest on his. Her blue-gray eyes were suddenly unclouded and amused. "Find the answer to that, and you might just find your killer."

True. He rose and crossed to the windows. Outside, rain had begun to sheet down, and on the street below, men and women scurried for cover. This street was always busy—surely someone, somewhere, had seen *something.*

The killer hadn't cut an escape hole in the smoke colored glass, so if their killer was a shapechanger, she certainly hadn't escaped that way this time. He headed into the doctor's office to check the windows there, but there was nothing. Nor did anything appear disturbed or out of place in the room itself. Meaning their killer had come in and out through the front doors—either in human or nonhuman form—and *had* to be on the security tapes.

He returned to the reception area. Sam was looking through the diary.

"Anything?"

She shook her head. "No appointments during lunch. Looks like the postman had just been here, though." She motioned toward a stack of mail, half of which had been opened.

"We'll track him down, see if he saw anything." He frowned and studied the corpse for several seconds. "Someone must have seen the killer leave this time. If she left in human form, she would have had blood sprayed all over her."

"Anyone checked the restrooms?"

"You up to it?" The trembling in her hands had definitely

eased and color was back in her face.

She nodded and walked from the room. He squatted next to the body again. It didn't make any sense. The killer had been so careful up until now, so why do this? And why up the time frame?

He shifted slightly and caught the glint of silver in the carpet pile, close to the woman's outstretched hand. He slipped on a set of gloves and reached across. It was a small medallion, depicting an eagle entwined in barbed wire. The insignia of the Hopeworth Military Base.

"Crimecorder, record evidence found in carpet near victim's right hand."

The black sphere buzzed into action. "Recorded," the metallic voice stated a moment later.

"Resume original position." He turned the medallion over in his hand. On the back was a number—zero four. It should be easy enough to check whether the victim had ever served with Hopeworth.

And if the medallion belonged to the killer, then he finally had his first real clue. The viaphone vibrated against his side. "Yes?" he said, flipping the medallion right side up. The eagle had a small cross engraved on its chest.

"Think you'd better come down to the restrooms on the twenty-first floor."

Sam's voice was devoid of all inflection, giving no hint as to what she'd found. "On my way."

He made his way over to the main door. O'Neal stared at his com-unit, viewing the security tapes.

"Anything?" Gabriel dug a plastic container from the crime kit and dropped the medallion inside.

O'Neal shook his head. "Nothing yet."

"Anyone check the restrooms on the floors above and below?"

"No, sir. Not yet."

Slack as well as dumb. Gabriel shook his head, took off his plastic glove and dumped it in the nearby bin. Then he headed downstairs. Sam was waiting in the foyer of the twenty-first floor.

"What did you find?" he said, the moment he saw her.

"A few spots of blood splattered across the mirror. A blood stained sweater wrapped in plastic and stuffed deep into the trash can." She led the way along the corridor. Her movements were still slow, but becoming steadier.

He could only shake his head in amazement. She shouldn't even be alive, for Christ's sake, and here she was, walking and talking almost normally. Whatever race she was, it was a damn strong one.

"So our murderer came down here to clean up?"

"It would appear so." She pushed open the bathroom door.

The trash can's cabinet door stood ajar. The plastic bag was easy enough to see, wedged about halfway down. Her viaphone sat on the nearby bench, light flashing to indicate record mode.

He put on fresh gloves, reached into the bin and grabbed the plastic bag, holding it by two fingers in an effort not to foul whatever prints might be available. Blood smeared the plastic inside and out.

"Military green," she murmured. "Available in any disposal store."

"Yes. But I found a medallion upstairs near the victim's hand. The insignia belongs to Hopeworth."

She raised an eyebrow. "Any hope of getting them to trace who it might have belonged to?"

"Depends how helpful Hopeworth feels like being."

"If they won't cooperate, why not just do a search through the computers?"

"We would, except it happens to be the one place SIU hasn't got full access."

Surprise flitted across her face. "Really? Why's that?"

"Don't know." He got out his viaphone and called O'Neal, instructing the young detective to bring the crime kit down. Then he glanced back at her. "Where are the blood spots?"

She pointed to an arc of five microscopic spots. Maybe the murderer had flicked her hair, spraying droplets across the mirror. But how had Sam spotted them? *He* could barely see them, and his hawk-sharpened senses were more attuned to things like this.

"The murderer is desperate." She stared at the spots, her expression becoming distant once again. "She knows we're closing in. She needs to get it finished. Needs to fulfill promises made."

Her voice was as distant as her expression. He'd seen this type of thing before—the SIU employed several psychics who could read the emotions that lingered in otherwise empty rooms. But Sam had been tested repeatedly for psychic gifts, and she had repeatedly come up negative. Until she reached SIU halls, where she'd registered as a neutral—a feat that should have been impossible.

Finley had said it suggested her abilities were so strong that she was able to void all tests done on her.

"What promises?" He kept his voice soft, not wanting to jar her out of her trancelike state.

"To the dead." She hesitated, frowning lightly. "To her twin sister."

Emma Pierce was listed as an only child. But she was also adopted. It might be worth checking back to see if a mistake had been made. "Why is she killing these people?"

"They should not exist."

Her breathing was becoming too shallow, too quick. As much as he needed the insights, he couldn't let her continue. Not after she'd barely escaped death.

"Sam." He touched her arm lightly, and she jumped.

Her gaze leapt to his, her expression confused, and just a touch frightened. "What happened?"

"You were reading the room. Or the emotions in the room."

A shudder ran through her. "It felt like I was a watcher in someone else's dream. I could see and hear what was going on, but I couldn't intervene."

He touched her cheek, gently wiping away a drop of sweat. "I think those psychic gifts you don't have are starting to come to the surface."

She stared at him and then shook her head. "Impossible. I was tested."

"Tests can be skewed. I think we should do more."

She reeled back, as if he'd hit her. "No more tests. You promised."

"I also promised to help you get answers about your past. That isn't going to happen unless you start cooperating."

"No." She crossed her arms, her look mutinous. "The last batch of tests almost killed me. I won't do any more."

She was talking about the cell-invasion tests that the bastard she'd once called her partner had performed. "Jack didn't care about you, only what you were and how he could use you."

"And are you so very different, Assistant Director?"

The barb struck home, and anger surged. O'Neal chose that moment to walk into the room, but he stopped abruptly, his gaze darting from Gabriel to Sam.

"Everything all right, sir?"

"Fine." He somehow managed to keep his voice even. "We found the bloody sweatshirt in the trash can. There are blood specks sprayed across the mirror. I want samples taken from both and sent to the labs ASAP. And next time, O'Neal, kindly make sure you do a proper sweep of the crime scene."

The detective flushed and nodded. Gabriel shoved his hands in his pockets and walked from the room. He heard Sam murmur something to O'Neal, and then her footsteps as she followed.

He punched the elevator button. She stopped behind him, her gaze burning deep into his back.

"If you've got something to say, then say it," she said, voice sharp. "Don't take your anger out on other people."

Normally, he didn't. But she had an uncanny knack of seeing what others didn't, and it both irritated and alarmed him. He turned to face her.

"I'm not Jack. I'm not using you for my own purposes. If I were, I'd keep you as a partner."

She crossed her arms, her expression cynical. "And that's supposed to make me feel a whole lot better about the situation?"

It wasn't supposed to make her feel anything. "Sam, that certificate Jack gave you might be a fake."

"I know that."

"Then you should realize that the only true clue we may ever get lies in uncovering whatever that unknown chromosome in your system is. Remember, someone looped Finley's computer to stop us accessing the test results. They may very well have bombed Central Security for the same reason." He hesitated, and then added, "Damn it, Sam, don't you want to know what you are?"

She rubbed her arms and stared at him for several moments. "Who I am, yes. What I am? I don't know." Her voice was soft, face troubled. "I really don't know."

"Then you'd better decide really quickly. People died because of the secrets in your past. How many more have to do so before you find the courage to face what you might be?"

She stiffened. "You're a bastard, you know that?"

"Maybe I am. But at least I'm a realistic bastard."

They waited in silence for the elevator, then got in and headed back down. She led the way out of the building. The rain pelted down, a cold gray curtain that quickly drenched them both. Not that she seemed to take much notice as she marched up the street to the nearest cab rank.

"What now?" she muttered, once they were both inside the cab.

"Now we go back to my place and view the security tapes from both Harry Maxwell's apartment building and this one." The address he punched into the console was hers—she'd catch a cold, or worse, if she stayed in her current clothes, and he didn't have anything that would even come close to fitting her.

"Well, gee, don't you know how to show a girl a good time."

He ignored the sarcasm in her voice. "We'll stop and get some takeout, too. There's not much in the way of edible food at my place."

"There's a surprise."

She crossed her arms and stared out the side window, as angry as all hell and fighting not to show it. He ran a hand through his wet hair, and half wished he could take back the words he'd said in anger. But, damn it, if she didn't start investigating just who and what she was, all hell could break loose. Her psychic gifts were coming to the surface. Why that was happening now, when she was almost thirty, he didn't know. But Sethanon had feared the emergence of those gifts enough to place at least one guard on her, though, oddly enough, he seemed reluctant to physically harm her.

It made no sense. Nothing about her past made any sense.

But he had a bad feeling they'd better start finding some answers. Jack had warned them that a war was starting, a war in which Sethanon planned to subjugate the human race, as well as any nonhumans who sided with them.

And he had a feeling she was a key in what might happen. Why else would Sethanon be so interested in her? And if she *was* a key, then he sure as hell was going to keep forcing her to chase her past and the memories she'd lost. Because they could be very, very important for everyone's survival. So perhaps she was right. Perhaps he *was* no better than Jack.

Except that she'd liked Jack. The same sure as hell couldn't be said about *him*.

Which was a damn shame, because if she wasn't his partner, he surely would have been tempted to explore what might lie between them.

***

Sam leaned back in the chair and stretched. She'd been sitting at this console for close to ten hours and her butt felt numb. As numb as her mind.

She rubbed her forehead. The ache had set in behind her eyes again, and her stomach was beginning to cramp. Probably a result of all the coffee Gabriel had given her in the last few hours.

It was time to give her eyes another break. Sighing, she turned away from the console. His apartment wasn't what she'd expected. Given his long hours, and the time he spent working on Federation projects, she'd expected his apartment to be sterile—a place where he came to sleep and regain strength, and nothing more.

Situated in Parkville, opposite the grand old Royal Park, the two-story apartment block was a carefully renovated leftover from the Victorian era. Gabriel owned the top floor, and the view from the front windows was a sea of green. It was like living in the treetops, she mused, and wondered if that was why he'd bought it. Perhaps it appeased some need in his hawk soul.

The color scheme within the apartment complimented the leafy view, yet stood apart. Sandstone colored walls and faded turquoise doors and frames. Brightly patterned rugs scattered across the polished floorboards. Dark blue leather sofas that had seen better times. Oddly enough, there were no photos of Stephan—no photos of any family. Maybe it was a precautionary measure. Maybe he didn't want to risk anyone breaking in and discovering just who he was related to. Certainly that information wasn't available on any computer—she'd checked the SIU files some weeks back.

Gabriel himself used the com-unit in the kitchen. His long legs, crossed at the feet, were stretched out under the table. No doubt he'd wander back in soon to fill her with more coffee to keep her awake.

The com-unit pinged softly. The tape had finished rewinding. She turned around. "Fast forward to twelve-fifteen, then play."

The murderer must have arrived sometime between then and twelve-thirty. The doctor had patients booked up until twelve. Allowing the usual ten or fifteen minutes per patient, the last appointment would have walked out around twelve fifteen. The postman had walked in at twelve-eighteen, and the doctor had been alive and alone.

"Playing," the com-unit intoned.

She leaned sideways against the desk, propping her head

up with her hand. This was the fourth time she'd watched this particular run of film. She could just about cue each person.

Yawning hugely, she watched the postman, dressed in a yellow raincoat, carry a handful of letters and a small parcel into the doctor's office. On the far edge of the screen, a man in a badly cut blue suit headed towards the stairs. Nothing for a good five minutes, then the lunchtime rush began.

The yellow clad postman walked back out. She glanced at the clock. Twelve twenty-two. After that, nothing. People moved in and out of the foyer, but no one went near the doctor's office. The initial report set the time of death as twelve thirty-one. Nine minutes after the postman had left. Given the extent of the doctor's wounds, and the fact that she'd died reasonably quick, it was doubtful whether the postie could have been involved. Besides, there wasn't a speck of blood to be seen on his uniform.

"Rewind tape to twelve-twenty two."

The computer hummed briefly. "Tape rewound."

"Find ID on this man." She pointed to the postman. His details were probably in the initial report, but Gabriel had the folder and she didn't want to walk across to check.

"Search started."

She yawned again and glanced at her watch. It was nearly two o'clock. Surely Gabriel would let her go home soon and get some rest. Twelve hours had just about passed and she seriously needed sleep. Her brain felt like mush.

The tape continued running. She leaned on her hand again and watched it. People flowed through the foyer. A sandwich trolley came out of the elevator and was briefly mobbed by those few who didn't go out for lunch. She rubbed her forehead again, trying to ease the growing ache between her eyes. It didn't help.

"Gabriel, you got any pain killers?"

"Yep. Hang on, and I'll get you some."

The chair scuffed against the floorboards then his footsteps moved across the kitchen. She returned her gaze to the screen. And saw the doctor walk out of the office.

At twelve forty-eight.

Seventeen minutes after she'd been murdered.

Five

The killer was a multishifter, Sam thought, staring at the woman on the screen. The counterfeit doctor wore a knee-length white coat and carried a plastic bag in her right hand. She kept her head down, loose brown hair all but covering her face, and headed quickly for the stairs.

"Rewind tape one minute then freeze," she said, and glanced up as Gabriel walked into the room. "I think I've found your killer."

He handed her two painkillers and a glass of water, then leaned over the back of her chair and studied the image frozen on the com-screen.

"A shapeshifter."

"A multishifter," she corrected. "Not that it comes as much of a surprise. You said in your report you suspected a shifter was involved."

He squatted down beside her chair, face almost level with hers. "We suspected, but this is the first evidence we've found to confirm it."

She frowned. "You found nothing on any of the other tapes?"

"No." His breath washed warmth across her face. "No evidence of anyone going in. The only form of exit appears to be the small hole cut into the bathroom windows."

"But that makes no sense." If the killer was a multishifter, how the hell was she getting away from the crime scene, if not through any doors? A small hole cut in a window pointed towards a shapechanger, not a shifter.

He scrubbed a hand across the dark line of stubble on his chin. "Did anyone enter the office close to the time of the murder?"

"Postman, but he came out at twelve twenty-two. I've begun an ID search."

"Good. Have you checked the tapes for the seventh floor?"

"Not yet."

He looked at the screen. "Display tape seven. Fast forward to twelve forty-eight p.m."

The screen briefly went blank. Gabriel went against current trends, having no cartoon character as the face of his com-units. No time for fun, she thought, even for something as minor as this.

The seventh floor tape began to role. The counterfeit doctor came into sight, quickly disappearing into the ladies restroom. She was out four minutes later, hair wet, but tied back off her face, and still wearing the white coat. The elevator answered her call almost immediately. The doctor joined several other people already standing in the lift and was whisked away.

"Why keep the coat?" She met his gaze. "Why not dump it with the sweater?"

"Maybe she had nothing else to wear."

"But why not? This woman is meticulous. She gets in and out of crime scenes without being spotted—at least not until now. She knows there's security cam's watching and she knows how to get around them. Her timing with the doctor was perfect. So why wouldn't she pack a change of clothes?"

A smile touched his lips. "There's a limit to what you can hide when you shift form, you know."

She raised her eyebrows. "There is?"

He nodded. "Clothes don't change. Nor do watches, or shoes or bloodstained sweaters. The body image is all that shifts."

"But what about shapechangers? You grow feathers and talons, for Christ's sake. I've never seen you wearing size ten boots in your hawk form."

His smile widened, touching the corners of his eyes. "Nor will you. The rules vary for changers. No one knows why. It's just a fact that whatever we carry on our person becomes integrated within the animal persona."

"What if you were holding a bag of some sort?"

"Then that would be gripped in my talons when I changed."

"Weird." She frowned at the screen for a moment. "That still doesn't answer my original question."

"You suggested in the doctor's office that the killer was angry. Maybe she didn't bring a change of clothes simply because she thought she was in control—until confronted by the doctor wearing a white coat."

"So our killer has an unpleasant history with doctors, might be a doctor herself, and is definitely a multishifter." She met his gaze. This close, flecks of green gleamed in the warm hazel depths of his eyes. "How many multishifters has the SIU got on file?"

"Several hundred, at least."

"I thought you said multishifters were rare."

"They are, by comparison to the numbers of shifters."

"Yeah, right." What other half-truths had he fed her? "How many of those have twins?"

He shrugged. "Twins run in families—it's not a side effect of being a shifter."

"So the first thing we do is search the files and see how many multishifter twins we have on record."

The warmth fled from his face. "The first thing you do," he corrected softly. "After you get some sleep, that is."

He was locking her out again. Not that she was entirely surprised. He'd warned her of his intentions, after all.

"You can push as far as you like. I'm not quitting." Despite an effort to keep her voice flat, a hint of anger crept in.

"We shall see," he said softly. "Ready to go?" He rose to his feet and held out a hand.

She ignored it and rose. She brushed past him, tried to ignore the tingling warmth that resulted from such a brief contact, and walked over to the coffee table to collect her bag. "There's a cab rank down the street. I'll catch a ride there."

"It's two-thirty in the morning."

"And I'm a cop with a gun. I think I can manage to survive a three-minute walk in the dark."

"I have no problem with driving you home."

"But I have." She snorted softly, then added, "You can't play it both ways, Gabriel."

He raised an eyebrow. "I am merely offering you a ride home. Nothing more, nothing less."

"Yeah, right."

"Fine," he muttered, and made an oddly violent motion with his hand. "Go, then."

She walked out. And for the second time in twenty-four hours, slammed a door shut with wall-shaking force.

***

Gabriel grabbed his coat and viaphone, and then he set his apartment's alarm sensors as he walked out the door. Once he reached the street, he changed shape and soared into the night skies.

He had no doubt Sam could survive the three-minute walk to the cab rank. Under normal conditions, he'd back her to survive just about anything the streets could throw at her. But in the last twenty-four hours she'd been given an overdose of Jadrone and had had very little sleep. Her reflexes, strength, even alertness, would be down. If someone *did* actually want her taken out, it would be the perfect time.

He spotted her within minutes—an angry looking shadow striding towards the cab rank. He circled slowly while she climbed into the vehicle, and then he followed it through the quiet city streets.

She got home without incident. He waited until the lights went on in her apartment, then wheeled away and headed for his brother's place in Toorak.

A bleary-eyed Stephan opened the door as Gabriel walked up the steps.

"Do you know what time it is?" Stephan asked.

"Yeah. It's time for a drink." He stopped on the top step and regarded his twin steadily. The shadows under Stephan's eyes were darker than ever, but at least he no longer looked like death. "Why are you up?"

"Lyssa's been throwing up half the night."

Gabriel raised his eyebrows. "She's close to term—shouldn't the morning sickness by over by now?"

"Should be. And the term morning sickness is definitely a misnomer." He stepped aside. "Head into the study."

He walked through the marbled entrance hall. It was hard to believe that only three months ago this house had been little more than a crater in the ground. Every thing was the same, right down to the knickknacks that lined the bookcase shelves.

Stephan closed the study door and walked to the bar. "Whisky?"

"Double. No ice."

Stephan raised an eyebrow. "Trouble with the case?"

"No."

"Then what?"

He accepted his drink and swallowed half of it in one gulp. The liquid burned its way down his throat, hitting his stomach with the force of a hot brick. "I hate being a bastard."

Stephan sat on the sofa and crossed his legs. "We're talking about your treatment of Sam?"

He nodded.

"Then the solution is simple. Stop being one."

"The solution is simple, all right. You can transfer her to another section. Or another agent."

"I've all ready told you that's not going to happen."

He met his brother's gaze. Stephan smiled, though it never

touched his eyes.

"You work too well together, Gabriel. It's almost instinctive, the way you two interact, and that's extremely rare."

"My partners have a horrible tendency to die in the line of duty. I told you the last time it happened that I will not go through it again." He downed more whisky.

"If she is fated to die, it will happen, whether or not she's your partner."

He finished the whisky and shoved the glass down on the desk. Thrusting his hands into his pockets, unable to keep still, he began to pace.

"It damn well almost happened today."

Stephan frowned. "I read a report that mentioned her involvement in a disturbance at a nightclub. The owner's in intensive care." He hesitated. "Did she put him in there?"

"No. She went there to interview him, as he was apparently Harry Maxwell's regular Jadrone supplier."

Stephan's frown deepened. "Harry was human. Jadrone shouldn't affect him."

"Exactly what I said. But according to her, she was regularly picking up an overdosed Harry. The only reason he never ended up with a rap sheet was because Frank kept getting the charges dropped."

"But Frank's human, and I'm pretty sure his wife is, as well."

"And according to Sam's profile, she's also human, but she was given enough of the drug to kill an elephant changer, and it affected her the way it would affect any changer. The doctors who looked after her have no idea how she actually survived."

"The fact that she was given Jadrone suggests that whoever did the administering knew she was something other than human. And that begs the question, how?"

Gabriel paused, thinking back to what she'd said. "I think the answer to that is simple. According to Sam, she ordered the owner to tell his girlfriend to change to human shape. Yet the owner hadn't told her his girlfriend was amongst the other birds flying around."

"And usually, only changers that can sense other changers." Stephan paused. "But why she was given Jadrone rather than simply being left to die in the fire like the owner?"

"That I don't know, and I'm afraid she was too washed out by the Jadrone to really remember anything useful about the attack."

"But you'll question her when she's recovered?"

"Of course." He walked across to the window and stared at the moon-washed garden. "Something else happened today, though. Something that worries me."

"What?"

He hesitated and briefly wondered if he was doing the right thing coming here tonight, in talking about this with his twin. If nothing else, it would open old wounds between them.

"I was in Melton when the attack on Sam happened," he said, after a moment. "But I felt the blow to her head, the pain of the Jadrone burning through her body, as if it were happening to me."

"Well, well," Stephan murmured.

Well, well, indeed. The ability to link minds, to psychically share thoughts, or, in this case, emotions and pain, was very rare—a bond seldom found outside the domain of twins. But it was a connection he didn't want with Sam—or anyone else. Not even his twin.

"So we come to the real reason you're here tonight," Stephan continued softly. "You are being forced to face what you have denied for so long."

He turned and faced his brother. "Apparently so."

Stephan's expression held very little sympathy. But then, Gabriel wasn't expecting a whole lot from him. Not when it came to something like this—something that had caused a rift between them for years.

"I told you it would happen some day. You cannot keep denying one part of your soul forever—not without consequences."

"And you're saying this link with Sam is a consequence of denying my link with you?"

"I'm saying it's possible. You may have developed shields strong enough to keep me out, but I am far from the strongest telepath."

"This isn't telepathy. This is something else."

"Then perhaps it simply a rerouting of your talent."

"It's not. It's unlike anything I've ever experienced—"

"You've experienced nothing," Stephan said, voice sharp. "You closed yourself psychically when you were eighteen, and you haven't allowed that part of yourself to experience *anything*."

He turned away from the anger—the accusation—in

Stephan's expression. "And you know why."

"Denying what you are will not change the events of the past. It will not bring Angie back to life."

"Don't you think I realize that?"

"Then why do you cut yourself off? Why bury yourself in your work? Why give nothing of yourself to your friends or family?"

"You're a great one to talk about burying yourself in work. How often do you see Lyssa?"

"Not often enough, that's for certain." The anger in Stephan's voice was stronger. "But at least *I* have a wife and a child on the way. You have nothing."

"I have friends."

"And a family. Yet when it comes to your dreams and desires, you confide in neither."

Because he had no dreams. No desires. Only a wish to some day glide upon the wind and see where she might take him. "It's safer that way."

"Safer for who?"

Safer for everyone. Him included. "I didn't come here to dissect past decisions."

"You never do," Stephan retorted. "But you might want to start talking to someone. If Sam has breached your defenses, and somehow created a link that is strong enough for you to feel her pain, we need to know how. And why."

"That's part of the reason I'm here. I want the Federation labs to go through her test results and see what they can find."

"What do you hope the Federation labs can find that Finley didn't?"

"The origin of that unknown chromosome. Maybe even the reason why, at the age of nearly thirty, she's beginning to develop psychic abilities."

A human normally developed psychic skills during puberty, and she was well past that. That it *was* happening now suggested nonhuman origins—as did her reaction to the Jadrone. Most nonhumans were slower in development, and for changers and shifters, at least, puberty hit at about thirty. So why hadn't Finley's tests revealed a nonhuman link? Or did Finley's tests only look for the obvious? Maybe they needed to go deeper. Much deeper, and look for things like gene-splicing.

"Send the disk to Martyn—he'll take care of it."

"I'm also sending her to Doctor O'Hearn." O'Hearn was a

nonhuman and rare species specialist, and though she wasn't strictly in Federation's employ, she often worked closely with them. "I want Federation to pick up the cost."

"Are you intending to ask Sam to join Federation?"

"No. We can't afford to, not until we know more about her."

"Keeping her as a partner would be a sure-fire why of discovering more about her. Certainly better than trying to get rid of her."

"I'm not trying to get rid of her," he said, a note of frustration in his voice. "I never said I want her out of my life. I just don't want her as a partner."

"But you said it once yourself—Samantha's work is her life. Get rid of her as a partner, and you risk getting rid of her completely."

And if that happened, it would be a shame, because even from the beginning it had been obvious they had the potential to be a whole lot more than friends. But he would not go there with a partner, not again. He'd made that mistake when he was eighteen, and it had damn near torn his world apart.

The study door opened, and he turned around. Lyssa, looking pale and drawn, looked in.

"Gabriel," she said warmly. "How nice to see you."

He smiled. Ever the lady, even at three in the morning. "Liar. Hope we didn't wake you."

Her smile was as pale as her face. "No, I was upchucking my heart out and heard your voices. Everything okay?" She glanced at the two of them anxiously.

"Everything's fine, Lys." Gabriel glanced at his brother and saw the worry etched there. Knew then that Lyssa was in more trouble than Stephan was letting on. He wasn't the only one refusing to confide in his brother.

"Can I get you anything?" she continued softly.

"Yeah. Go back to bed and get some rest." He met his brother's gaze. "I can contact Karl later this morning, if you like. See what he recommends."

At the very least, he should have something to stop Lyssa's vomiting. If she lost any more weight, the child she carried would weigh more than she did.

"I'd appreciate that." Stephan rose from the sofa and placed his half-finished whisky on the table. "I'll see you out."

"I know the way by now. You take care of Lys."

Stephan gripped his shoulder, squeezing lightly. "See you

tomorrow, then."

Gabriel nodded and walked away. On the front steps, he stopped and looked up at the stars. He wasn't ready to go home, nor did he feel like going to the office. The breeze tugged at his hair, throwing dark wisps across his face. Sometimes the answer to a problem could only be found when the mind was free from the clutter of thoughts.

It was a good night to surf the breeze, to relax and just enjoy the freedom of the skies. Changing shape, he let the wind tuck under his wings and rose swiftly into the starlit sky.

***

Sam dreamed again of Joshua. This time, he ran ahead of her, up the moonlit slope, a phantom she could see but not hear. When he reached the crest, he flopped on the grass, staring up at the stars.

She lay beside him, puffing like an express train. Joshua breathed so softly she could barely even hear it.

"The Southern Cross," he said, pointing to a kite-shaped formation. "A symbol of freedom."

"Not our freedom," she muttered. Only at night were they free to roam, and only then when the moon was down.

"People died under that symbol. They will die again." He hesitated, and she felt his shrug. "Soon."

She stared at him. His face was remote, cold. She hated that face. Feared it. "What do you plan?"

"Revenge. Freedom for us both."

"They will never let us go."

He smiled, but there was nothing pleasant about that smile. Just as there was nothing pleasant behind the fire that sprang to life across his fingers. She knew *exactly* what that fire could do. "They will have no choice."

She shivered, then sat up and rubbed her arms. "I don't want anyone to die, Josh."

He didn't answer. She looked at him. A smile touched the corners of his lips. "You don't know what you want."

Yes, she did. A home. A mom and dad. Friends. A normal life. Everything she didn't have now.

"Dreams that can never be achieved. Not with what we are."

"And just what are we, Josh?"

She woke with a start, her heart racing even as the question seemed to reverberate through the semidarkness. For several seconds, she didn't move, simply stared up at the ceiling. Just

who the hell was this Joshua she kept dreaming of? Someone
close, of that she was certain. Maybe a brother or a friend.
Someone from the time she couldn't remember, the years
between her birth and her arrival at the state-run home.

But if these were true memories, and not some form of
subconscious yearning, why were they coming back now? What
had happened in the last few months to crack the wall that had
hid her past from any scrutiny?

As usual, she had no answers to her questions. Sighing
softly, she threw the bedcovers to one side and climbed out. It
was nearly eight-thirty. Time she got moving. Given Gabriel's
terseness last night, he'd probably put her on report if she was
late for work.

She grabbed a coffee, and then she got ready, barely catching
the nine-thirty tram into the CBD.

Her dim little hole certainly hadn't improved any in the
brief time she'd been away. She threw her bag across the back
of the chair and sat down.

"Computer on."

Izzy's image flicked to life. "Good morning, sweetness.
Have a good trip in?"

"Absolutely wonderful," she muttered. There was nothing
nicer than being wedged between a guy reeking of garlic and a
woman who tried to pick her up. "How'd the searches go?"

Izzy sighed dramatically. "Do you know how many people
have purchased *Heat* in the last month?"

"I don't really *want* to know."

"Two thousand four hundred and eighty."

She raised her eyebrows. Given the sales hype surrounding
the perfume, she'd expected the figure to be much higher. "Any
chance of cross referencing those people? I need to find a
doctor."

The purple boa swung into action. "You do like delving
into haystacks, looking for needles, don't you, sweetie?"

"Favorite pastime. Just do it."

"As long as time is something you have plenty of."

Right now, it was the *only* thing she had plenty of. "Got
another search for you, as well."

"Well, hallelujah!"

"I want you to search SIU records for multishifters with
twin sisters. And do a separate search for multishifting quacks
while you're at it. "

"By quacks, I presume you mean the medical profession?"

"You presume correctly."

"Human or animal?"

She raised her eyebrows. She hadn't thought of that—there was nothing to say a vet couldn't have the knowledge to cut up a human efficiently. "Both. And cross-reference the results against the *Heat* results; see if we come up with any similar names."

"Your wish is my command."

She snorted softly. Izzy's tone was anything but compliant. "You found any history on the four men in the photo?"

"I certainly have."

"Show photo and results on screen."

Izzy disappeared, replaced by the photo Sam had found in Frank Lyle's apartment. It came as no real surprise that the four men had been in the military and worked alongside Frank Lyle at Hopeworth. Hal White, the oldest of the four, had died a month before Lyle's murder. The other three were listed as retired. Their pensions were generous, even by military standards.

"Any details on Hal White's death?"

Izzy reappeared. "Checking police files."

If Izzy had gone directly to police files, Hal White's death was listed as something other than natural. While she waited for the results, she leaned back in her chair and massaged her temples. If this damn headache didn't go away soon, she might have to visit a doctor herself. Something she normally tried to avoid.

"Hal White's file remains open, sweetie. Cause of death unknown."

Interesting. Maybe it was fate that two of the five friends had been murdered within a month of each other. Then again, maybe it wasn't. "Grab a copy of the case report for me. And send the current addresses of the three remaining men to my viaphone."

"Proceeding. Anything else I can help you with?"

"Yeah, the results for the priority one search."

"Results being displayed."

There wasn't much to see. Of the four men listed on the birth certificate, only one—Mark Allars—was still alive. Interestingly, he lived only one block away from Roy Benson, one the three remaining men in the photograph. None of the women were still alive. All eight had worked at the illusive

Hopeworth.

She tapped a finger against her lips. "We have photos of any of these people?"

"Nothing available on file."

"What about their life before they joined the military?"

"Nothing available there, either, sweetie."

She raised her eyebrows. There should have been school and medical records, at the very least. "Why not?"

Izzy gave an exasperated sigh. "I'm a computer, not a mind reader. How would I know?"

"Have you tried requesting Hopeworth for details?"

"No. And I wouldn't back your chances of getting an answer if I did."

Neither would she, but she had nothing to lose by trying. "Put in a formal request for information on these eight, as well as the four men in the photograph."

"I'm requesting."

"Good." She pushed the chair back and rose. "If you happen to get any results back from the other searches, forward them to my viaphone."

"Consider it done, sweetie."

"And check out a car from the pool for me."

Izzy tapped a chicken-like foot for several moments. "Car nineteen on standby."

"Thanks Izzy."

"Have a nice day," Izzy said, before the screen went blank.

She snagged her bag off the back of the chair and headed down to the car pool. An attendant handed her the keys and a pass-out to sign. She scrawled her signature across the bottom, then threw her bag into the back of the car and climbed in.

After joining the late morning traffic, she cruised through the city streets, headed for Kensington. Roy Benson, like his three friends, lived in a suburb befitting the image of an independently wealthy retiree. Only Frank Lyle had made an attempt to hide his wealth—though not very successfully, given he had million dollar paintings all over his walls.

It took her twenty minutes to get to Kensington. She stopped under the shade of an old plane tree, then climbed out and studied the two-story building across the road. It wasn't, as she'd expected, a house, but rather a retirement home—and an expensive one at that, if the gold fittings on the front door were anything to go by.

She collected her bag, slammed the door closed and walked across the road. She'd barely reached the steps when heat flashed across her skin, a white-hot rush that exploded her senses outward.

A kite was close. So close his evil itched at her skin and turned her stomach.

Her gaze went upwards. The kite was on the roof somewhere, moving to the left. She'd have to find the stairs and get up there—the thought was cut off as glass shattered.

A second later, the screaming began.

Six

Gabriel glanced impatiently at his watch. John Hartwell, the postman who'd delivered the mail to the doctor thirteen minutes before she'd been murdered, should have been back from his rounds by now. Hopefully he was just late and not the victim of some careful after-the-event cleanup by the murderer.

He crossed his arms and leaned a shoulder against the wall. Around him, machines hummed, sorting through the mail, watched by disinterested men and women of various ages. No one talked—probably couldn't be bothered, given the noise and the fact they all wore ear protection. A lonely job, and not one he would have ever opted for. The lack of human interaction would have driven him crazy. Despite what his twin seemed to think, he wasn't a loner. Not by a long shot.

"Oi! Agent Stern!" He glanced around. A big man in a sweat-stained brown shirt pointed towards the back door. "Johnny just came in."

Gabriel waved his thanks and headed toward the back. John Hartwell was a weedy looking character with slick black hair and pockmarked skin.

"Heard you were looking for me," he said, opening a locker that had seen better times. "What can I do for you, Agent Stern?"

"Just a routine follow-up. You heard about Doctor Brandon being murdered yesterday?"

Hartwell nodded. Gabriel could almost see the grease flying off his hair.

"Yeah, shame that. She was a nice lady."

"When you delivered the mail yesterday, did you see or hear anything suspicious?"

"Nah. She was alone. The receptionist usually heads out for lunch after twelve, and the doc's generally handling the calls when I come in."

"No patients?"

"Not yesterday."

Gabriel shoved his hands on his hips. This was great. They finally get someone who was actually at the scene minutes before the murder, and he didn't see one damn thing wrong.

"What about the mail? Was there anything unusual?"

Hartwell pulled off his tie and threw it in the locker. "Hey, it was just mail. I never take much notice."

"What about the parcel?"

"Parcel?" A frown briefly creased his brows. "You know, *that* was strange."

"In what way?"

"I think it was live cargo. I mean, it's illegal to send live cargo through regular mail, but it happens, and it's not always picked up. Odd thing to send to a people doc, though."

Live cargo? The murderer had *posted* herself to her victim? Now *that* took balls. "You mean it was an animal of some sort?"

"Yeah. I could hear it scratching round. The poor thing didn't seem to have an air hole. It was a wonder it survived."

"Is there any way we could find out who sent the parcel?"

Hartwell shook his head again. "As I said, it was sent ordinary mail. Unless a signature is required, we have no way to trace it."

Great. Just great. "What did it look like then?"

"I dunno. Ordinary, I suppose. Brown paper wrapping, green and white string holding it together."

"How big?"

He shrugged. "Maybe six inches in diameter."

Big enough for a mouse or a rat. Even a small bird. "So the creature was definitely alive when you delivered it."

"Yeah, as I said, I could hear it scratching about."

"Did the doctor open the parcel while you were there?"

"Nah. We chatted for a while, 'bout the weather and stuff, and then I left. Simple as that."

And as simple as that, they were presented with another clue that didn't lead anywhere. Still, it might be worth checking to see if any of the other victims had a parcel delivered just before their murder.

"Well, thanks for the help. We'll be in contact if we need anything further."

Hartwell nodded. "No prob."

Gabriel headed back to his car. After punching in the code for auto drive, he set the course for SIU headquarters. Then he leaned an arm against the window, blindly watching the traffic slide by. The killer was a multishifter, that much was obvious. But maybe, just maybe, she was also a rare shifter-changer hybrid.

He scrubbed a hand across his jaw and then reached across to the onboard computer.

"Access sweep report for Emma Pierce."

"Identification required."

"Assistant Director Stern. Badge number 5019."

"Voice patterns correct. Report on-line."

Emma Piece had died of a massive heart attack. There was no evidence that the attack was anything but natural. Interestingly, the autopsy also showed that Emma had no ovaries. Tests indicated they'd been surgically removed somewhere between twenty-five and thirty years ago.

Which was when Emma was still a part of Hopeworth. Maybe the killer knew Emma. Maybe she knew the reasons behind the removal of Emma's ovaries. Maybe these killings were some form of revenge.

Though why attack four people who were barely a gleam in their mothers' eyes twenty-five years ago?

Unless, of course, their parents were somehow connected to Hopeworth and what had been done to Emma Pierce. Though that didn't make much sense, given that with the first two victims, at least, Emma Pierce was listed as their birth mother.

He read through the rest of the sweep report. Cell and DNA samples taken from clothes and other personal items in the second bedroom indicated the boarder was closely related to Emma. Probably a sister or mother.

Only Emma reportedly was an only child. Both her parents died in a car crash when she was three months old.

Again, that didn't make sense.

But he knew someone who just might be able to shed a little light on the confusion. Mark Allars. A childhood friend of his father's, and a man who'd spent thirty-five years working at Hopeworth.

He was also one of the four men listed on Sam's birth certificate—and undoubtedly, she'd be furious that *he* hadn't mentioned knowing the man behind one of the names. But, damn it, the old adage of leading a horse to water was correct. He could push all he wanted, could lead her to names, but in the end, it wouldn't matter unless she *truly* wanted to uncover her past.

That said, it might be interesting to see the old man's reaction to Sam.

He reset the auto control for Kensington, then got out the viaphone and dialed Sam's number.

* * *

The screams were coming from the first floor. Sam flashed

her ID at security and ran for the stairs, taking the steps two at a time. By the time she reached the first floor, all the nursing home's residents seemed to be milling in the corridor. Many more screams had joined the first, and the sound was almost deafening.

"SIU, folks. Please clear the area." She had to shout to be heard above the din being made, and even then, it did no good. Everyone ignored her. Perhaps they had their hearing aids turned down to cut out all the noise.

She pushed her way through until she reached the room at the far end of the corridor. Inside, the kite had sheeted its victim. Two nurses were gamely attacking the creature with brooms, alternatively sobbing and screaming for help.

"SIU. Ladies, step away!"

The two women looked up, relief etched across their faces when they spotted her. When both stepped away, she fired the stun laser at the creature's head. It looked up and snarled.

She kept firing. The creature rose, shaking its head as it backed toward the window. Then it turned and jumped out. She ran over. The creature was fleeing for the nearest tree, white flesh billowing in the breeze.

There was a fire escape to the left of the window. She clambered out and hesitated, glancing back. The nurses, their faces still white, were beginning respiration on the victim. Given the bloody condition of his face and chest, she didn't give them much hope, but at least they were trying, no matter how gruesome the task was.

"I'll call an ambulance," she said.

One nurse nodded. Sam rose. As she ran down the rusting metal stairs, her viaphone vibrated against her side. She pulled it out and hit the answer button.

"What?" She jumped past the remaining five steps and hit the ground running. The kite had taken to the treetops, jumping from one to the other like some great white bat.

"What wrong?" Gabriel's voice, instantly on edge.

She inwardly groaned. The man definitely had a knack for catching her at the wrong moment. "A kite just attacked one of the four men in the photograph I took from Lyle's."

"Where is it now?"

"Heading west up Racecourse Road"

"Where are you?" His voice had a resigned note. He obviously had a pretty good idea where she was.

"Right on its tail, figuratively speaking."

"I see you now."

He did? Why the hell was he in Kensington? A gray ford slewed to a stop beside her and the door flung open.

"Get in," he ordered.

She did. After securing her seat belt, she leaned forward and watched the kite jump across the treetops. "It appears to be heading for the race course."

"Probably has some type of escape route there."

"I thought you said these things were brainless."

"Brainless, but programmable. More programmable than we'd thought, obviously."

"Are you admitting the SIU doesn't know everything?" she said, slipping a note of shock into her voice.

His quick glance suggested he was not amused. She grinned and continued to watch the kite. If any of the pedestrians noticed the monster above their heads, they gave little indication. Nor did the passing traffic. Maybe monsters had become such an everyday event, or maybe they simply thought it was a sheet tumbling along in the breeze.

The creature leapt over the race course ground's fence and disappeared from sight. Gabriel swore, then spun the wheel and aimed the car straight at the nearby gates.

"Hang on," he said, almost as an afterthought.

The engine roared as the car accelerated. As the gates loomed close, she closed her eyes, braced her feet, and hung on grimly to the seat belt. The car slammed through the gates, the impact smashing the front of the car and throwing her forward, then back, as the air bags popped.

He swore as the car skidded sideways and came to a jarring halt. "Can you still see it?"

She couldn't see a damn thing above the white balloon of the air bag. She opened the door and climbed out. The kite was running through the trees, its white body dappled with shadows.

"I see it."

"Good. Catch."

She looked around in time to see him toss a laser rifle her way, and then he slammed the trunk shut.

"Aim for its neck," he said. "Cutting its head off is the only way to kill it."

Just like a vampire, she thought bleakly. Maybe they *were* some sort of vampire family offshoot.

They tracked the kite through the parking lot. The creature was running on all fours, and it was amazingly fast. She ran flat out, but she could barely keep up with Gabriel, let alone the creature.

"Listen," he said. "Can you hear that?"

Who could hear anything past her labored breathing and pounding footsteps?

She frowned, concentrating, and after a few seconds, caught it—the soft whump, whump of rotor blades. A helicopter, approaching fast. "Sounds like someone's coming to collect their pet."

"Maybe we should let them, then."

"Thought SIU policy was to kill on sight?"

"It is. But these things keep appearing. I think it's about time we learned from where."

The kite stopped and stared skyward. Gabriel halted behind the cover of several old elms. She stopped beside him and tried to catch her breath. So much for thinking she was fit. Maybe she'd better start heading back to the gym.

The helicopter came into sight—a long red and silver bird that gleamed in the afternoon sunlight. She shaded her eyes and stared up at it. Was that some sort of canon hanging out the side of the helicopter...

"Fuck, they're going to shoot it." Fear burned through Gabriel's voice. He flung an arm round her waist and pushed her to the ground, holding her tight as he covered her body with his.

Behind them, hell exploded. Asphalt and dirt fired into the air, and then a wave of heat burned over them, thick with the smell of burned flesh. She threw her arms over her head and cowered under the protection of Gabriel's warm body. Another bomb exploded, closer this time. Huge clumps of black asphalt rained around them. Gabriel's shudder ran right though her, then she gasped as a sharp twist of pain ran along her calf.

Then nothing. For several long minutes, they simply lay there. The sound of the helicopter faded into the distance. All she could hear was the crackle of flames as they licked through the trees behind them, and the thunder of her heart, beating in rapid time with Gabriel's.

"You okay," he whispered, his breath tickling warmth past her ear.

"Think so. You?"

"A rock has torn a hole in my jacket, but other than that, I'm fine."

She smiled. He sounded more aggrieved about the jacket than he did the fact he was probably cut as well. He rolled to one side, allowing her to sit up. Obviously, beheading wasn't the only way to kill a kite. Blowing the shit out of them worked fairly well, too. Two gaping wounds now marred the parking lot, one where the kite had stood, and the other just before their row of trees. The old elms had no doubt saved their lives.

Gabriel got his viaphone from his pocket, and called in the fire brigade and an SIU cleanup team. When he'd finished, she motioned towards the craters.

"Someone didn't want to risk anyone following their pet."

He nodded. "They must have been watching with binoculars. Interesting that they chose to blow up the kite, rather than us. They must have an abundant supply of them."

"Now, that's an ominous thought."

He rose and held out a hand. She let him pull her to her feet, her fingers almost lost within the heat of his.

"So, what happens now?" She gave his hand a light squeeze and then pulled hers away.

"Normally, we'd go back to headquarters and fill in the required mountain of paperwork."

She raised an eyebrow. "I sense a but coming here."

"I think it's more important right now that we go visit old uncle Mark."

She frowned? "Who's Uncle Mark?"

"Mark Allars."

Anger rose, and she had to clench a fist against the sudden urge to whack him across the ear. "You know him?"

His gaze, when it met hers, held absolutely no expression. She might well have been staring at hazel granite. "He's an old friend of my father's."

"And you kept that from me? Knowing Allars was one of the names on my birth certificate?"

"You told me not to push you."

"But I didn't tell you to hold back vital information!" She stopped, and shook her head. "My future lies in my past. You said that yourself. You keep saying you want me to discover who and what I am, yet you hold back something like this, something that could provide a vital clue. Why?"

"Because if you were ready to know, you would have done

something. How long did that certificate sit in the drawer before you gathered the courage to even do a search on the names?"

"You tell me. You obviously went through my drawers to find it."

His gaze slipped from hers. "I was looking for a pen to write you a note."

A note she never got. "Why? Email go down that day?"

He shoved his hands in his pockets and turned away. The left shoulders of his jacket and shirt were torn, revealing several cuts. Blood oozed down his lightly tanned shoulder blade.

"Maybe," he said, after a moment, "I just wanted to say hello in person."

"More likely berate me for not finishing some inane task you'd set me." She glanced over her shoulder as the wailing sirens drew abruptly close. Two fire engines had entered the parking lot. Behind the trucks came several gray Fords.

"I'm not always a bastard, Sam."

No, sometimes he could be infuriatingly nice; other times just infuriating. Then there were the times when he just looked at her, as if contemplating a fantasy he would never allow.

The two Fords pulled to a halt in front of the strand of trees. Three men and a woman climbed out. Gabriel walked across and chatted to them for several minutes, then came back, carrying two plastic bags.

"Here's a pair of pants to change into." He tossed her a bag. "I want that leg seen to before you do, though. You're bleeding fairly heavily."

She glanced down. Her right boot was covered in blood, yet she hadn't even felt any pain. It was amazing what fear and anger could do. "Whose clothes are we borrowing?"

"No one's. I asked Sandy to pick us up something."

"Sandy being the blonde, I gather?"

"Yes."

"So how does she knows my size?" She didn't bother asking how Sandy knew *his* size. That was patently obvious.

"I told her you're roughly the same size as her." His voice was as cold as the look in his hazel eyes. "She's got a medikit in the car. Get over there and let her look at that wound."

"Immediately, sir," she said, and saluted him.

His gaze narrowed, and he muttered something she couldn't quite catch before turning away. Good, she thought. It was about time she started getting some of her own back. She walked over to the second car. Sandy was your average model type—leggy, a figure to die for, and sapphire-colored eyes. Stunning, in other words, though the term *bitch* also lingered in Sam's thoughts.

"Agent Ryan," Sandy greeted, a warm smile touching her full red lips. "You'd best sit down while I tend to that wound. You're loosing a fair amount of blood there."

Sam felt her hackles rising and couldn't understand why. The woman was being nice, for Christ's sake. Maybe *that* was the problem. It was something she wasn't entirely used to, especially given her partner's behavior of late.

She sat on the back seat and pulled up her pants leg. "I'll survive."

Another white smile flashed, revealing teeth that were as perfect as the rest of her. Sandy knelt, medikit in hand. "Yeah, I suppose you're used to it, being Gabe's partner."

Gabe. Not Stern, not even Gabriel. Gabe. "You two are friends, I gather."

"Old friends," Sandy agreed, without looking up.

No dark roots, she thought. Either the dyeing techniques had improved dramatically, or the woman was a natural blond. "You still go out?"

"Occasionally. When we've both got free time."

Which confirmed what she'd thought earlier. And shot to hell the opinion she'd had that Gabriel was little more than a hermit who lived for work. "That's nice."

"It usually is," she agreed, glancing up.

The look in her blue eyes left Sam in no doubt that she was referring to horizontal rather than vertical pursuits. And somewhere deep inside, a vague spark of jealously stirred. This woman saw a side of Gabriel she probably never would. But it was a side she *wanted* to see, and with a fierceness that was totally surprising.

Of course, to have a chance of seeing *that* side, she'd either have to stop being his partner, or stop constantly sniping at him. She wasn't sure which was the lesser of two evils.

"You can change in the car, if you like. I'll make sure the men don't bother you."

Like that was going to worry her, especially after ten years of sharing locker rooms with the men in State. But she nodded and swung her legs into the car. Sandy picked up the medikit and shut the door, then minced across to the fire trucks to join Gabriel and the three other agents.

The pants turned out to be a pair of black denim jeans that fit like a glove. She wondered how Gabriel had guessed her size so precisely, because she and Sandy definitely weren't the same size. He'd certainly never got into *her* pants, and waist size wasn't something she'd felt inclined to mention. She threw her dark gray slacks into the bag, then climbed out of the car.

Sandy had finished tending to Gabriel's wounds, and she was currently standing shoulder to shoulder with the man. They made a good-looking couple, she thought, and resolutely stomped on the desire to run over there and wedge them apart.

Instead, she leaned against the trunk of the car, crossed her legs to take the weight of her injured calf, and waited. He finally walked over about ten minutes later, but not before giving Sandy a nice little kiss on the forehead.

God, anyone would think the man meant more to her than just an attraction that was never going to happen.

"Ready to go?" he said, stopping several feet away and regarding her somewhat warily.

She waved a hand. "After you."

He didn't move. "Sandy's just a friend."

"Look, it's really none of my business, is it? Let's just go."

He regarded her for a moment, then nodded. "We're taking Sandy's car. Mine's probably too bent to drive."

Just like its driver. The retort tingled on the tip of her tongue, itching for release. But if she annoyed him too much, he was likely to give her some inane task and send her hiking back to headquarters. She climbed into the front seat and slammed the door instead. Slamming doors was undoubtedly childish, but right then, she was feeling particularly childish.

He started the car and headed back to Kensington. A third gray ford sat outside Roy Benson's retirement home—obviously, Gabriel had called in a cleanup team to tend to the second kite attack. She wondered why. Surely it was a task he would normally have forced her to handle, especially given it might be connected to Lyle's murder.

He drove on. Mark Allars lived a block away from the retirement home in a single fronted Victorian-style house that was probably worth a fortune, despite its rundown appearance. She studied the building as she climbed out of the car. The small front yard was filled with gate high weeds, and the window to the right of the door was boarded up with wood. It looked abandoned—until you looked up and saw the state-of-the-art satellite dishes sitting on the roof.

The gate creaked when Gabriel opened it. She limped through and knocked on the door.

"Who the hell is it?" a rough voice demanded.

She raised her eyebrows and glanced at Gabriel.

"He's your average, cranky old recluse," he said, then raised his voice slightly. "It's Gabriel Stern. Charles's son."

Footsteps shuffled towards the door. Seconds later it was flung open. An old man stood before them, wearing blue pajama bottoms and a battered, smoke-stained sweatshirt. His feet were bare, toenails yellow and a good inch longer than his toes.

He leaned forward, peering at Gabriel with red ringed, weepy eyes. "So it is. Fancy that."

His gaze turned to her and recognition flickered through the rheumy eyes. He stiffened, his knuckles white as he clenched the door.

"You," he breathed softly. "You're dead. They said you were dead."

Seven

Sam glanced briefly at Gabriel, then back to Allars. "I have to say, I don't feel dead."

The old man blinked, and then he smiled. "You don't look it, either." His red-rimmed gaze went back to Gabriel. "What game you playing here, son?"

"Mark, this is my partner, Sam Ryan."

Allars studied her for a moment. "No relation to Meg Moore, then?"

Hope leapt. Meg Moore was one of the four women listed on the birth certificate. "I might be. I'm not really sure."

"Interesting. You look the spitting image of her." He hesitated and leaned close. His breath was a lethal combination of whisky and salami. "Except for the eyes. Meg had real pretty green eyes."

Gabriel touched the old man's arm, drawing his attention away. She took a deep breath of fresh air.

"Mark, do you mind if we come in?" he asked. "We have a few things we need to discuss with you."

"Sure thing, son. Just don't mind the mess." He stepped back and opened the door wide. "First door on your right."

She limped in after Gabriel. The air in the old house was a combination of staleness, sweat, and "old person." Dust lay thick on the skirting boards and telephone table, and in the hallway, spiders hung in ropes from the ceiling. The old man obviously spent most of his time in the living room, because the dust and webs were absent there. Newspapers and betting slips were scattered all over the coffee table and small sofa. A TV dominated one corner, and a comfy old recliner sat several feet back from it, one arm lined with remotes.

Gabriel swept the newspapers laying across the sofa into a pile, and then he stacked them in one corner. She sat down in the cleared space. He sat next to her, his thigh brushing hers, sending little tingles of electricity up her spine. She ignored it, though part of her wanted to confront it—confront him—about the awareness, and what could be happening between them. If he ever let it.

Damn it, what was so wrong with her that he didn't want her as a partner and wouldn't consider her as a potential lover?

Allars shuffled across to the recliner. "Now, what can I help you with, son?"

"Emma Pierce. You recognize that name?"

"Sure thing. She worked at Hopeworth, same as Meg and me."

"What on?"

Allars' smile slightly. "Secrets act, son. Even now, I can't talk about it."

"Can you remember who else you were working with at the time?" she asked quietly.

"It's just the body that's gotten old, girlie, not the mind." He hesitated, rheumy eyes distant. "Let's see—in my project there was Meg, Mike Shean, David Wright, Jeremy Park, Alice Armstrong, Rae Messner, and Fay Reilly."

She crossed her legs, not just to ease the ache in her calf, but to keep in check the sudden rush of excitement. Those names were all on the birth certificate. Finally, she'd found someone who might know *something*.

"And Emma?" Gabriel asked.

Allars shook his head. "No. She was several years younger than us. Completely different project."

"Different how?" Gabriel's voice held a touch of impatience. "And don't quote me the secret's rubbish, Mark. You haven't worked at Hopeworth for a good twenty years, and the project's probably obsolete by now."

Allars' smile was jovial, but there was something almost cunning in his eyes. "You'd be surprised."

"Mark, four people have been murdered in the last week. The only connection we have between any of them is Emma Pierce and Hopeworth. We have to find out what Emma was involved in. It may provide our only real hope of finding the murderer."

Allars' gaze was assessing. "Why don't you put in a request to Hopeworth itself?"

"I have," she said, and Gabriel gave her a brief look of surprise. Why, she had no idea, when it was a logical next step. "But you and I both know I'll only get the runaround. We need to catch this woman before she kills again, and we need you to help us."

"I like you, girlie. You've got guts."

She raised an eyebrow. "Does that mean you intend to help us?"

"Not sure that I can." He shifted slightly, bumping one of

the remotes onto the floor. "But what's in it for me if I do?"

"Maybe your life."

Allars' rheumy gaze met hers. In it, she saw a shrewdness that spoke of sharp intelligence. The aging body was definitely no indication of the mind trapped within.

"Now what makes you say that?"

"Do the names Hal White, Frank Lyle and Roy Benson mean anything to you?"

"Yeah. Benson lives a block away."

"Lived," Gabriel corrected bluntly. "He was murdered about an hour ago."

The old man raised an eyebrow. "And you're thinking I might be next?"

"We don't know, Mark. Nor do we know if the murder of White, Lyle and Benson is related in any way to our serial killings."

"But they could be?"

"Maybe."

The old man sighed. "Lyle, White and Benson were three of the eighteen scientists involved in our project."

"What about Cooper and Haynes?"

Allars nodded. "Them, too."

So did that mean someone was going after people who worked at Hopeworth? And how did the murder of Emma Pierce and the scientists link to the serial killings? Because she was sure they were linked. It was just too much of a coincidence for both these killing to be happening at the same time.

She leaned on the arm of the sofa, and covertly massaged her temple. Her damn headache had sprung into high gear again. Maybe it was working in sympathy with her calf, which had at least died down to a muted ache. "What project were they working on?"

"In truth, I can't really say. It was real hush-hush. All I know is that it went by the code name Penumbra."

Penumbra? Where in hell did the military get these names? "How were you involved?"

Allars smiled. "I was a specimen, much the same as the others. Took cell samples, semen samples, stuff like that."

If Hopeworth was taking cell and semen samples, they were obviously delving into the genetic side of human anatomy. "For what reason? Isn't Hopeworth a weapons development center?"

"Yeah, they are. But there's all kinds of weapons, girlie."

Meaning Hopeworth was developing human—or rather, nonhuman—weapons? Wasn't that a fantastic thought?

Gabriel rubbed a hand across his chin, his expression thoughtful. "Were the other seven people involved in your project shifters as well?"

"No. I was the only shifter. David was a changer; Meg a werewolf ; and Alice a vampire. Not real sure about the other four. Didn't really have a lot to do with them."

Or didn't really want to talk about them, for whatever reason. She tried a different tack. "What about the other scientists on the project? You said there were eighteen in all."

"They died some fifteen years ago. A massive fire took out half of Hopeworth. It destroyed our project and half a dozen others."

She remembered her dreams, remembered the fire that had danced across Joshua's fingers, and a chill ran down her spine. Were the two connected? Was she—they—Hopeworth brats?

"Why was the fire so extensive? And surely they had backups of everything?"

"That's the thing no one can figure out. There was plenty of fire prevention in place, but none of it worked. Everything was destroyed. The buildings, the computers, every scrap of data on Penumbra—backup systems, storage areas, everything—including the personnel who were in the buildings at the time. Nothing escaped."

"Nothing except five men." If the motive was revenge, why leave five alive? She glanced at Gabriel. "Maybe someone's making amends for a past miss."

"But why wait fifteen years? It makes no sense."

"That it doesn't, lad. Especially when whoever set fire to Hopeworth managed to get in and out without ever being seen. If they could do that, they could finish it off properly."

"Could it have been an inside job?"

"Doubtful. Everyone in Hopeworth is microchipped. Every move is tracked."

Someone had microchipped her. Was that confirmation that she'd been a part of Hopeworth?

"Were there many families at Hopeworth?" Gabriel asked, obviously following her line of thinking.

Allars snorted. "Hopeworth is no place for kids, believe me."

"Then why do they employ a gynecologist?"

The old man shrugged. "The military has many strange ways."

"What about you, Mark?" she asked. "Did you ever have kids?"

Allars smile held more than a little bitterness. "Couldn't. Some of the tests they did on us back then made us sterile. They compensated us, of course, but I know the women, Meg in particular, were real resentful."

There was an edge in his voice that made her ask, "Just how well did you and Meg know each other?"

The old man shrugged, yet the sudden grief in his eyes belied his casualness. "We might have gotten married, if we hadn't been in the military. Marriages between personnel weren't allowed."

"Still aren't, in some sections, from what I hear," Gabriel commented.

Allars nodded. "As I said, the military has strange ways."

"What about Emma Pierce, then? Where does she fit into all this?"

"Emma was a friend of Meg's. Came to Hopeworth about three years after us."

"What sort of project was she involved in?"

He shrugged and dug a handkerchief out of his pajama pocket to wipe his watery eyes. "We didn't really share info. It was code-named Generation Eighteen, and I know everyone involved was either a shifter or a changer."

"Did they take cell samples from Emma, as well?"

Allars snorted. "Took a damn sight more than cells. They took her damn ovaries."

She blinked. "They *what?*"

"Yeah, real nice of them, wasn't it? Emma wasn't aware of it until much later, of course. At the time, all the women were on medication to prevent ovulation, anyway."

"But how could you not know you'd undergone major surgery like that? Surely there would have been a scar, at the very least.

"They were cutting into her, and the others, all the time. Taking little sample of skin, pieces of this, pieces of that. It was part of the job. Emma had volunteered to be a specimen, like me and Meg. The pay and living conditions were top rate, even for Hopeworth. But so were the costs, as we later discovered."

"What price did you pay, Mark?" Gabriel's voice was soft

and held a hint of compassion. "Besides losing Meg, I mean?"

"I'm seventy-eight years old, and look at me. Shifters have a life span almost double that of humans, and here I am, ready for the scrap heap. But I'm luckier than some. Many developed cancers. Meg—" Allars hesitated, his gaze drifting to the photo of a gray-haired woman sitting on the top of the TV. Sam could see nothing of herself in that photo, despite Allars earlier statement that she was the spitting image of her. "Meg developed skin lesions all over her. It wasn't pretty and it wasn't quick." He hesitated, and wiped his eyes again. "I never saw her die, you know. The military came and took her away from me."

"What about Emma," she asked softly, and rubbed her aching head again.

"She had a rare muscle cancer." Allars shrugged and swiped at his eyes again. "Ate away at her until she couldn't walk, could barely even move."

Gabriel drew a small container out of his pocket and pressed it into her hand. Painkillers, she saw with surprise. So much for covertly rubbing her forehead. "Thanks," she murmured.

He nodded, his gaze meeting hers briefly before returning to Allars. "So who looked after Emma when she lived at Melton?"

"Her sister, of course."

"Emma Pierce was an only child."

Allars snorted. "The only child who survived the accident, but definitely not the only child. Rose had heart trouble and was in the hospital at the time. The family was on their way to see her when the accident happened. Both became wards of the state and were adopted separately. The two sisters never caught up with each other until Emma was at Hopeworth, and by that time, it was a secret that could not be revealed. Em would have been thrown out had they known she had relatives."

She frowned at him. "Why would having relatives make any difference?"

"Hopeworth policy. I guess they wanted to make sure no one could sue them if the tests went wrong." A shudder ran through Allars' slight frame. "Which they did, quite often."

"Can you tell us anything about the sister?"

Allars frowned. "Not really. She was the spitting image of Em, that's for sure. Looked about the same age, too. I only met her the once."

"Don't suppose you have any idea of her adopted name, or

where she lived?"

Allars shook his head.

Gabriel swore softly. "And you really can't tell us anything else about the project Emma was on?"

"As I said, we didn't dare talk about what we were involved in. But why don't you go have a chat with Haynes or Cooper, if either of them is still alive?"

"Were they involved with Emma?" she asked.

"Those two, as well as White, Benson and Lyle, were the men in charge of Generation Eighteen."

"Then we'd better get to them before our murderer does," Gabriel said, and got his viaphone out.

She studied Allars for a moment. The old man was staring at the photo again. He had the look of a man who'd seen more than enough of one lifetime. The look of a man who waited for death.

Then she frowned, remembering what he'd said earlier. "You said the military took her away. Do you know why?"

He shrugged and wiped his eyes again. "Precautionary measure. They said the lesions could be contagious."

"But how did they know about them? Did either you or Meg tell them?"

He studied her for a long moment, his rheumy gaze intense. "No. We didn't."

And yet the military had known. Either the house was wired, or Meg and Allars had been. She was betting on the latter. "Would you mind standing up for a moment?"

The old man considered her request, then nodded and slowly climbed to his feet. She rose, and lifted his grimy sweatshirt.

"What you looking for, girlie?"

She raised a finger to her lips. His gaze narrowed slightly, but he nodded. Maybe it was a stupid precaution, especially after all they'd asked, but right now, it was better safe than sorry. Besides, Allars was the one who'd said all military personnel were microchipped—and if they were chipping employees, why not ex-employees involved in important projects?

"I'm looking for something to squash that great big spider about to run up the arm of your chair," she said, just in case there *were* listeners.

She carefully pinched the skin along his left side, working her way up towards the armpit. His flesh hung loosely from his skeletal frame, indicating he'd lost a lot of weight recently.

Perhaps premature aging wasn't the only complaint he had.

Then she found it—something round and hard just under the skin near his armpit. She glanced at Gabriel.

"What?" he said, putting the viaphone away.

"Want to pass me one of those newspapers? The ones here are to flimsy to squash that spider with."

He raised an eyebrow, but did as she bid before approaching Allars. She showed him the lump and then removed her fingers.

Gabriel pressed the old man's flesh. "Quite ugly, isn't it?"

"Nasty," she replied. She grabbed the rolled up paper and thumped the arm of the chair with it. Remotes jumped and rolled off onto the floor.

"Hey, watch them things," Allars said. "They're expensive to replace."

She glanced at him. "Missed it. You got anything in the kitchen we could use?"

His gaze met hers, his expression shrewd. He knew she wasn't talking about fly spray. "Yeah, in the cupboards, under the sink."

She left the room and went in search of the kitchen. It was at the far end of the house. Dirty dishes lay in the sink, but otherwise, the kitchen was relatively clean. She found a sharp knife and then grabbed a pot. After putting the knife into the pot, she filled the pot with hot water. Lighting the stove, she leaned a hip against the sink and waited for the water to boil and clean the knife.

Crossing her arms, she stared out the window. The old man's property was on a slight slope, and from the kitchen you could see the traffic on the nearby road.

Though it was early afternoon, a steady stream of cars rolled past. The constant, droning hum would have driven her mad had she lived here. But perhaps the old man liked it—liked the reminder he wasn't entirely alone in this world.

When the knife was sterilized, she hunted around for some antiseptic and a Band-Aid, and then she headed back to the living room. It barely took a minute to remove the chip from the old man's armpit. The cut wasn't very deep—like hers, it had been planted close to the surface. She patted away the blood, dabbed on some antiseptic and stuck a Band-Aid across it.

Gabriel dropped the knife back into the pot of water and held the microchip up to the light. It was bigger than the one they'd found in her, though—about the size of a small pea. He got out his viaphone, scanned its image, then dropped the bug to the floor and crushed it under his heel.

"You mean them bastards have been listening to me all these years?" Allars said immediately.

"I'd say so," Gabriel said. "How else would they have found out about Meg?"

"Bastards." The old man squinted at the circuitry remains on the floor. "But why would they bother doing something like that? I retired, for Christ's sake. Why would they want to keep track of me?"

"Maybe they were worried that some aspects of the tests they performed would have ill effects later in life." Gabriel got a small bag from his pocket, then knelt and swept the remaining bits and pieces into the bag. "Of course, destroying the chip will warn them something is wrong."

"That's how they knew about Meg," Allars murmured.

"And maybe even Emma," she suggested. Though why would they take Meg from Allars care and simply leave Emma to die? She glanced at Gabriel. "Did you find a chip in Emma?"

"Not something we normally look for," he said. "I'll get them to check."

She nodded, picked up the knife and water and headed back to the kitchen. On the road below, a green army truck slowly cruised past.

Her heart leapt. It couldn't be a coincidence, nor could it be a reaction to the microchip being destroyed. The military were fast, but they weren't *that* fast. Either they'd been intending to pick up Allars anyway, or they'd swung into action the minute she and Gabriel began questioning him. And that might mean the old man knew more than he was currently telling.

She waited, watching the traffic roll by. Eight minutes later, the truck did another drive by. She walked back to the living room and went over to the window. Through the grim-darkened lace, she could see a military green Ford parked in the shade of a tree two houses down.

"We have company." She stepped back, out of sight. "One out front, and one out back."

"Damn, they moved fast." Gabriel looked at the old man. "Do you want to go with them or not?"

Allars snorted. "I've spent half my life with them, lad. I don't want to spend what's left with them."

"Then you come with us." He dug the keys out of his pocket

and dropped them into her hand. "Take the car around to the back street and meet us there."

"There's a truck around the back, cruising past every eight minutes."

"Wait for the next pass, and then give me a call."

She nodded, grabbed her bag and headed for the door. Not looking at the Ford down the street, she climbed into the car and started it up. The green Ford didn't follow as she moved off. They wanted Allars, obviously.

She turned left and stopped in the shadows of a gum. Four and a half minutes later, the truck rolled past the far end of the street.

She quickly dialed Gabriel's number. "Truck's just gone past. Moving into position now."

"On my way."

She turned onto the main street and cruised down to Allars' back fence. A minute dragged by, then the fence rocked and several palings were torn away. Allars squeezed through the gap, followed quickly by Gabriel. He helped the old man into the back seat, and then he climbed into the front.

"Where to?" She turned the car around to avoid running into the truck on its next drive past.

"We get away from this area as fast as we can. Then you take Mark to a safe house, and I go get Haynes and Cooper."

She glanced at him. "I thought you put a watch team on them?"

"I requested one. Doubt if it's there yet."

And Gabriel could fly there faster than any car could drive. She put her foot down, and sped away from the area. If they wanted answers, they had to get to Haynes and Cooper. And she had a bad feeling time was running out.

***

Gabriel glanced skyward as he climbed out of the car. The wind was freshening, and the clouds hung low. Hopefully, the impending rain would hold off until he got to Haynes. He hated flying in foul weather.

"Contact me when you get there," she said.

Gabriel bent and met her gaze. "When Mark's safe, I want you to go back to headquarters and go through the search results. There has to be some link between the murders other than Emma and Hopeworth."

"Will do," she said. Though her voice was tightly controlled, he could feel her annoyance at being given another desk job. But this time, he wasn't doing it in a deliberate effort to get rid of her. The simple fact was, she couldn't fly and he could. Had it been the other way around, he would have gladly let her go. Dealing with cranky old men was not his favorite pastime.

He closed the door, and she sped off, tires squealing. He shook his head and called the SIU, ordering the team meant to protect Cooper to pick him up and bring him back to headquarters. Then he asked for a location on Haynes' team. They were apparently caught in traffic and could be up to half an hour away. After hanging up, he shifted shape and soared skyward. But the wind buffeted his wings, making any sort of speed difficult. He half wished he hadn't spent most of last night airborne. His muscles were beginning to ache long before he'd reached the halfway point.

Mulgrave finally came into view. He dove down, skimming the treetops, looking for Haynes' house. He wasn't the only one. A military vehicle cruised slowly down the road. He could see two men inside, the passenger holding a street directory open on his lap. It might have been a coincidence, but he never had been one to believe in them overly much. Especially since similar vehicles had been sent after Allars.

But the fact that they were close meant there was no time for finesse. With a flick of one wing, he swung left, diving down to Haynes' well kept red brick home. He lined up with the kitchen window and arrowed directly at it.

Glass shattered, flying everywhere. He changed as he hit the floor, and he rolled back to his feet. Though hawks had relatively thick skulls, the impact left him a little dazed. He shook his head, trying to clear his thoughts. Shards fell like rain from his hair, chiming softly as they hit the tiled floor.

"What the hell...?"

A tall, thin gentleman wearing glasses walked into the room. Gabriel smiled in greeting and then swung a clenched fist. The blow took the old man on the chin and knocked him out cold. Gabriel caught him before he hit the floor, and he swung him up over his shoulder. Luckily, he didn't weigh all that much.

He headed out the back door. A dog barked loudly to his left, running back and forth along the fence line. He ignored it, heading for the rear of the property and the adjoining back yard. After ducking behind the cover of a tin shed, he peered over the fence. No dog, and no sign of movement from the house.

He carefully hoisted Haynes over the fence and then quickly followed. After lifting the old man back up, he ran for the front of the property. The gate was shut but not locked. He opened it and casually walked out into the street. There was a bus stop several houses down. Gabriel headed for that, and he eased the old man into the seat. Holding him upright with one hand, he dialed the SIU with the other.

"Christine, I need a mobile unit at my current location ASAP. And tell the team on the way to Haynes' place to return to headquarters."

"One moment, please."

The old man began to groan. Gabriel held the viaphone to his ear with a shoulder and got out his ID, showing it to the old man as he opened his eyes.

"I don't care who you are," Haynes growled. "What right do you have to come busting into my home and beating me up?"

"We've reason to believe your life may be in danger, sir."

"And you couldn't tell me this in my own home?"

"No, sir." Gabriel glanced up the street. It wouldn't take the military boys long to discover Haynes wasn't home. No doubt they'd then turn to the tracker.

"Unit four is thirty seconds away, Assistant Director. And team three-five are returning to headquarters, as ordered."

"Thanks, Christine."

As he hung the viaphone, a dark gray Ford turned the corner. Gabriel waved them down and returned his attention to Haynes.

"I'm sorry about the force used. But we don't know who's behind the threats and didn't dare take a chance with your safety. Lyle, White and Benson have all recently been murdered, and we've reason to believe both you and Cooper are next on the list."

"We all worked together," Haynes murmured, face pale.

"We're well aware of that, sir." Gabriel gripped the old man's arm, helping him up as the Ford pulled to a halt beside them. Haynes climbed in. Gabriel slammed the door shut then walked around to the other side.

"Where to, Assistant Director?" The driver, a red haired freckle-faced youngster, asked.

"Headquarters." Gabriel glanced at the driver's dark skinned partner, recognizing him from a recon trip they'd done several years ago. "How's that knee, Ford?"

He smiled. "They have me teaching brats how to drive. Scarier than missions, sometimes."

Ford had taken several bullets in his left knee when the mission went sour. Though doctors had replaced the shattered joint, he'd been left with a permanent limp. At only 35, he'd been too young too retire, and too young to send to the vaults.

Like he'd sent Sam to the vaults. Gabriel ignored the momentary stab of guilt. "Still carry that knife in your boot?"

Ford smiled. "Yeah. Comes in handy when the brats get uppity."

The youngster driving grinned. Obviously, knives and dour instructors didn't worry him. Gabriel returned his attention to Haynes.

"We're taking you into SIU headquarters. You should be secure there until we find out who's behind these murders."

Haynes scrubbed a hand across the back of his neck. "What about Cooper?"

"I've sent another team out to retrieve him."

"Why couldn't you have told me this at home? Why did you have to knock me out and haul me away?"

Gabriel wasn't about to tell him the truth, especially if the military were listening in. "Because I believed we had very little time to play with."

Haynes grunted. "I left the damn heater on at home. Probably burn the place down, you know."

Gabriel glanced at Ford. "You able to secure Mr. Haynes' place once you drop me off?"

"Yeah. No problems."

"Thanks," Haynes muttered.

Gabriel nodded, and leaned back in the seat, watching the traffic roll by. It didn't take that long to reach the city and SIU headquarters. The redheaded driver swung the car into the underground parking lot and stopped next to the elevator.

"Nice driving, kid." The youngster looked seriously insulted at the compliment. Gabriel half smiled and looked at Ford. "Be careful at Haynes' place. You could have company."

Ford's brown eyes narrowed slightly. "What type?"

"Kite." He hesitated. Though there were scramblers down here that should prevent their conversation being overheard, he didn't want the powers-that-be behind the chip knowing the SIU was well aware of what was going on—at least where the microchips were concerned. But, by the same token, Ford needed to know there might be trouble. In the end, that point won out over wariness. "The military might also be present."

"Treat them as hostile?"

"Unknown."

Ford nodded. Gabriel climbed out and walked around to assist the old man out of the car and into the elevator. He swiped his security card through the elevator slot and pressed B25. Not only did that floor have short-term apartment cells, but it also possessed the latest in both electronic and psychic deadeners. The military would not be able to hear or track them.

The elevator swept them downwards. When the doors opened again, Haynes made a surprised noise.

"It looks like an upmarket hotel," he murmured, as they walked out onto the plush mauve carpet.

"It is, in many respects." Gabriel strode towards the desk. "We've found over time that people cooperate more fully if you look after them."

Haynes gave him a sidelong look. "And if they don't...cooperate?"

Gabriel met his gaze. "We make them."

Haynes' gaze narrowed at the threat. Gabriel looked at the security officer. "Mr. Haynes needs a room. Full service."

The blonde nodded. "Room 25-4 is ready."

"Thanks. Tell me when team nine brings in Jake Cooper." He hesitated and glanced at his watch. "Has Agent Ryan reported in yet?"

The blonde pressed the com-screen. After several seconds, she looked up. "No, sir."

"Let me know when she does."

"Yes, sir."

Gabriel escorted Haynes down the corridor. Like the rest of the cells, room four was divided into three areas—bedroom, living room and bathroom. There was no need for a kitchen, as meals were provided. Every room was monitored twenty-four hours a day.

Haynes dropped down onto a well-padded armchair and regarded Gabriel somewhat stonily. "Now that we're here, you going to tell me the truth?"

Gabriel swung a chair around and sat down, resting his arms on the back. "I told you. We believe your life is in danger."

"And like I said, you could have told me that at home. You bought me here for a reason, Assistant Director."

He raised an eyebrow. "Are you aware that the army put a tracking and listening device in your side while you did service at Hopeworth?"

Haynes snorted. "Yeah, it was policy. But that was twenty five years ago. They removed it when I retired."

"We have reason to believe they didn't."

Haynes stared at him for several minutes, brown eyes sharp. "Are you saying the military are trying to kill me?"

"No, I'm not. But I have reason to believe they'd do what it takes to prevent you from helping me."

Haynes crossed his arms, a hint of confusion in his expression. "I don't know what you mean."

"Does the name Emma Pierce mean anything to you?"

"Emma Pierce." Haynes frowned. "She...worked with us in Hopeworth."

"She was one of your test subjects," Gabriel corrected. "On something called Generation 18."

"How did you know that? No one's supposed to know about those projects."

Those projects? There'd obviously been more than just a couple of attempts to manipulate life. He wondered how many of them had been successful—and what exactly they'd created. A kite monster, perhaps?

"I've been talking to Mark Allars."

"Allars?" Again the frown flicked across Haynes thin features. "The name seems familiar."

"Should be. He worked with you on something called Penumbra."

"Damn fool." Haynes shook his head. "The military will kill him for speaking, you know. As they'll kill me if I say anything."

So the military were willing to murder to protect their secrets. Interesting. "This room is fully shielded. They won't know."

"It won't matter."

"Why not?"

"The mere fact you've bought me here will be enough."

"Better here than out there. As I said before, Lyle, White and Benson have recently been murdered—and by a creature I doubt is nature-made." He watched the realization dawn in the older man's eyes. "If that's true, the military might well be after you already."

"That makes no sense. I mean, the projects were shut down years ago."

"But Hopeworth staff are still experimenting, aren't they?"

"Probably."

"Then they might simply fear any word about their projects getting out into the general population."

"They wouldn't fear that, because most of us can't speak about them."

"Why not?"

Haynes tapped his head. "Blocks have been placed on our memories."

Blocks could be removed, but it would take time. Time they didn't have. "So, you can't talk about the projects at all?"

"Wouldn't think so."

"Mind if I test?" When Haynes shrugged, he added, "Tell me about Penumbra."

Haynes frowned. "Nope. Can't do."

"Lyle, Benson and White, along with you and Cooper, are the only survivors from the fire that destroyed the Penumbra project—that true?"

Haynes nodded.

"From what Allars said, it sounded like an inside job."

"Impossible. We were tagged and watched, twenty-four hours a day."

"What was Penumbra?"

"I can't say…I can't."

"The five of you also worked on Generation 18, that right?"

Haynes nodded. Yes and no answers were outside the limits of the blocks, it seemed.

"Emma Pierce was one of the test subjects?" Again a nod. "From which you took her ovaries?"

Haynes looked uncomfortable and dropped his gaze from Gabriel's.

"Generation 18 test subjects were either shifter or changers. What were you hoping to achieve?"

"Hy…Hyb…" Haynes scrubbed a hand across the back of his neck, his expression uncomfortable.

"Hybrids?" Gabriel finished. Haynes nodded.

So the military were trying to develop shifter-changer hybrids—something that occurred only rarely in the natural order of things.

"What about Penumbra? What were you trying to create

there?"

Haynes could only shrug. The conditioning was stronger for that project than the more recent one. Gabriel wondered why.

"Did the Generation Eighteen project succeed?"

A brief, sharp nod. And a hint of pride in the old man's eyes.

"How many successful crosses did you achieve?"

The other man shrugged. Either he wasn't sure of exact numbers, or he couldn't say.

"Were there many failures?"

"All experiments have failures."

"What happened to them? Did they all die, or did some live?"

Another shrug. Haynes either didn't know or didn't care. Maybe both.

"Would the Military have adopted the failures out?"

"I don't know. I was not privy to that sort of information."

Gabriel rubbed his chin. Emma Pierce had entered the military at an early age and lost her ovaries in Generation Eighteen. She couldn't have had children before entering Hopeworth. If what Allars said was true, that one fact would have disqualified her from the tests. And yet, the first two victims listed Emma Pierce as their birth mother. They had to be rejects from the project.

Question was, why did the military adopt them out rather than simply killing them? If they were worried about security, surely death would have made more sense.

"Is it possible that one of the hybrids has gotten loose and is going after her less successful sisters?" A hybrid certainly fit the puzzle pieces in the doctor's murder, at least.

Haynes somehow managed to force an answer. "Tagged...Alarmed."

If not a rogue hybrid from Hopeworth, then who? The SIU had no hybrids currently on register for Victoria, and within Australia, there were only three listed. There was a forth, one the SIU didn't know about. He and Stephan intended to keep it that way. Their old man wouldn't have been involved in these murders anyway—not without consulting both him and Stephan first.

He glanced at his watch again. Half an hour had passed. Sam should be back by now, and hopefully she had finished the search. He wasn't going to get much more from Haynes until the conditioning had been neutralized.

"I think you'd better rest for a while." He rose and walked to the door. "I'll send someone back with some food."

Haynes nodded and picked up the remote near the chair. He was taking his confinement well—maybe a little too well. Gabriel walked down to the security station. "I want a breakdown team assigned to Mr. Haynes. And get him something to eat."

The blonde nodded.

"Has agent Ryan checked in yet?"

"No, sir. Not yet."

He swore softly and glanced at his watch. An hour and a half had passed since he'd left her. More than enough time to deposit Allars at a safe house and get her butt back here. Unless, of course, something had gone wrong. He strode over to the elevator. He'd call the safe house and see what was going on. And if she didn't have a real good excuse for her tardiness, she'd be banished to the vaults permanently. At least that was one way to ensure she was damn safe.

***

Sam glanced at her watch. An hour had passed since she'd left Gabriel. Given his desire to get rid of her, he'd no doubt hit her with an official warning about her tardiness. Three warnings and you were out, she'd been told.

She slammed the door shut and ran down the stairs. Allars had been almost impossible to accommodate. The old fart had insisted on the latest in TV and satellite connections, and, because of his inability to walk very far, had required an apartment with few steps. Unfortunately, most SIU safe houses tended to be in buildings that had no elevators—simply because a would-be assassin might make more noise climbing stairs than taking the elevator. In the end, she'd told the watch team to carry him up to his room.

Why the hell Gabriel simply didn't house him in the short-term accommodations back at Headquarters was beyond her.

The green-eyed security officer near the front door looked up from the monitors as she approached. "The grump settled in okay?"

"Yeah. Give him what he wants—within reason, of course. And don't fall asleep, Wright. We don't want the military getting their hands on him until we have time to question him some more."

"How likely is it that the military will try to spring him?"

That depended on several factors—what the military thought Allars might tell them, how much they knew about the SIU, and how quickly they could hack into SIU programming and get a list of current safe houses. "We don't really know. Priority is given to getting him out of here if it happens, though."

Wright nodded. Sam swiped her ID through the slot. The front door opened and the wind gusted in, thick with the promise of rain. She lifted the collar on her jacket and headed out to her car.

Rain spotted across the pavement. She raised her face, enjoying the feel of the cold droplets against her skin. There was something almost soothing about it.

"Samantha."

She froze. The voice was deep and warm, yet held a hint of caution. It was the voice of the man who'd once saved her life. The voice of the man who wanted Gabriel dead.

The voice of a man who was neither friend nor foe, but something in between.

Eight

Sam turned around slowly. The hirsute stranger leaned against the apartment building's brick wall, half-hidden by the shrubs and bottlebrushes that overhung the pavement.

"Just who the hell are you? And why do you keep popping up in my life?"

The stranger smiled, though how she knew this, she wasn't entirely sure. She couldn't see his mouth through the forest of his beard.

"When you are ready to know, you will find the answer here." He pressed a grimy hand over his heart.

She raised an eyebrow. "What are you? Some kind of mystic?"

This time she did see his smile. "Some days I believe I am. We must talk, Samantha. There is a small cafe just around the corner that serves excellent coffee. It would be ideal."

He made a sweeping movement with his hand, indicating she should precede him. She didn't budge.

"Tell me one good reason why I should go with you."

The stranger regarded her for a moment, brown eyes intense and somewhat sad. "The answers you seek will not be found in the man you protect within this building."

She glanced briefly at the building. "What do you know about Allars?"

"I know he cannot help you." He hesitated and crossed his arms. It was an oddly defensive gesture. "At the very least, you owe me ten minutes of your time, Samantha."

She owed him a hell of a lot more than that, because he'd saved her life. But that didn't mean she had to trust him.

"Ten minutes, then."

He nodded and then smiled when she motioned for him to go first. She fell into step behind him. Despite his disheveled, unwashed appearance, there was nothing of the streets in his walk. He had the stride of a soldier—purposeful, balanced, powerful.

A man ready to move, to fight, at a second's notice.

The cafe came into sight. The stranger chose a table under the awning, out of the rain. He sat down with his back to the street, letting her take the chair near the wall. Not that she felt any safer for it. She had an itchy feeling that this man could kill her faster than she could react.

Once they'd placed their orders, she leaned on the table and regarded the stranger steadily. "So what did you want to talk about? And how do you know so much about me?"

Her hirsute friend leaned back in the chair. He looked relaxed, almost asleep. It was an appearance that deceived. She could see the tension around his eyes, if nowhere else.

"We are two of a kind, Samantha. Two halves of the one whole."

"What is it with these riddles? Can't you speak plain English?"

He smiled again. "When you are ready for the answers you will see them. In your dreams and in your heart."

She licked her lips. This man knew about her dreams of Joshua. Maybe he was even responsible for them. "What are you doing to me?"

"I do nothing. I merely watch and wait to see what side you fall on. Though I think, perhaps, the answer is already clear."

"Not to me." She leaned back in her chair, smiling as the waitress placed her coffee on the table. "Why did you say Allars can't help me?"

"Allars was little more than a piece of meat the scientist's were using. He was one of eight. He was told nothing and knew nothing."

"His name is on my birth certificate. He must know something. A conception involves both male and female, you know."

"But not eight men and eight women. How do you explain that?"

"I can't." This man knew too much about her. And though he could read her thoughts, she sensed he wasn't doing that now. "How do you know about the certificate?"

"I sent it to you."

His eyes were as shuttered as his face, and yet she could almost taste the wariness in him. Its touch was so strong she might have named it fear in any other man.

But this man didn't fear. Didn't care.

And how the hell she knew that she couldn't honestly say. "Jack gave me that certificate."

"Yes, I know." He tilted his head to one side. "You cared for him, didn't you?"

She dropped her gaze. "He was my friend." He might have

been assigned to watch her, might have tried to use and kill her, but somewhere deep in his murderous heart, he had cared. Otherwise, he wouldn't have offered her the choice of joining him—something that had gone against his nature.

"And now?"

"And now I have only my work." And a partner who didn't want her.

"Sometimes it is better that way."

Only a workaholic or the dead would think that. But her private life was not something she wanted to discuss with this man.

"Jack said he got that information from Sethanon. Are you he?" If he was, she should be shooting him rather than talking to him. Especially when Sethanon was villain number one on both the SIU's and the Federation's hit lists.

"Sethanon is not a name I have ever called myself."

Truth or lie? She couldn't tell, and that worried her.

"Allars told me he was involved in a project called Penumbra. That four of the eight involved were a changer, a shifter, a vampire and a werewolf."

"And the other four were psychically endowed. Mike Shean was a strong telepath and empath. Jeremy Park was a fire starter. Rae Messner's gift was psychometry, and Fay Reilly was an emotive."

She stared at him. "How the hell do you know that?"

"Simple. I was there."

"You were one of the scientists?" She couldn't help the incredulous note in her voice. She could believe he might have been in the military, but a scientist? No way. This man was a killer, born and trained.

But then, with what she was beginning to learn about Hopeworth, maybe that wasn't so far off the mark.

He laughed. It was an oddly familiar sound that scratched at the back of her mind.

"Not a scientist. Not even a test subject."

"Then what?" If he'd been involved with security, surely he wouldn't have known so much about the project?

"Samantha, you have all the answers you need. All you have to do is look for them."

"So, we're back to the riddles again." She sipped at her coffee. It was strong, and sweet, with just a hint of hazelnut.

"Your favorite, I believe," he said softly.

This time he was reading her thoughts. She put her coffee down, and leaned back, crossing her arms. "Tell me your name."

He hesitated. "I go by many names these days."

"Give me your birth name, then."

He looked away, but not before she'd caught the hint of anger in his eyes. "I was never given a name at birth. The names I have are ones I've collected over the years."

"Give me a name, or I get up and walk away."

His hesitation was briefer. "Call me Joe Black."

"What are you, a funny man? Joe Black was a character in a movie of the same name."

He shrugged. "When you have no name of your own, you steal others that appeal. You asked for a name, I gave it to you."

"Okay then, Mr. Black—"

"Joe," he murmured.

"Mr. Black," she continued, ignoring his almost bitter smile. "What do you know about Jake Cooper and Alan Haynes?"

He sipped at his coffee for a minute. "Both worked on the Penumbra project. Both worked on the Generation Eighteen project."

"What can you tell me about Generation Eighteen?"

"Nothing your partner doesn't already know."

He said the word *partner* like it was a curse. She raised her eyebrows slightly. "Why do you want him dead when you haven't even met him?"

"That would take longer to explain than we have."

Not that he intended to explain. She rubbed her arms. "What makes you so certain Gabriel knows anything about Generation Eighteen?"

"Because the logical step after the first three murders is to pick up the two remaining men. Stern is nothing if not logical."

"How do you know about the three murders? The SIU has a media blitz on it. And how do you know that there are two men remaining?"

"I'm a mystic, remember?"

"Yeah, right. Maybe you'd better accompany me downtown for some questioning."

"That I cannot do."

"I think maybe you will."

"Do not push me, Samantha."

Though there was no threat in his voice, no threat in the way he sat, fear surged. She swallowed. This man could reach out and kill her without even moving. Could snuff out the flame of her existence with merely a thought. How she could be so certain about something like that, she couldn't really say. But she *was* certain.

"If you wish to find some answers," he continued, "look at the pin I gave you."

The pin? The one he'd given her when he saved her life? She frowned, trying to remember where she'd put it. "Do you mean answers to the murders, or answers about myself?"

"Perhaps it would be a start for both paths." He drained his coffee in one gulp and rose.

"We shall meet again, soon," he said. "In the mean time, be careful. Your abilities will not protect you from the kites if you get too close."

"The kites? What do you know about them?"

A smile ghosted across his face. "I made them," he said, then raised his arms to the sky. His body shimmered, then began to blur, briefly resembling putty being molded by unseen hands. Then he leapt skywards on black wings.

A crow. The harbinger of bad news. The messenger of death. An oddly fitting choice for the stranger.

Could he be believed when he said he'd made the kites? She'd sensed no lie in his words, and yet, it hadn't seemed the entire truth, either.

And that made a whole lot of sense, didn't it?

Snorting softly, she finished her coffee, then picked up the bill and paid for it. She glanced at her watch. Another hour had passed. Gabriel was going to kill her.

It took half an hour to get back to headquarters. By that time, her head was pounding again. She headed down to her dark little hole.

"Computer on." She threw her coat over the back of the chair and sat down.

"Afternoon, sweetness. How's your day been?"

"Just peachy. You got those test results back yet?"

Izzy swung her boa, her expression a little startled. "My, we are a bit abrupt right now, aren't we?"

She rocked her chair back against the wall and rubbed her eyes. Now her damn com-unit was telling her off. These things were definitely becoming *too* human. "Sorry Izzy. I've got a bitch of a headache."

"Perhaps you should see a doctor."

There was something almost coy in Izzy's voice. She opened her eyes and stared at the pink fuzz-ball. "And can you recommend one?"

"I can recommend five, actually. Funnily enough, they've all bought *Heat* in the last month."

"Izzy, you're a doll. Did you cross reference the results with our shifter records?"

"Certainly did, sweetie. There's one match. Our doctor is a multishifter, but that's it, I'm afraid. Definitely no sister."

She tapped her fingers against the desk. The murderer was definitely a shifter, that much they knew. But that didn't explain how she was getting in and out without being seen. There was something else, something they were missing. "Make an appointment with her for me."

"Might want to reconsider that. The doctor in question is a vet."

"Then I'll hire a dog to take. What about the Jadrone search? That finished yet?"

"I've been working my butt off here, darlin'. Of course it's finished."

"Was Emma Pierce listed?"

"No. But Harry Maxwell was."

Sam let her chair thump back. "What?"

"That's right, sweetness. Also listed were Raylea Burns, Anna King and Dr. Brandon."

"These recent prescriptions?"

"Yes. Though all four have been taking the drug since their mid-teens, from the look of it."

Sam rubbed her forehead. "Do a check on the prescribing doctor. And get me his address."

"Consider it done, sweetie."

"Thanks." Sam watched the purple boa rotate for several seconds. "Izzy, are any of the four victims on file as being shifters?"

The boa twirled a little faster while Izzy searched the records. "Not a one."

Then why the hell were they being prescribed Jadrone? Especially at such a young age? "Get me the autopsy results for King, Burns and Brandon."

"On screen."

The three reports tiled onto the screen. She quickly read through them. No evidence of Jadrone had been found in the toxicology or blood reports. So why were they being prescribed the drug if they weren't actually using it?

"Izzy, who performed the autopsies?"

"Warren Michaels."

"Get him on vid for me."

Izzy tapped his foot for several seconds, and then he disappeared, replaced by a dark haired man in his mid-forties.

"Agent Ryan. What can I do for you?"

"You handled the serial killer autopsies, didn't you?"

"Yep. Why?"

"I just found out that all of them were being prescribed Jadrone. Would you have any idea why?"

Michaels frowned and scratched his shadowed chin. "If they were taking it, I found no evidence of it."

"So I read. And yet all of them had been prescribed the drug since puberty, from what I can gather."

"Can't see why. They weren't shifters." He hesitated and frowned. "Though I did notice severe bone degradation in both Maxwell and King."

"What sort of degradation? And how might it be connected to Jadrone?"

"Shifting puts severe stress on the body's organs, particularly bone and muscle. As the shifter gets older, the bone and muscles become less pliant, more brittle. Arthritis and other, associated diseases become a real problem. In a shifter, this doesn't normally happen until they are well into mid-one-fifties, one-sixties. Even in humans, it doesn't normally happen until your late sixties."

"Is there a history of this sort of degeneration in either King's or Maxwell's family?"

"That we don't know."

She frowned. "Why?"

Michaels snorted. "They were adopted, same as Burns and Brandon. Don't you read follow-up reports?"

The edge of derision in his voice stung. "Obviously not." Nor had Gabriel mentioned that fact. "Let's presume there's no history of this in their background. What else might be the cause?"

Michaels shrugged. "Random chance. It happens. Kids as young as five get arthritis, you know."

Yeah, but their killer wasn't attacking kids as young as five. There was some sort of pattern here, one they just couldn't quite see. "What about the other two?"

"Minor degradation. A little more than what you'd expect for their age, but nothing extreme."

"Did you do a cell investigation on the four?"

"No need to. They were human."

"Do it. And tell me what you find."

Michaels raised his eyebrows. "By whose authority are you ordering this?"

"Assistant Director Stern's." She looked up as the man in question stepped into her office. He raised an eyebrow and walked the two steps over to the desk.

"Sorry, Agent Ryan. I can't order that sort of investigation without authority from the man himself."

Gabriel placed a hand on the back of her chair, his face close to hers as he stared at the com-screen. "Then you have it, Michaels. Please proceed."

Michaels nodded and signed off. Gabriel sat back on the edge of her desk. "What did I just authorize?"

"Cell investigation on our four victims."

He crossed his arms and regarded her for a minute. The intensity of his gaze made her want to squirm like some errant ten-year-old faced by a headmaster. And that, more than anything, annoyed the hell out of her. What was it about this man that got to her so easily?

"Really? Why?"

She tilted her chair back. Her knee brushed against his and warmth surged across her flesh. He didn't move, nor did she. "All four were being prescribed Jadrone, and yet they were not on record as being shifters."

"Jadrone has no effect on humans."

"Exactly. And yet Maxwell was a junkie who got high on it regularly, and the others had been prescribed it since their teens. I think we need to find out why."

He frowned. "I agree. But there was no mention of Jadrone being found in their systems."

"Which makes me wonder why, especially with Maxwell. He was a junkie for years—surely it would have had some effect on his body."

"You'd think so. You doing a trace on the prescribing doctor?"

"Izzy's handling it now. Why didn't you mention all four victims were adopted?"

"Why were you going through the files?" he countered. "You're supposed to be handling the kite murders."

"You can't have it both ways, chum. Either I'm helping you or I'm not."

"You do what I tell you to do. And right now, you're my research assistant, nothing more."

His face was remote, eyes cold. She felt like strangling him. God, the man was aggravating. As he no doubt intended.

"Why are you here, Assistant Director? Planned to leave me another nice note, did you?"

His arms flexed, as if he were clenching his fists. "You left the safe house more than an hour ago. Where the hell were you?"

"Having coffee with a friend."

"You have no friends."

"Obviously not." An edge of bitterness crept into her voice. She took a deep breath and crossed her legs. Warmth still tingled where their knees had touched. She scratched at it irritably.

"That's not…" Gabriel looked away from her gaze. "Next time, report in first."

"Yes, sir." This time she resisted the urge to salute.

His anger washed over her, a blanket that briefly smothered. She shuddered and leaned back, trying to get some fresh air.

Concern flitted briefly through his hazel eyes. "You okay?"

"Yes. Fine." She rubbed her forehead briefly. She really had to go see a doctor. Not only about the headache, but the weird sensations that kept washing over her.

Izzy choose that moment to reappear. "You have a five-fifteen appointment with the animal quack, sweetness."

"Thanks Izzy."

Gabriel gave her com-unit a somewhat disgusted look. But then, he wasn't into cartoons. Or com-units with character. "You're visiting a vet? Why?"

"Dog's sick." She'd be damned if she'd tell him the truth. He'd probably go interview the vet himself and leave her here in this shoebox doing another inane task.

"You don't have a dog."

"I will tonight."

He studied her thoughtfully. "The crosscheck came up with her name, didn't it?"

"Yeah." She rubbed her forehead again, and waited for the axe to fall.

He was silent for a few seconds. Then he sighed and rested

his palms on the desk. "When are you going to see a doctor about that headache of yours?"

Consideration when she'd expected an axe was definitely cause to be wary. "What do you mean?"

"I mean you've had that headache for the last few days. I think it's time you got it checked out."

"I will." She barely kept her irritation in check. Lord, it was bad enough that he was ordering her around at work. Now he was trying to run her private life, as well.

"When?"

"Soon."

Gabriel shook his head and looked at the com-unit. "Izzy, make an appointment for Sam with Doctor O'Hearn at the Collins Street clinic."

"Sorry, sweetie, but you're not the boss in this shoebox."

Surprise and annoyance flitted across Gabriel's features. She smothered her laugh and would have hugged the cyber character, if she could have. "Who's Doctor O'Hearn? SIU employed?" If he was, she was staying well away. A SIU doctor meant Gabriel could access her records. He knew more than enough about her already.

He shook his head. "No. Federation. She specializes in nonhuman medicine."

She snorted softly. "Federation. So you could get access to my medical files, anyway."

"Not with Doctor O'Hearn, I can't. The old girl's a stickler when it comes to patient confidentiality."

"Then why are you sending me to her?"

"Because she's not only the best, she's also the only one who might truly be able to help you."

Because they didn't know what was she was, other than the fact she was not entirely human. She glanced at the boa twirling fuzz ball. "Do it, Izzy."

"Right away, darlin'."

"Tell Dr. O'Hearn I recommended you. She'll forward the bill to Federation."

She raised an eyebrow. "I'm not a part of Federation."

He crossed his arms. "You could be, if you wanted to."

"What's this, a recruitment attempt?" And why now, a good month after she'd found out about Federation?

He shrugged. "No. Just something for you to think about."

"Why? I don't know a thing about Federation, apart from

what you've told me."

"I've already told you the important stuff."

"You gave me a brief background. That's hardly the same as knowing the current goals."

He shrugged. "If you're interested, let me know."

She considered him for a moment. His face, as ever, was neutral. It was hard to judge whether he was actually serious or not. "I thought you were trying to get me out of your life?"

His smile seemed almost bitter. "I don't want you out of my life. I just don't want you as a partner. It's nothing personal."

Yes it was—at least to her. And if he did want her in his life, then if not as a partner, what? A friend? It certainly couldn't be as a lover—not if his determined lack of reaction to physical touch was anything to go by. Or was he merely reacting that way because she *was* his partner? Did he perhaps believe in the adage of not combining work and play?

Izzy twirled onto the com-screen. "There's a call from a General Frank Lloyd on vidscreen. You want to take it?"

She glanced at Gabriel. He slid off the desk and stood near her chair—close enough to see the screen but out of direct line of sight.

"Patch it through, Izzy."

General Frank Lloyd came on screen. "Agent Ryan, I presume?" His voice, like his appearance, was powerful.

She nodded. "What can I do for you, General?"

"I need to know why you have requested information on these thirteen people before we can go any further."

"We have a number of murder victims that may be linked with Hopeworth. They're certainly linked with an Emma Pierce, who worked at Hopeworth for a number of years, and was supposedly the mother of at least two of them."

The general's sharp blue gaze narrowed slightly. "I see." He rested his elbows on the desk in front of him, fingers interlaced. "I'll be in the city this evening, attending the opera. Perhaps we could meet afterwards?"

Gabriel grabbed a pen and paper, quickly scribbling. She glanced at it. "I've heard there's a very good restaurant in South Bank—Han's, I believe it's called. Shall I make reservations?"

"Around eleven should be suitable."

She nodded. "See you then, General."

The screen went dead.

"Well, well," Gabriel murmured. "A call from a General,

no less. Your request for information certainly raised a few alarms."

"Have you heard of the General before?"

"No. But a doctor Frank Lloyd attended the birth of both Raylea Burns and Anna King."

She raised her eyebrows. "Same man, you think?"

"Too much of a coincidence, otherwise."

"Why meet at a restaurant? Why not at Hopeworth? Or even here?"

Gabriel shrugged. "Neutral territory, perhaps. I doubt they'd let us near Hopeworth, anyway. The place is level ten security."

Which meant top of the tree. Not even Stephan's Byrne persona would get in there.

"I gather you intend coming with me tonight."

"Yes. I'll contact Han and arrange for us to be in the dragon room." He hesitated. "The restaurant is upmarket. Nothing casual allowed, I'm afraid."

She raised an eyebrow. "You think I don't know that?"

He looked away. Though his face was still neutral, she had a sense of his embarrassment.

"I'll pick you up at nine-thirty."

"It's a date, Assistant Director."

He flashed her a grim look. She smiled and watched him walk from the room. Sometimes, he was extraordinarily easy to rattle.

And that, just maybe, should be her line of attack. Damn it, there was something between them, and he had to be as aware of it as she. Rather than sit back and wait for him to make a move, as she usually did when it came to men, maybe she needed to take the reins and lead the way. The worst that could happen was that he'd say no.

And he was already doing that in other areas—what was one more?

"Izzy, do a search through the personnel files. I need to find an agent who has a dog or a cat I can borrow."

"Searching now, sugar."

Good. Her next major worry was finding an outfit to wear tonight. Something subtle but stunning. She might not be able to stop him from thrusting her from his life, be it professional or personal, but she sure as hell could make him regret it.

Tall, curvaceous blondes weren't the only ones who could look like sex on legs.

***

Sam grabbed the box restraining the growling cat and climbed out of the car. Heat tingled across her skin, standing the small hairs at the back of her neck on end. Then her senses exploded outward, tasting the secrets within the clinic.

The shifter inside was more than just a shifter.

Frowning, wondering what the hell that was supposed to mean, she headed in.

After filling in a bunch of forms, she sat down. The cat, safely parked two seats away, had a claw through one of the air holes and seemed intent on shredding the seat.

"Doctor Francis will see you now," the receptionist said after a few minutes.

She collected the box, ensured the killer claw was pointed away from her body, and walked through the door indicated by the white-haired receptionist.

Doctor Francis, like the woman out front, was in her mid-fifties. She wore what Sam called a power suit under her unbuttoned white coat—a tight fitting, no nonsense outfit that acknowledged her femininity but said hands-off. Her hair was a rich chestnut, and undoubtedly dyed. Her face was natural, unmarred by makeup or face-lifts. A woman proud of her looks and her age.

A woman whose very presence itched energy across Sam's skin.

"And what can we do for you and Kahn today?" The vet's voice, like her looks, was striking and powerful.

She placed the box on the table and carefully pulled the cat out. It continued to growl its displeasure. "He's overdue for his shots."

The doctor nodded and walked across to the cupboard. "Haven't seen either of you here before, have we?"

"No. We just moved here."

"Oh yes? Where from?" The doctor's voice was flat. Making small talk through habit, not interest.

"Elwood." She hesitated. The doctor slipped a white glove on and moved back to the table. "Park Street. You know it?"

"Lovely area," O'Hearn murmured, bending to examine the squirming, hissing feline.

Sam regarded her steadily. No reaction whatsoever to the location or street name. She'd have to push a bit harder. "I used to think so. But a neighbor of mine was murdered the other day."

The doctor glanced up. The shock in her face didn't quite reach her eyes. "How horrible. Did you know him well?"

She raised her eyebrows. "Yes, I did. I have an interview with the cops tomorrow."

She continued to examine the cat. "Nasty."

"Yeah, I'm not looking forward to it."

"Nor would I. Kahn's in excellent condition."

"That's good. He's been a little off his food. Not impressed by the change of housing, I think."

"Just keep him inside a while, and he'll be fine. Hold him down, will you?" She took a needle out of the cupboard. "Why do the police want to interview you?"

She grabbed the cat by the scruff of the neck. It responded by trying to twist around and shred her hand. "Routine, I think. I was just unlucky enough to be in the building at the time."

"Did you see anything?"

"No." She hesitated again and frowned. The doctor watched her almost too carefully. "Though I saw the postman arrive. I swear he had something live in one of the parcels. I could hear it scratching around."

"It's illegal to send animals through the post. They should hang the person who did that."

"They'll probably get a pat on the head and a warning not to do it again."

"Yeah, the courts don't seem to care these days." She injected the growling cat, somehow avoiding the razor sharp claws it flung her way.

"That's it. If you both head back to reception, I'll write up the bill and send it out."

She nodded and put the squirming feline back into the box. It was easy to see why this particular cat hadn't had any recent shots. Kahn was definitely a killer. She just had to hope the box would hold up till she got him back to his owner.

She headed back to reception and paid the fee. All the while, the back of her neck itched. Someone watched her. Someone with death on her mind.

After seat-belting the cat carrier into the back seat, Sam climbed into the front and got out the viaphone. The SIU's digital receptionist answered on the second ring.

"Christine, could you patch me through to workstation 1934?"

Izzy appeared onscreen. "This is a new experience, sweetie."

"Hate for you to be bored, Iz. Listen, do a search on Doctor Francis. I want a complete history—if she lives in an apartment, include surveillance tapes from her home if you can get hold of them."

"Will do. You have a six-thirty appointment with Doctor O'Hearn."

O'Hearn certainly didn't waste time. She glanced at her watch. She'd just have enough time to return the cat and get there. "Thanks, Izzy."

"Have a nice evening."

Sam started the car and headed out of the parking lot. All the while, the eyes watched, burning into the back of her skull.

Nine

Gabriel leaned back in his chair and glanced at his watch. Seven-thirty. He wondered how Sam was doing with O'Hearn. He'd phoned the doc earlier, calling in a favor and getting Sam squeezed in. He just hoped O'Hearn could discover the reason for Sam's continuous bout of headaches.

"Search completed," the com-unit intoned.

Gabriel rubbed his eyes and then studied the com-screen. "Results?"

"All four victims were adopted from the same state care center. All four victims were placed in care on the same day."

Coincidence? Not likely. "Did you find the birth certificates for Harry Maxwell and Carmen Brandon?"

"Yes."

"Who's listed as the mother?"

"Emma Pierce."

So Emma *was* the link. "Is there a complete list of all children handed into State care that day?"

"Searching. One moment please."

Gabriel tapped the desk and watched the blank screen. And couldn't help thinking a pink fuzz-ball twirling a purple boa would definitely be more interesting.

"Seventeen children were entered into the care of the Greenwood center that day."

He shook his head. Seventeen children and no one had thought that odd? "Get me the complete list of names, their adoption records, birth certificates and current location."

"List and adoption records onscreen. Searching for birth certificates and location."

The list was in alphabetical order, with the adoption details beside each name. Gabriel scanned through the list. One name, half way down, jumped out at him. The air left his lungs, as suddenly as if someone had punched him in the gut. Miranda Jones, now Miranda Stern. His sister.

He reached for the viaphone and quickly dialed Stephan's secure number.

"Byrne speaking."

Obviously he wasn't alone in the office, or he would have used the vidscreen. Gabriel swore softly. "We need to find Miranda, quick."

"Why?"

"I just discovered all four murder victims had Emma Pierce listed as their mother, and they were adopted from the Greenwood State care center. Miranda's one of seventeen children that came in on the same day."

"She's moved. Charles will know where she's at." Though there wasn't the slightest change in his voice, he could feel his brother's sudden alarm. Felt it, because it was in him as well.

"Maybe not. The reason Miranda moved in the first place was the almighty argument she'd had with him."

"Give him a call, and then let me know. This meeting will be finished in ten."

"Will do." Gabriel hung up and quickly dialed his old man's number.

"Stern residence."

His father's familiar, suntanned features came on-line. Though close to a hundred years old, he barely looked fifty. His skin, like his still black hair, showed little sign of aging. It was only when you looked deep into his green eyes that you saw the truth. They were the eyes of a man who'd seen too much death, too much destruction, for one normal life span.

"Father, I need Miranda's new address and phone number."

The welcoming smile faded. "What's wrong?"

"Stephan's updated you on our current investigations, hasn't he?"

Charles nodded. "Several days ago. There wasn't anything we'd consider a Federation matter, so it wasn't in-depth."

"I've just discovered a link between our murder victims. They were all fosterlings at the Greenwood State Care Center. Miranda came into care the same day as the others."

"And you think she's in danger?"

"I sure as hell don't want to take a risk."

Charles rubbed his chin. "I haven't heard from her in over a week."

That didn't surprise him. Miranda could hold a grudge with the best of them. She'd once gone two months without saying a word to *him*—just because he'd had the audacity to call her date an idiot, which she had been, as Miranda had admitted later.

"What about mom?"

"She's still in New York. Flights out of Kennedy have been delayed by storms. I'll phone her and see. If not, Jessie will know."

Jessie was his oldest sister, and she had been something of

a surrogate mother to the much younger Miranda. "I want full protection on her."

"That goes without saying. I'll contact you when I have the address."

The vidscreen went blank. Gabriel leaned back in his chair and scrubbed his chin. He didn't like this. They might not know where Miranda was, but that didn't mean the killer wouldn't. She'd been ahead of them every step of the way so far.

The com-unit beeped. "Director Byrne on vid one."

"Display."

Byrne's familiar features came on-line. "How'd you do?"

There was a slight buzz overriding Stephan's voice. He had the scramblers up, just to ensure no one listened in. "He didn't know, and mom's still overseas."

"I thought she was due back yesterday?"

"Yeah, she was. He's contacting Jessie."

"She'll know." Stephan ran a hand through his hair. "I can't go look myself. I promised Lys I'd be home early tonight."

"Nor can I. Sam and I have got a meet with a General Frank Lloyd of Hopeworth Military Base at eleven."

Gabriel glanced at his watch. If he didn't get moving, he'd be late to pick up Sam. He wanted to ensure they arrived at Han's well before the general. He had an uneasy feeling about this meeting. Given the security surrounding Hopeworth's activities, the general had been too quick in agreeing to meet them.

"Hopeworth? How's that tie in with the murders?"

"Emma Pierce used to work with them. She was listed as the mother of all four victims, even though Hopeworth took her ovaries for tests. From what we've learned, Hopeworth's been experimenting in genetics."

"I've heard whispers of that over the years. Nothing concrete, though."

"I'd like to know if the kites are a by-product of their experiments."

"We would have been advised, especially given the spate of recent attacks."

Somehow, he doubted that. The military were not inclined to admit mistakes, just get rid of them. "Have we got enough manpower available to put watch teams on the remainder of the Greenwood fosterlings?"

"I'll have to pull some teams off other work, but yeah, we can manage. Send the list through and I'll arrange it."

The com-unit beeped. "You have a call on vid-line 2, Assistant Director."

"Hang on a minute." Gabriel switched lines. His father's features reappeared. "Did you get hold of Jessie?"

"Yes. Miranda's living in a house out Strathmore way. Jes and Alain are heading over there."

Alain was Jessie's shapechanging husband of six months, and, quite literally, a bear of a man. "You told them to bring her back to the compound?"

"Kicking and screaming, if they have to."

"Let me know what happens."

The old man nodded. "Take care, son."

Gabriel switched back to Stephan. "Jes and Alain are picking up Miranda."

"Good. At least she'll be safe back home. You have any idea how the murderer is getting in and out of the victims' homes yet?"

"I've several ideas. Nothing concrete yet."

"Well, you'd better start finding something concrete. Our killer is about due to strike again."

Like *that* was something he wasn't fully aware of. He held back the surge of annoyance. "I'll send the list through now. The quicker we can get surveillance teams on these people, the better it will be."

"Keep me informed."

"I usually do." The retort held a hint of hostility. He scrubbed a hand against his jaw. Getting angry with his brother wouldn't achieve anything. "How's Lyssa?"

"The herb Karl suggested is working. She only threw up once last night."

At least that was an improvement. "Send her my love. I'll be in touch."

He broke contact and glanced at his watch. Ten to eight. He'd better get going. He collected his jacket and headed down to the car.

Two hours later, he ran up the stairs to Sam's second floor apartment. He'd showered and changed, but he still felt like shit. What he needed was a good night's sleep. Something that wasn't likely to happen until they caught the murderer.

"Door's open," Sam yelled from inside her apartment.

He raised an eyebrow. It could have been anyone coming up those stairs. Maybe he'd have to sit her down and explain the basics of security—though as a former cop, with over ten years experience, she should know them. He pushed the door open and entered the apartment. It was starker than he'd remembered. The walls were bare of paintings, and she'd yet to replace the shelving and knickknacks lost in the bombing. He wondered whether she still had all the books in the bedroom.

"You're late," she said, her voice coming from the direction of the bathroom.

"Working on the case." He walked across to the window and stared out over the ocean. If he ever moved, it would be for something like this. Something close to the sea. The wash of waves across the sand was hypnotically soothing.

"Anything new?"

"Yeah, the four victims entered the Greenwood State care center on the same day as thirteen other kids. How'd you do with Dr. O'Hearn?"

"She took some blood and skin samples. I have to go back tomorrow." Sam came out of the bathroom and walked towards him.

He did a double take. She wore what was becoming standard dress for her—a jacket and shirt, this time teamed with a knee length skirt rather than pants. Only there was nothing conservative, or even normal, about *this* little dark gray number. Both the jacket and skirt appeared to be made from *Contour,* the latest in textile development. It clung like a second skin, displaying every curve with loving detail. The skirt was slit on one side to her thigh, revealing plenty of tanned leg.

She looked stunning. Sexy. And it sure as hell would be difficult to see her in *any* suit the same way again. He cleared his throat. This was not a good development. Not when he was trying to ignore his attraction to her.

She collected her purse from the coffee table, a smile touching her full, red lips. It was then he realized she'd done it deliberately—had dressed to shatter his reserve and get some reaction.

"The cut on your leg has healed rather nicely," he said lamely.

Indeed, it was little more than a pale pink scar. She definitely healed way too fast. The three scrapes he'd received across his shoulder had barely scabbed over. As a shapechanger, he healed a good two or three times faster than a human. He'd have to call O'Hearn and mention it.

"Yeah, it has. Shall we go?"

He waved her ahead of him, locking her door and following

her down the stairs. But he kept his eyes on the shining beacon of her red-gold hair rather than the enticing sway of her hips.

They drove to the city in silence. It was neither uncomfortable nor tension-filled, just the easy silence that existed between two people who understood each other very well. Even if they were still relative strangers—something he had no intention of changing, no matter how sexy she was, no matter how comfortable he felt with her.

He found street parking, and they walked the block to the restaurant. Han's eldest son, Michael, made his way across to them as they entered.

"Hey, Uncle Gabriel, how's it going?"

He smiled and shook the big man's hand. Like his father, Michael towered over him by a good four or five inches and almost doubled his width. "How's Danni and the kid?"

Michael beamed. "We finally decided on a name. Katie Jane, after Danni's mother."

"About time. I was beginning to think she'd have to choose her own name when she went to school. Michael, this is my partner, Samantha Ryan."

"Whoa! If I knew partners could look like this, I would have joined the force." He grinned and stuck out a hand. "Pleased to meet you, Samantha."

She grinned. "Please, call me Sam."

"Dad's put you both in the Dragon room. You have sole ownership tonight."

"Thanks." He glanced around as two more people entered the restaurant. It looked like Han was having another good night. Already the place was so crowded you could barely move between the tables. He'd have to buy Han an extra large bottle of bourbon for doing them such a huge favor. "We'll make our way there. You look after your customers."

Michael nodded. "Dad'll be with you in a few minutes."

Gabriel lightly placed his hand against Sam's back, guiding her through the tables to the private function room near the back of the restaurant. The holographic dragons played across the ceiling of the room as they entered, the creatures diamond bright in the candlelit darkness.

"Lord, I still can't get over how real they look," she murmured, a smile touching her full lips.

Gabriel watched a sapphire blue dragon flame a butterfly that danced near its tail. Warmth washed over his face, followed quickly by a hint of acrid smoke. The butterfly emerged from the flames unscathed, and the dragon looked miffed. "Han's always working on the holographs. His aim is to make them as real as possible."

A golden dragon dove for her head and she ducked, then smiled ruefully. "He's just about achieved that."

He motioned her toward the table set up in the middle of the room. She sat at one end. He sat to one side of her, but the table was small enough that his knee brushed hers. The touch sent warmth rushing to his groin. He might not be willing to admit his attraction to his partner, but his body sure as hell had no such inhibitions. Just as well he was sitting.

A door opened near the back of the room. Han loomed out of the shadows, his smile almost lost in the bushiness of his moustache.

"Gabriel. Samantha. It is good to see you both."

Gabriel clasped the big man's hand. "You, too, old friend. Thanks for giving us the room when you're so busy."

"For you, anything. I have the deadeners on full. No one will eavesdrop on your conversation."

"Good. The general should be here by eleven. Just keep an eye out for me. I don't really trust him."

Han nodded. "You wish a drink while you wait?"

"Just iced water for me, thanks," Sam said.

"That is very boring, and I do make the best cocktails in town, you know."

She grinned. "I'm still on duty. Water will do."

Han looked at Gabriel. "And you my friend? Are you playing by the book?"

"The SIU would go into shock if I did. I'll have a beer, thanks."

Han nodded and walked away. She interlaced her fingers and leaned her chin on them. The ring of smoke around the blue of her eyes gleamed like ice in the candlelight. But there was nothing cold about the smile that teased her lips. A moment later, her bare foot slid up his shoe and under his pants leg. The skin to skin caress had his muscles—and other parts of his body—jumping in delight.

"Why don't you trust the general?" she asked.

When had her voice gained that sexy edge? "I just have a feeling about the man. He agreed to this meeting far too fast."

"Maybe he just wants to help."

Her foot was sliding up and down, up and down, and he was beginning to find it extremely hard to concentrate.

"The military is not known for its helpful nature," he said dryly. "He's got his own agenda for agreeing to this meeting."

"Then why come here? Why not somewhere more secure?"

"Han's is as secure as we'd ever get, and the general might just relax his guard here."

She nodded. Han walked in, and her foot stopped it's teasing. Gabriel wasn't sure whether to be relieved or annoyed.

"Thanks, Han," he said, once the big man had placed their drinks on the table.

"I have ordered a tray of savories for you both." A hint of amusement ran through Han's voice. "Complimentary, of course."

"Thanks," he said, and knew he'd get the third degree from his friend later. But what could he say? That his temporary partner was pushing boundaries in a way she'd never pushed before? That while he was attracted to her, he had no intention of heading down that path while she was his partner?

Han left. She raised her glass and slowly sipped. Moisture glistened like tears on her mouth. God, it would be so easy to reach across the table, to wrap his arm around her neck and his mouth around hers, and kiss those droplets away.

But he could not. Dared not.

She raised an eyebrow, and for a minute he wondered if she'd somehow caught his thoughts.

"So, what do we talk about until the general gets here?"

"How about the weather?" he said, keeping his voice bland.

She smiled that smile again, and heat twisted through his veins. "How about we talk about us?"

"There is no us," he said gently, even though he wished it could be otherwise. "Not while we're partners."

"Then you're not denying the attraction between us?"

"Only a fool would do that. And while I may be many things, a fool is not one of them."

Amusement warmed the silver in her eyes. "I'm tempted to disagree with that statement."

He smiled. "Undoubtedly."

"So, is this reluctance to get involved with a partner the reason why you're trying to ditch me? So you can feel free to play?"

He hesitated. "In truth, no. I have a habit of killing partners. I don't want you—or anyone else—to join the list."

She nodded. "Then this 'no involvement' rule is one you've had from the beginning?"

Again he hesitated. "Not really."

She raised her eyebrow. "Then you have been involved with a partner?"

"It went badly," he said. "And I realized my mistake. Hence the rule."

"How badly?"

"Very." He paused, not wanting to get into a discussion about an event that had happened long ago, even if that event still haunted his actions today. "While you're my partner, nothing will happen between us."

"And if I did happen to ask for a transfer? What then?"

Then he'd definitely be tempted. But to what end? He wasn't looking for anything more than a casual relationship—which was exactly what he had with Sandy. Free and easy, with no commitment or restraint on either side. In the brief time he'd known Sam, he'd learned one thing—she wasn't the casual type of woman.

"And are you considering asking for a transfer?" he asked

"At this point, no."

"Then it's a moot point, isn't it?"

His viaphone chose that moment to ring. Almost gratefully, he dug it out of his pocket and flipped it open.

Stephan's grim feature's greeted him. "There's been another murder."

Something clenched in Gabriel's gut. *Surely not Miranda.* "Where?"

"Up in Greenvale. Neighbors reported hearing two women screaming. The local cops have called us in."

Tension flowed from his body. Greenvale was no where near Strathmore. "So it's definitely connected to our serial killings?"

"From what they said, yes."

"Damn." Gabriel glanced at Sam. "There's been another murder. You able to handle the general alone?"

"I've been a cop for ten years. I don't think an interview with a general is beyond me."

He wasn't worried about her interviewing techniques. He was worried about leaving her alone with a man instinct told him they couldn't trust. He looked back at the viaphone. "I'll head there immediately. Have you heard anything about Miranda?"

"No. I called the old man, and he's still waiting to hear from Jes and Alain. You?"

"Nothing." If he didn't hear something soon, he'd call Jes and see what was going on. "You home?"

"Yes. Call me if anything happens."

He meant Miranda-wise, not case-wise. "Will do."

Gabriel put the viaphone away and met Sam's gaze. "Miranda's one of my adopted sisters, in case you were wondering."

She smiled slightly. "One of? How many do you have?"

"Four adopted, and two full sisters." And two dead brothers, he thought grimly. Lord, he did *not* want to lose anyone else. He guzzled the rest of his beer and stood up. "I have to go. Be careful with the general. Remember, he probably has his own reasons for being here."

She nodded. "I'll give you a call and let you know what happened."

"Do that." He dug the car keys out of his pocket and dropped them into her hand. "Take my car. You can pick me up in the morning."

She nodded. Gabriel walked from the room. Han was in the process of heading into the kitchen and stopped in surprise.

"You're leaving your pretty lady so soon?"

"She's not *my* pretty lady, or anything else, for that matter."

Han's smile was disbelieving. "I saw you together, my friend. Lie to yourself, if you wish. I have seen the truth."

"What you've seen is the natural attraction of a man for a beautiful woman in a form fitting outfit. Half the men in this restaurant looked at her that way."

Han's smile was gentle, almost mocking. "As you wish, my friend. What can I do for you?"

"Keep an eye on her for me. As I said, I don't trust the general, but I've no option on leaving."

"She will come to no harm in my restaurant. I shall monitor them, if you like."

"I like. Thanks Han." He clapped the big man on the shoulder and quickly left. In the shadows of the bridge he shapechanged and headed for Greenvale.

***

So much for dressing to kill, Sam thought, watching Gabriel's retreat. Even if he had admitted his attraction, he'd actually taken about as much notice of her as he would have a gnat doing the cancan.

She leaned back in her chair and toyed with her drink. As a seductress, she'd been a miserable failure. Beyond his initial surprise, he'd given no reaction, made no comment, about how she looked. Nor had he had any obvious physical reaction to her caressing him suggestively with her toes.

Maybe he really did prefer tall, leggy blondes to short, slender redheads.

She sipped her water and stared at the dancing dragons. After a while, a waitress came in and placed a platter of hors d'oeuvres on the table. She nodded her thanks and glanced at her watch. Ten past eleven. The general was late. She hoped he wasn't reneging. The evening would be a total waste if he did.

As if on cue, the door opened. Han came into the room, followed by two men. Heat tingled a warning across her skin.

The general wasn't human, nor was the man who accompanied him.

"Would you gentleman like a drink?" Han asked.

"Two coffees," the general replied, tone almost offhand.

"Two coffees it is." Han's gaze touched hers. "I'm only a call away if you need anything else."

She nodded. It was good to know Han was close. There was something about these two men she didn't trust, and it was more than just the warning itching her skin.

Somewhere, sometime, she'd met the general before. There was something horribly familiar in the way he walked.

The two men sat opposite her. The general's companion was in his mid-twenties, with red-gold hair and green-gray eyes. He could have been Harry Maxwell's brother. Could have been her brother.

Maybe he was.

If Hopeworth was playing with genetics, and if she was somehow connected to Hopeworth, then anything was possible.

"Samantha Ryan, I presume?" the general said.

She took a sip of water and nodded. The general glanced at the man beside him. "My attaché, Duncan King."

The younger man held out his hand. For a second, she regarded it warily, and then she reluctantly clasped it. Power tinged through her fingertips—a power that was similar, and yet different, to the kind of energy that she felt in storms. It was a little "earthier" than the ethereal energy of the storms, though.

One other thing she noticed—part of the power that surged between them had a sucking feel—like he was a drain and everything she was swirled towards him. King was psychic, and he was attempting to read her. She tore her hand away.

The general's eyes narrowed slightly. "You mentioned a

murder case on the phone. Are the thirteen men you requested information on suspects?"

"No, but they may be victims." She scratched her palm under the table. Her hand burned were King had touched.

"Ten of the thirteen men are dead. Why would you consider them possible victims?"

So the general knew about the recent kite murders. Knew, too, that the other seven men were dead. "We have two separate murder cases involved here. Benson, Lyle and possibly White were killed by a vampirelike creature we call a kite. We believe Cooper and Haynes are the next likely victims."

"Which is why the SIU currently have both under protection?"

She nodded. "We thought it best for their safety."

The general's smile suggested he didn't believe that excuse. "And the other eight men you requested information on?"

"Their names came up during our investigations on a recent series of murders." She hesitated, meeting King's icy gaze. "All the victims were in their mid-twenties, were adopted from Greenwood state care, and had red hair. Just like your friend here."

"I see." If he detected her slight lie, he gave no indication of it. "Then you have heard of the Generation Eighteen project?"

She raised her eyebrows. Gabriel was right—the general was just a little too eager to talk about military secrets. He had an agenda of his own. If the heat washing a warning across her skin was any indication, it boded her no good.

"It's been mentioned, yes."

The general leaned back in his chair. "By who? Allars or Haynes?"

He was direct, if nothing else. She shrugged lightly. "We pieced together details from what they've both said. Which wasn't much, believe me."

"Nor should it be. Both had behavior modifications." He hesitated, as if waiting for a reaction.

She crossed her arms and returned his gaze steadily. After a few seconds, he continued.

"The first eight people on your list—Allars included—have nothing to do with Generation Eighteen."

A point she already knew, as Allars had already told her that those eight—the names on her birth certificate—were test subjects rather than scientists. But for his safety, and maybe even her own, it was best to pretend ignorance. "Then what were they involved in?"

The general considered her for a moment. "Have you ever heard of the Penumbra project?"

She didn't bat an eyelid. "No."

He continued to stare at her, his expression neither believing nor disbelieving, just blank. As if, in that moment in time, there was absolutely no one at home in the general's mind. King had a similar blankness. Were the two conferring mind to mind?

"The two projects," the general said, "were only connected by the fact that the same five scientists worked on both."

A waitress came in, carrying two coffees. Sam waited until she'd left before continuing. "But from what we can gather, Emma Pierce did not. She was only a part of the Generation Eighteen project."

"That's true."

"Then what, exactly, was Generation Eighteen?"

The general picked up his coffee and sipped at it slowly. Then he reached for the tray of savories, sampling several. Obviously trying to decide just how much to tell her.

"King here is a product of Generation Eighteen."

So he *was* Maxwell's brother—or, at the very least, his test tube brother. She raised an eyebrow. "So Hopeworth is breeding children?"

"Special children, with special gifts. Not all weapons are mechanical, you know."

The hint of pride in his voice rolled revulsion through her. Tiny children growing in a bloodless, emotionless vacuum, pawns to the military's whims? What madness was that? No wonder King acted like a robot. He'd probably had any sort of humanity hammered out of him. "And the seventeen children placed into Greenwood twenty-two years ago?"

"Failures. Nowadays, we place them into care."

Meaning that in the past they'd been discarded with the other rubbish? God, what sort of monsters were these men? "Why were they considered failures?"

"Because they were born human."

And that was a failure? That they'd even managed to survive made them successful, surely. "But why adopt them out? Why not keep them in the military environment? Surely even mere humans could find a place of worth in Hopeworth?"

His smile was cold. "If we wanted human soldiers, we could recruit them. Besides, we don't have the facilities to raise children."

Yet they had the facilities to raise "gifted" children? What was the damn difference? "Then why were the failures being prescribed Jadrone? The drug has no effect on humans."

The general raised an eyebrow. "The SIU system is better than we thought."

Meaning, she gathered, such information would be buried deeper in the future. "The autopsies revealed severe bone degeneration in King and Maxwell. Why would that be?"

The general exchanged a glance with King. The younger man's eyes went curiously blank again, and then life returned as he glanced back to the general. It was almost as if the general was asking permission to explain.

Maybe that explained King's presence here. He was the link back to base. Which might also mean every word they said was being monitored.

But how, if Han had the scramblers up?

The general met her gaze again. "Though our failures could not shift or change, they still carried the genes. In manipulating them in the manner we did, we accelerated some of the problems shifters face."

"But only two of our four victims had the degeneration."

He nodded. "It depends on which genes were matched. Some got lucky."

Or unlucky, depending on your view. "Then why were the two without the degeneration being prescribed Jadrone? The drug is dangerous long term, and kills changers outright."

"We discovered a mix that hybrids can take with no ill-effects."

She wondered how they'd discovered it. Wondered how many had died in agony before they did. "Do you know if there's a drug in development that can take Jadrone's place?"

The general exchanged another glance with King. "No. Why do you ask?"

"Harry Maxwell was a junkie addicted to Jadrone. Yet a week before he was murdered, he gave up cold turkey. His supplier said he'd found something to replace it."

"I know of no such drug."

Was he lying? She wasn't sure. Either way, it was obviously time to change the direction of her questions.

"Why do at least two of our victims have Emma Pierce listed as their birth mother, when Hopeworth took her ovaries long before she was ever able to produce children?"

The general smiled. "You've certainly done your research,

young lady."

"I'm trying to save lives, General. We think someone is going after your failures."

"It could be just coincidence."

The look in his eyes told her he didn't believe it was. "Answer the question, General."

He smiled. A crocodile toying with his prey, she thought.

"We never did anything without the permission of people involved. In Generation Eighteen, the sacrifice was one they made willingly."

Not if what Allars said was true. "Then why was Emma Pierce listed as birth mother to at least two of your failures when in truth the children were conceived and raised in a test tube?"

"Because, in a sense, she *was* their mother. If the eggs from her ovaries resulted in successful births—and by this I mean children evolved from the initial procedure and reached full term—then she was listed as birth mother on the certificate."

Given a woman's ovaries carried all the eggs she needed to see her through her years of menstruation, it left open the possibility of there being hundreds of children out there who owed their existence to the unknowing Emma. It also meant that there could have been literally thousands of children who began their journey to life only to have it snuffed out by natural or military causes.

Her heart ached at the thought. But maybe it hurt more simply because she could never have children of her own. "And the seventeen children placed into Greenwood? Were they the only failures from the project?"

"The only ones that survived, yes."

"How many of them can Emma call her own?"

The general hesitated. "Nine, I believe. But surely that is something you can discover yourself."

She smiled. Of course she could, but it was easier to ask the source directly. "What about successes? How many of those belong to Emma Pierce?"

"Five."

"Are they still with Hopeworth?"

"Yes."

And would be forever, if the general's tone was anything to go by. "How were people like Emma selected for these projects?"

"They volunteered. We had criteria, of course."

"Was one of those criteria to have no family outside of

Hopeworth?"

The general began to tap the table lightly. It was the first sign of annoyance she'd seen in him. His stern features were as impassive as ever.

"People join Hopeworth with the knowledge that, once accepted, it becomes your life. Only with retirement can you walk away. The 'no family' policy is more a general policy for Hopeworth itself than one related to the projects."

From what they'd learned, even retirement was no guarantee of escape. "Did Emma Pierce have a sister?"

"No. Her family was killed in an auto accident when she was a child." He hesitated, staring at her bluntly. "As you surely know."

"We do. Only Allars swears Emma had a sister. Claimed to have met her once."

"Impossible." But his quick frown told of his uncertainty.

"Why was Emma chosen for the project?"

"As I said, she volunteered."

"Yeah, but surely all volunteers are not automatically selected."

His quick grin conjured more images of crocodiles. "No. Emma Pierce had the right qualities."

"Those being?"

The tempo of his finger tapping increased. "Her father was a shifter. Her mother, a changer. Emma herself could do both."

She stared at him, uncertain at first whether she'd heard right. "What do you mean, she could do both? I thought you had to be one or the other?"

"Hybrids are very rare—I think the figure is something like a one in a million chance."

"Did Generation Eighteen defy the odds?"

"We were more successful than the quoted figure, yes."

So the military had hybrids at their disposal. Her gaze went to King. Hybrids with psychic abilities. "Why wasn't Emma listed as a hybrid?"

The general's smile was disdainful. "Because those who do the testing do not know what to look for. Generally, the hybrid is stronger in one area. Emma was listed as a changer simply because that was her strongest ability."

Which meant, more than likely, that Emma's sister had also escaped the net. They had a definite suspect. Now all they had to do was find her—and stop her.

"Is it possible for one of your hybrids to have escaped and

be killing her less successful brothers and sisters?"

"No. As I'm sure you're aware, everyone at Hopeworth is tagged. All movements are monitored. Even mine."

She nodded. "The question had to be asked."

"I'm sure it did." He leaned back in his chair, regarding her through slightly narrowed eyes. "You have very unusual eyes, young lady."

The tension level jumped several degrees, though why she wasn't entirely sure. She took a long drink of water and nodded. "A few people have commented on that."

"Inherited from your mother or father?"

"I was placed into state care as a teenager. I have no memory of my parents." Her smile was grim. "As I'm sure you already know, general."

He flashed his reptilian smile again. "I admit to doing a little checking myself."

"Why?"

"I thought you might be one of our rejects. I wondered if, perhaps, the programming had slipped and you were using this case to learn more about Hopeworth. Something similar happened recently with another project's reject."

So Hopeworth knew how to reprogram babes. The place was definitely the stuff of nightmares. "I was not a Greenwood attendee."

"No. And we never did use the Ashwood center."

He'd definitely done more than a little checking if he knew she'd been in Ashwood's care. She took another sip of water to ease the sudden dryness in her throat. Was it just nerves, or had the temperature jumped by several degrees?

"There *are* natural redheads in this world, general," she remarked, voice dry.

"Oh I agree. But your hair is not just red. It is more a red-gold, and in certain lights—this candlelight, for example—appears molten. It is something of a signature for our creations."

She glanced at King. Molten was an apt description for his hair. "Coincidence, general."

"Maybe."

His tone suggested he didn't think it was so. "General, I'm nearly thirty. Too old for the Generation Eighteen project by about five years."

"I'm well aware of that. There were other projects, of course."

"Like Penumbra?"

"Penumbra was our only true failure." The finger tapping hesitated slightly. "Though sometimes I wonder."

He glanced briefly at King. Again, she had the sudden impression of information exchanged, though neither man moved or spoke.

The general pushed back his chair and rose. "I don't believe there is much more we can help you with."

Meaning there wasn't much more he *intended* to help her with. She nodded. "Thank you for meeting me, General. You've cleared up a few problems."

"Yes, it's been most…interesting. Please call if you need anything else."

If she needed anything else, Gabriel could do the calling. "I will."

He nodded, and walked from the room. Tension flowed like water from her limbs, and she took a deep breath. She hadn't realized just how uneasy the general had made her feel.

She took another deep breath, and then she doubled over in the chair as cramps knotted her stomach. Cursing softly, she grabbed her bag and stumbled to the restroom.

And discovered, at the grand old age of nearly thirty, she was getting her first period.

Ten

Gabriel ducked under the police tapes and walked toward the house. The red and blue lights of the emergency vehicles washed across the white walls of the two-story building, providing color to an otherwise lifeless looking landscape.

Unlike the houses surrounding it, the owner here had gone for the minimalist look—no trees, no grass, just white concrete to every corner. It was a landscaping trend he hoped didn't catch on.

He showed his badge to the gnarled looking police officer manning the front door, then walked inside. The smell of blood hit him immediately. Its odor was rich and sweet and almost fresh. Obviously, the murderer had been violent again.

The scent led him into the kitchen. Warren Michaels and his autopsy team were already present. Warren himself was near the body. Annoyance flickered through Gabriel. His brother must have called them in, even though he knew Gabriel preferred to be first at the scene—it was easier to imagine what had happened without the inference of others.

The crimecorder hovering in the middle of the room spun round. "Identification, please."

"Gabriel Stern, SIU," he intoned, almost absently.

The first victim lay halfway between the cooking units and the bench. Her body was all angles, like a doll some child had broken and abandoned. Blood gleamed darkly on the white tiles, and it had splashed against the glass-fronted cooking units. In the pool of blood near the victim's head, something metallic glittered.

A dart, he realized, and looked across at the window. The finger size hole was plain to see. But why had the murderer tried to drug her victim first? That was out of pattern—and obviously hadn't worked, if the torn apart state of the kitchen was anything to go by. The victim had put up quite a fight before she'd succumbed.

He knelt next to Michaels. "Anything new?"

Michaels snorted softly. "Yeah, the whole method of killing. She's getting more violent each time." He pointed to the purple bruising around the woman's neck. "Strangled her until she was unconscious, and then stabbed her several times before gutting her. We're dealing with a very sick person here."

Or an extremely angry person. "How did the killer get in?"

"Glass door in the dining room."

"Forced?"

"No. Can you believe they'd left it open? In this day and age?"

He smiled. Michaels had obviously never made a similar mistake. "No tray of cigarette butts this time?"

"She barely had time to escape. She must have been going out the back door as the State coppers were breaking in the front door."

"Where's the second victim?"

"Upstairs bathroom." The com-unit Michaels held beeped. "ID confirmed on this one. Margaret Jones."

Hopeworth had no imagination when it came to names, that was for certain. "Adopted parents been notified?"

"Unit being sent there now."

He nodded and rose. Red droplets led away from the body of Margaret Jones, leading back into the entrance hall. There was a small cluster near the base of the stairs, as if the murderer had stopped, and looked up. Perhaps the second victim had come out to investigate the noise, only to see the bloodied killer and her knife.

But if that were the case, why retreat to the bathroom rather than heading for the nearest window? Even if she'd broken a limb in the jump to the ground, she might well have saved her life. The killer wasn't likely to come after her in the middle of the street.

He walked up to the first floor. There was another gathering of droplets at the top of the stairs, indicating the killer had stopped once again, perhaps to listen. Which in a sense contradicted Warren's theory that the killer was angry. Someone in the middle of a blood rage wasn't this cautious.

So why was she becoming more brutal with each murder?

He headed towards the first doorway. It turned out to be the main bedroom. The pillows bore the indentations of two heads, and the rumpled state of the queen-size bed gave evidence to the fact that not a lot of sleeping had been going on recently.

He moved on. The next room was another bedroom, which was in the process of being turned into an office. The bed still had a place but it was squashed in on corner while desks, chairs and filing cabinets, all new and still wrapped in plastic, filled the middle of the room.

The killer hadn't bothered to stop in either room. The droplets moved on, evenly spaced. He frowned. The killer must have injured herself in the fight downstairs. The blood was too consistent to be dripping from a knife.

He finally came to the bathroom, and he realized the second woman must have fled here because the door was lockable. The wood bore heel marks, and the catch had been torn from the frame. A second Crimecorder hovered in the doorway. Gabriel showed his ID and stepped past it.

Only to stop cold.

The second victim was his sister, Miranda.

**

Sam dialed Gabriel's number. All she got was an engaged signal—something she'd been getting for the last half-hour. Frowning, she put the viaphone back in her pocket. Something was wrong. He wasn't in danger, but something was definitely wrong. There was an ache close to her heart—an ache that was his, somehow echoing through her.

She studied the car's onboard computer for several seconds, wondering what she should do—go home, as he'd ordered earlier, or try to find out what was happening. And really, it was a no-brainer. How could she sleep knowing something was wrong? She punched Gabriel's address into the computer.

As the vehicle spun around and headed back to the city, she leaned back and watched the traffic roll by. That was the nice thing about these auto-drives. You could be as tired as all hell and it didn't matter. The auto-drive would get you to your destination regardless of the condition you were in. Of course, if the satellites ever malfunctioned, there was likely to be the biggest damn accident in recorded history.

She yawned hugely and closed her eyes. It seemed she'd barely gone to sleep when the car pulled to a halt and beeped softly.

She climbed out and looked up. There were no lights on in Gabriel's apartment. She climbed the steps and leaned on the buzzer for several seconds. No response. Frowning, she stepped back, staring up. If he was still at the murder scene, why wasn't he answering his phone?

She got back into the car, dug out the viaphone and tried his number again. Same result—engaged. Maybe his phone was charging. She dialed SIU. Christine answered on the second ring.

"Christine, Agent Ryan here. Can you check and see if A.D. Stern's viaphone is working?"

"One moment please." She turned away from the screen. The overhead lighting caught her hair, turning the black strands a rich dark blue. They'd certainly worked on making her realistic, Sam thought. Wisps of hair swayed with every move, and if you looked hard enough, you could see her breathe.

"A.D. Stern's phone is currently offline."

"Turned off?"

"Yes."

In the time she'd known him, that phone had never been turned off. "Who's on the cleanup team at Greenvale?"

"Agents Michaels and James."

"Could you patch me through to Michaels?"

"One moment please."

Christine disappeared, to be replaced a few seconds later by Warren Michaels' drawn features.

"Agent Ryan. What can I do for you?"

"I'm looking for A.D. Stern. He still there?"

"Left about forty minutes ago. Why?"

She hesitated. "He asked me to report in. I'm just trying to find him."

"Tried his viaphone?"

"No, I thought I'd call you first, just to piss you off."

Michaels raised an eyebrow, a slight grin twitching his mouth. "Yeah, dumb question I suppose. I guess you've tried his home number too, in which case, I can't help you."

She bit her lip. Gabriel was fine when he'd left her at Han's, which meant something must have happened on the way to the murder scene or at the scene itself.

"Did anything strange occur while he was there?"

Michaels snorted, and rubbed his eyes. "If you can call discovering your sister was one of the victims strange, then, yeah, I guess it did."

"*What?*"

"Yeah. He was shaken, as you would expect. Left pretty much immediately after."

She rubbed her eyes. "You got an official ID?"

"Yeah. Miranda Stern, current address fourteen Hillsyde Street, Strathmore."

Miranda. The sister he'd been desperate to find. Her name must have been on the list of Hopeworth adoptees. Christ, what a mess. "Who's listed as next of kin?"

"A Jessie McMahon."

"Got an address or number?"

"Yeah, hang on a sec."

An almost fierce look of concentration came over his face. After a second, Jessie McMahon's address and phone number appeared on a slip of paper from the side of her viaphone. She shoved it into her pocket. She had no right, and no real reason, to call just yet.

"That fax through okay?" he said. "I hate these things. I'd only just got the hang of the old phone."

She grinned. "Came through perfect. What about the murders? Anything different from the first four?"

"Yeah, she's getting more violent. She tried drugging her first victim, only it didn't work. Both women put up a good struggle before they died."

"What was the entry/exit point?"

"Came through an open back door and left through the bathroom window as the cops were breaking in the front door."

"What was the first victim's name?"

Michaels glanced down for a second. "Margaret Jones."

The killer certainly wasn't selecting her victims by alphabetical order, yet there had to be some sort of system. These weren't random picks off the list—the killer knew precisely what she was doing.

"Other than the violence, was there anything different in the murderer's actions?"

Michaels scratched his chin. "Well, she had no time for a ciggy, that's for sure. But she didn't with the doc, either." He hesitated, and frowned. "She injured herself this time. Right hand. And pretty badly, if the constant flow of blood is any indication."

"When you do an analysis on the blood, could you patch me through the results?"

"Sure thing."

"Thanks, Michaels." She hung up, then redialed SIU and got put through to Izzy.

"This is becoming a habit, sweetie. Don't you ever sleep?"

She rubbed gritty-feeling eyes. "Not lately, I don't. Iz, did you finish the search on Dr. Francis?"

"I surely did. She was born in New South Wales in 1987, the third child of a Meg and John Francis."

Which made her sixty years old. Only slightly more than she'd guessed. "No relation to Emma Pierce then?"

"No, honey child. Afraid not."

Damn. Every clue they'd had pointed to Emma's elusive sister. If Dr. Francis wasn't the sister, how was she connected to the case? She *was* connected, of that Sam was sure. "Were you able to acquire the surveillance tapes from her building?"

"Yes."

"Any visits from anyone connected to this case?"

Iz twirled the boa for several seconds. "Max Burton and Harry Maxwell were regulars until the time of Harry Maxwell's death."

She raised her eyebrows. Max had moved from his lair? It had to be love. "What hospital is Max holed up in?"

"City central."

"His condition listed?"

The boa twirled again. "Critical but stable."

"Great. Iz, can you do a search of the case file and grab the list of children placed into Greenwood's care?"

"List grabbed, sweetie."

"Patch it through to my viaphone, will you?"

"Consider it patched."

The viaphone beeped, indicating it was receiving information. "Thanks Izzy."

"Have a nice night, sweetness."

She hung up then glanced at her watch. It was nearly two in the morning. The hospital wasn't going to let her interview Max at this hour, no matter how vital it might be. She'd have to wait until morning. All she could really do now was head home, and get a few hours sleep.

***

Sam woke with a start. Her heart thundered, a rhythm that spoke of fear. Heat crawled over her skin, warning of danger. She glanced at the time. Four fifteen. She'd been home for nearly two hours, and asleep about half that.

She stared into the darkness that filled the living room. She'd fallen asleep on the sofa, as she did most nights. The TV had tuned itself off, and the only sound to be heard was the wind sighing through the window she'd left slightly open.

So what had woken her so abruptly?

She wasn't sure. Frowning, she rose and headed to the bathroom. But halfway there, she heard it—a slight beep outside her front door. An inconspicuous sound unless you knew what it meant. Someone was using a key-coder to break into her apartment.

The sensation of danger crawled over her skin, so intense it burned. But before she could move, the door handle turned. She caught her breath, barely daring to breathe, and hoped like hell the shadows would hide her.

The door opened slightly. A figure appeared, dressed in black, features covered by a mask. A woman.

She hesitated in the doorway, and then she threw something towards the bedroom. It landed with a soft thump, the impact obviously cushioned by the thick carpet. The woman stepped back and closed the door.

Sam stepped towards the object on the floor. It was round and metallic, and it had numbers that glowed into the darkness. Numbers that were counting down from ten...nine...eight...

A goddamn bomb.

She swore and dove for the window. The bomb beeped and then exploded. Heat sizzled across her bare feet as she crashed through the window. Glass and flames followed her into the night as she tumbled down to ground. Only, like a cat, she somehow landed not only on her feet, but unhurt. She wasted no time on reflecting how or why this was possible, running instead for the front of the building.

A car engine roared to life. She cursed and pounded around the corner. Lights cut into the darkness. She threw up her arm to protect her eyes, and then she realized the lights were drawing close. The engine roared and tires squealed as the driver accelerated—directly at her.

She threw herself sideways, but not fast enough. The car swiped her side, and pain leapt like fire through her body. She hit the concrete with a grunt. Darkness surged through her and she knew no more.

***

Gabriel leaned back in his chair and rubbed his eyes. They ached, like the rest of him ached, his heart most of all. But there was no time to rest, no time to contemplate *what if*. Not until he caught the bitch who'd murdered his sister.

Behind him, his father paced, his strides long and somehow furious. Grief was something that hadn't fully hit the Stern clan yet—anger, and the need to find Miranda's killer, were uppermost in everyone's mind.

Which was why they were here. Though Federation's headquarters was supposedly on Collins Street, this small bomb shelter was its true heart. One of a dozen built within the city during the new millennium, when the race wars were at a peak. The shelter was a two-story deep complex that housed the Federation's information gathering center. The SIU might pride itself on having an extensive network system, but the Federation had operatives in every government, every union, and every rebellious group currently on record. Though officially the Federation was not terribly active these days, it kept its finger on the pulse and was ready to intervene when and where needed. No matter whether that intervention meant direct or verbal assault.

Right now, those resources were concentrated on finding his sister's killer.

The door behind them opened. Gabriel glanced around. Stephan walked to the table and dropped a sheaf of papers on the glass-topped desk.

"That's everything we can find on Hopeworth and its projects." He collapsed into a chair and rubbed his eyes. Though family members currently manned the info center, the image Stephan retained was the image the world knew—black hair, green eyes. The Stephan that was the image of their father rather than his true self, Gabriel's identical twin. Even here, in the true heart of Federation, they had to be careful. "Our contact in Hopeworth wasn't able to help—security has been tightened since these murders began."

Gabriel raised an eyebrow. "Since they began? Did he say why?"

"Security breach the day before the murders started, apparently."

"Someone got into their system," he mused. "That's how the killer found out about the Generation Eighteen adoptees."

"And probably why the General was so anxious to meet with you. He wanted to know how much SIU knew."

He nodded, and glanced at his watch. "I'll call Sam at seven and scc how the meet went."

Stephan's gaze narrowed. "Why not call her now?"

"Because it's four in the morning, and she deserves to get a few hours sleep before I start hounding her again."

"Miranda is dead—doesn't finding her killer take precedence?" There was an almost accusatory note in Stephan's rich tone.

He clenched his fist and somehow restrained the urge to launch across the table and belt his brother. "I know Miranda is dead. I found her, remember?"

"Enough, both of you." Charles slapped a palm down on the table. The sound ricocheted through the abrupt silence, as sharp as a gunshot. "Fighting between ourselves is not the answer. And as much as I want to find this murderous bitch, I agree with Gabriel. What young Samantha has discovered can wait until morning. I have a feeling that we have all the clues we need right here."

He nudged the case reports with a finger. Gabriel stared at his twin for several seconds, saw the anguish and guilt in his eyes, which was no doubt a mirror of his own. Like him, Stephan felt he could, *should*, have done more to prevent Miranda's murder. He sighed and reached for the top folder. "We've been through these. There's nothing here."

Charles pulled a chair out and sat down. "How is the killer getting in and out from the murder scenes?"

"I think she's a hybrid; one we haven't got on record."

Stephan raised an eyebrow. "The SIU tests are pretty intensive. It's doubtful that we missed one."

"But it's only in the last ten or so years that our tests have become so precise. Before that, it was hit and miss, with most hybrids being allocated shifter or changer status, depending on which was their strongest trait. Emma Pierce was sixty-one. So was her sister. There's no record of Emma coming in for tests since puberty. "

Stephan frowned. "If she was part of Hopeworth, that's not surprising. As for the sister, we haven't been able to find anything on her yet."

"A little too convenient, don't you think?"

"Erasing records is not something an everyday hacker can achieve—not without setting off alarms."

"If they got into Hopeworth, we're dealing with someone a little more skilled than your average computer hacker."

"True." Stephan rubbed his chin thoughtfully. "You know, it might also indicate someone who has regular access to records. How else would they get into the system without raising alarms?"

"A government employee?" It was certainly a distinct possibility. As Stephan said, anyone without clearance hacking into the file system would have raised alarms. It was doubtful they could have erased data so completely without getting caught.

"You might even be looking for a cop," Charles said, deep voice somber. "They have access to all manner of records, and who would have a better understanding of how to avoid detection at a crime scene?"

Gabriel frowned. "If our killer was a cop, her hybrid status would have been picked up in the six month checkups."

"They never picked up Sam's extra chromosome," Stephan said. "It might just be possible they'd miss this. Race is not something checked every six months, unless the officer has noted his or her desire to become a vampire."

"True, but still…" He hesitated as the door opened.

Jessie walked in and dropped several sheets of paper on the table. "We traced the birth certificates for every one of the Greenwood adoptees. Emma Pierce is listed as birth mother for nine of them." She hesitated, tears suddenly welling in her green eyes. "The killer is working straight down the list. Miranda…"

She broke off. Stephan stood, gathering her in his arms and holding tight. Gabriel reached for the papers. Emma Pierce's children were highlighted. Miranda was number five of nine. He looked up.

"Then we know the next victim. Jeanette Harris is number six on the list."

Charles smiled grimly. "Get protection on her right away."

"Already done," Stephan said. He handed Jessie a handkerchief, then met Gabriel's gaze. "If our killer is a cop, she'll know about the safety measures we've taken."

"It won't stop her. She's a hybrid—if she's in animal form, more than likely our people won't even see her." He hesitated. "But Sam might be able to."

Charles studied him through narrowed eyes. "Why do you say that? I thought she didn't have any talents?"

No talent or too much talent? He was beginning to think it was the latter. "Test results to date indicate no psychic inclination, but I've seen her in action. In certain situations, she can sense the presence of other nonhumans. She sensed the shifter who'd attacked Finley in the labs, for instance, even though no alarm had been given."

"And didn't she sense the fact that Mary was a vampire long before either of us were aware of it?" Stephan said.

He nodded. "And yet she *didn't* know you were a shifter and that Martin was also a vampire."

"As if she could sense the evil in people, more than what they were," Charles murmured. "How very interesting."

"And useful, if that is the case," Stephan said. He glanced at Gabriel, gaze hardening. "Assign her to Jeanette Harris immediately."

Gabriel stared at his brother for several seconds and then reached for his viaphone. In that instant, pain hit, a sledgehammer that belted him sideways. He hit the floor hard, clutching his head, desperate to break the connection running fire up the left side of his body and into his brain.

"Gabriel!" Fear and confusion ran through his brother's voice.

Hands grabbed him, touching his neck, feeling for a pulse. Darkness welled, a tide that threatened to overwhelm him. "I'm okay. It's not me," he managed to gasp out.

"Sam?" Stephan's voice, close by his side.

He somehow managed to nod. In that instant, as fast as it had come, the pain eased, becoming a muted throb in the back of his mind. He took a deep breath and shook off his brother's grip and struggled to his feet.

"What the hell was that all about?" Charles demanded, lean face pale.

"It appears Gabriel and Sam have formed a telepathic link of some kind," Stephan said. "What you just saw is him experiencing what has happened to her."

Though Stephan's voice was tightly controlled, Gabriel nevertheless felt his twin's anger. It was as if the link being forced with Sam had somehow unfettered the link with his brother. Neither of which he wanted.

He reached for his viaphone again and quickly dialed her home number. No answer. He tried her viaphone, and got the same result. "She's not answering."

"I'll arrange for a team to go and check her apartment." Stephan's phone beeped. He moved away slightly and answered it.

Jessie touched Gabriel's arm, catching his attention. "You can use the link to find her, you know."

He met his sister's compassionate gaze. Knew she could taste the worry in his mind. Jes had taken after their mother, and she was both an empath and a clairvoyant. "What do you mean?"

Her quick smile was sad, and in some ways, an echo of the almost bitter smile Stephan had given him last night. "I mean your connection with this woman must be strong if a link has been forged despite your determination to avoid all such bonds." She hesitated and tucked a wayward brown curl behind her ear. "If you open fully to the bond, you can use it to track her down."

Once opened, never closed. He didn't want that sort of closeness with anyone ever again. Death was bad enough in itself, but when you could feel it within every pore and fiber of your being...

"Andrea was a long time ago," she said softly.

A long time, yes. But forgotten, never. In the worst of his dreams he could still feel the bullet that had torn through her heart and shattered his world. Could still feel the hand of death as it reached for her soul.

Jessie touched his face gently, like a mother calming a frightened child. "Such fear was perhaps understandable when you were eighteen. But you are thirty-four, and you have hurt Stephan more than you can ever imagine."

He glanced at his twin. "I know. But blocking him out has become such habit that I'm not even aware of it anymore."

"Until this Sam of yours came along."

"She's not *my* Sam." Why did people keep calling her that? Shit, the truth was, they barely even knew each other. "She's my partner, and if I have my way, won't even be that for much longer."

Jes raised a dark eyebrow. "Are you denying your attraction?"

"When you can read the truth in my mind?" He smiled a little grimly. "I'm not that foolish. But it's an attraction I have no intention of following through. I don't want to lose another partner."

"Such things cannot always be controlled, Gabriel. As evidenced by this bond you're forming."

"If I can cut my twin from my thoughts, I can cut an unwanted connection with Sam, believe me."

Her smile became a little sad again. "You will end up a very lonely old man if you're not careful, Gabriel."

He briefly cupped her cheek with his palm. "How will I end up lonely when I have a sister who'll nag me senseless?"

"You're hopeless, little brother." She leaned forward and

placed a light kiss on his cheek. "And soon you will learn to watch what you wish for."

Gabriel glanced up sharply. She met his gaze with a cryptic smile and stepped back as Stephan approached.

"That was headquarters." His face was grim. "Sam's apartment has just been bombed."

Jessie gasped softly. "Is she all right?"

"A question Gabriel can no doubt answer."

He ran a hand through his hair. "She's alive. She wasn't caught in the bombing, that much I know."

"Then you'd better figure out how to find her. She's probably our best shot of stopping this murderous bitch fast." Stephan glanced across the room. "Meantime, dad and I will search the State Police recruitment records and see if we can find anything suspicious."

He watched the two men leave the room and then looked at his sister. "How do I use the link to find her?"

***

Sam groaned and held her head. There were a thousand tiny madmen in there, all intent on beating drums out of sync with each other. The headaches she'd experienced before had nothing on this. The noise created by the madmen vibrated through every nerve, every cell—it even seemed to gain form and dance around her. Her whole body thrummed to the beat of its tune.

Slowly, she realized the noise was real, not imagined.

Slowly, she realized she was not alone.

She lifted her head. Dr. Francis, the vet she'd taken her borrowed cat to, stood four feet away, her arms crossed and a contemptuous look on her face. Behind her, though cloaked in darkness, Sam could make out a series of tumbledown brick walls. No light broke the darkness, and the air had a stale smell. All around them, noise hummed. Machinery, she realized. They were on a building site.

But what kind of site operated in the middle of the night?

"You should be dead," Francis said. Her voice was still ultra polite, still disinterested. "First you managed to overcome a lethal dose of Jadrone, and then you somehow survive a car accident that would have killed most."

"*You* were the budgie in Max's office," she murmured. The men in her head were beginning to find some rhythm, making some semblance of thought possible. "Why did you think injecting Jadrone into me might stop me?"

A smile fluttered across the doctor's brightly painted lips. "I can sense others of my kind, as you also appear able to do."

If she thought her a changer, at least that explained the dose of Jadrone. "But why try to kill me? And why try to kill Max? Wasn't he your lover?"

"He was nothing more than a weak fool." Contempt dripped from the doctor's voice. "He would have told you of our partnership. Would have implicated me in Harry's murder. With Max all but dead, I thought I was safe until you showed up at the office."

So the doctor had known who she was all along and had simply played along. She must have followed her to O'Hearn's and then home. Obviously, the doc had no idea that Harry's murder was tied in with a serial killer. Maybe she didn't read the newspapers.

She tried to ease the ache in her left leg by shifting her weight slightly and realized she couldn't even move. Her legs were wrapped in something cold and heavy. Chains.

Fear rose, but she thrust it away. There was no time for fear, only escape. And if she didn't do that soon she would die, of that much she was sure.

"How were you involved with Harry?"

"He was nothing more than a test subject."

"For your new drug," she guessed. "An addictive and expensive replacement for Jadrone."

"Yes." She hesitated. A siren blasted through the hum of machinery. "Time to go, I'm afraid. You are in the basement of the old South Melbourne Hospital. A fitting place to die, I think,"

At least that explained the predawn activity. Because of the hospital's proximity to a large number of office buildings, the demolition team had only been given clearance to work between midnight and dawn.

"The chains that contain you are silver-coated," Francis continued. "You cannot change shape until you escape them, my dear. And by then, death will be falling around your ears."

"You won't get away with this, Francis. The SIU doesn't take kindly to someone killing their operatives." She had no idea whether this was true or not, but hell, it sounded good.

"By the time they find out you didn't die in your apartment bombing, you will be dead and I will be long gone."

The doctor stepped back and raised her arms—her body

blurred, briefly resembling putty being squeezed into a too-small tube. Then she became a budgie and flitted away through the darkness.

Sam glanced down at the chains. The two ends ran off in the darkness, one to her right, and one to her left. They were connected to hooks in the wall that kept the chains taut. All she had to do was unlatch one and she'd be free.

She lunged sideways. The chains around her waist bit deep, and breathing became difficult. She ignored it, and tried to flick the end of the chain off the hook on the wall. It didn't even budge. Cursing softly, she sat back up and grabbed hold of the chain. Taking a deep breath, she pulled back as hard as she could.

A muffled thump ran through silence, followed by a thick wave a dust. She coughed, and glanced up. A shudder ran through ceiling above her, and cracks began to appear, spider-like lines that raced from the edges toward the middle.

Fear surged. Time was running out. She swore and pulled back on the chain again. The hook on the wall shifted slightly. Another muffled thump ran through the silence. Dirt and plaster began to rain down on her.

"Come on, you mother, come *on!*"

The hook came free with a sudden "pop," and sent her sprawling backwards. At the same time, another muffled thump ran across the shattering darkness, closer this time. The ceiling above her groaned. The spider-like lines intermingled and the whole ceiling dropped.

She screamed and threw herself sideways. But the chains still restricted movement and all she could do was throw her hands over her head and pray for a miracle.

Eleven

Gabriel hit the ground running. Part of the old hospital building had already been demolished. Dust rose in a wave, stinging the night sky with the scent of decay and death.

He wrenched open the door to the command center. The two men inside turned around, surprise evident in their expressions. He flashed his badge. "You have to stop the demolition. We have an agent trapped inside the building."

"I can't. It's automated."

He grabbed the man's shirt and dragged him close. "Listen very carefully. I have an agent trapped inside. I want the demolition stopped, and I don't care how you do it."

"Okay, okay," the man stuttered. "We'll try."

"Don't try. Just do it." He thrust the man away from him, grabbed the flashlight that was sitting on a bench, and headed back outside.

Another muffled explosion ran across the silence. The old building seemed to shudder, and then the west wing came down in almost graceful silence. More dust rose into the sky.

He swore and ran for the central building, the area that had once housed the hospital's administration and emergency services. That's where she was.

The main doors were boarded shut, but several well-placed kicks soon fixed that. Dust rolled out to greet him, as thick as the darkness beyond the doorway.

He coughed, and turned on the flashlight. Another explosion rolled through the night, followed quickly by a muffled scream.

Sam. As yet unhurt by the falling debris.

He picked his way down the shattered corridor, heading for the emergency exit sign that gleamed brightly in the beam of the flashlight. The stairs beyond were a tangle of wood and jagged plasterboard. He shone the light upwards. Part of the ceiling had collapsed. It wouldn't take much to bring the whole lot down.

He continued on. Dust caught at his throat, making him cough, and the air became stale, almost hard to breathe.

"Gabriel?" Her voice rose from the darkness, full of sudden hope.

"Here." He swung the light to the left. Her voice had come from beyond the row of disconnected walls.

"I'm trapped," she said. "Hurry."

Another explosion ran through the darkness. He swore and wondered why the fools in charge hadn't yet stopped them. Surely they could throw a power switch. No power, no computer to regulate the charges.

Plaster and brick began to rain from the ceiling, deadly missiles that drew blood every time they hit. He ran through the maze, dodging and weaving the best he could. The flashlight danced across the darkness, briefly illuminating shadowed corners. None of them held Sam.

"Talk to me, Sam!"

"Here!" she said.

She was close, so close. He kicked his way through a doorway. "Again."

"On your right, through the door, I think."

There were two doors on his right. Letting instinct take control, he booted open the second of the two. The light picked out her dust-covered face.

He knelt by her side. The ceiling had half collapsed, covering her in plaster and wood. But that wasn't what held her. Chains did. Anger rose, swift and hard. The would-be assassin had better hope he wasn't the one who caught her.

"You okay?" He pushed the debris away from her body, grabbed the end of the chain and began to unwind it.

"Fine," she said. "How did you find me?"

He met her gaze briefly. Confusion and relief mingled in her smoke-ringed blue eyes. She wasn't aware of the bond she'd forged. Good. Perhaps he'd be able to close it before it got too strong.

"Long story." He unwound the chains from her legs and tossed them to one side. "Can you move?"

"I think so." She grabbed his hand and pulled herself up. No sooner had she put weight on her left leg than it collapsed under her.

He grabbed her before she could fall back down. "Looks like you've done some damage to your leg." He slipped an arm round her waist, taking her weight—what little there was of it. "Let's get out of here."

She didn't argue. They made their way back to the stairs, their progress agonizingly slow. Though she made no complaint, her pain was an ache that itched at the back of his mind.

Another muffled thump ran across the darkness. A shudder

ran through the bricks around them, and the dust became a wall thick enough to carve. The flashlight's bright beam flared against the soupy swirl, unable to penetrate more than a yard or so.

They struggled up the stairs. Behind them, it began to rain bricks and wood, gently at first, but increasing in volume and strength. The building was coming down.

He swung Sam up into his arms and ran like hell for the front entrance. The collapse was a tidal wave that raced behind him. He could feel the strength of it pushing at his back, urging him to fall. Plaster and wood crashed around them, and the dust was so thick he could barely breathe, let alone see.

He stumbled past a mound of wood and bricks and out the front door. A deep groaning filled the silence—the final scream of a dying building. He kept on running.

The old hospital came down with an almost silent sigh, and a sudden rush of wind battered at him, thrusting him to the ground. He twisted as he fell, so that he cushioned Sam's body with his own. For a few seconds, all he could hear was the thunder of her heart, and all he could feel was the warmth of her body pressed against him. And all he wanted to do was keep on holding her, because it felt so right, so real, somehow.

The two men scrambled out of the control room.

"Jesus man, are you all right?"

The sandy haired worker he'd threatened stopped several feet away. Which was just out of reach. "Yeah. Call an ambulance, will you?"

"I'm okay," she murmured, struggling against his hold on her.

He released her, and she rolled away from him and sat up. Though she made no sound, her teeth caught her bottom lip. Beads of sweat broke out across her brow.

"Sure you are." He took a handkerchief from his pocket and began wiping the dust from her face. Her left cheek was badly scratched, and blood oozed down to her chin. "Tell me what happened."

"I pissed off that budgie again." She took a deep, shuddering breath. "And I'm gonna sell my damn apartment. People keep insisting on bombing the damn thing."

He half-smiled at her indignant tone. "Are we talking about the budgie that tried to shit all over you in Max's office?"

"The very one. Dr. Francis. Ex-lover to one Max Carter, and would-be supplier to Harry Maxwell."

"But no relation to Emma Pierce?" he guessed.

"Unfortunately, no. She's not our serial killer, just a would-be drug mogul who hasn't taken the time to see the bigger picture. I'm going to take great delight in throwing her well-manicured butt in prison, I can tell you."

He grinned. "I almost feel sorry for Dr. Francis."

Her grin briefly echoed his. "Sure you do." Then she hesitated, her smile fading as her gaze searched his. "I'm sorry to hear about your sister."

An ache cut through his heart. An ache he'd been trying so hard to ignore. "How did you find out about it?"

It came out more abruptly than he'd intended, and she raised an eyebrow in surprise. "You weren't answering your phone, so I called Michaels to see what was going on. He told me."

"Why were you calling in the first place?"

"You asked me to report in, remember?" She leaned back on her hands and studied him for a moment. "Why the third degree?"

He thrust a hand through his hair. He hadn't meant to be so brusque, but he didn't want the whole world knowing about his sister's death, either. Not until the Stern clan had time to deal with her loss, time to say good-bye. "Sorry. I guess I'm not ready to talk freely about her murder just yet."

"Especially with me, I suppose."

Her words were a whisper he barely caught, and her expression suggested a loneliness as deep as anything he'd ever experienced. He half reached out to comfort her, and then he dropped his hand. This is what he wanted, he reminded himself fiercely. The more she thought him a bastard, the more likely it was she'd walk away. More than ever, he wanted her to remain safe.

Silence reigned as they waited for the ambulance to arrive. He itched to get back to searching for his sister's killer, but he wasn't enough of a bastard to simply walk away from Sam before she'd received medical attention.

After a few minutes, she ran a hand across her bloody chin, and asked, "How did you find me?"

He shrugged. "Local's took note of Francis' car as it sped away from your building. We traced it to here."

"Really?" There was disbelief in her face, in her voice. "Then how did you know which building I was in?"

"It was the only one left standing. I took a chance."

Her gaze searched his face. "Why are you lying to me?"

"I'm not." A siren finally sounded in the distance. He glanced past her, watching the red and blue lights of the ambulance draw close. "The ambulance is here.'

"I want to go home, not to the hospital."

"Your home's been bombed, remember?" He brushed a strand of hair from her forehead.

She jerked away from his touch, expression annoyed as she glared up at him. "I don't care."

"Okay. But let the doctor examine you first."

"Fine." She crossed her arms and stared at him mutinously.

He knew her silence would only last until they were alone. Then she'd want answers—answers he had no intention of giving.

The ambulance officers trotted across, medical bags in hand. She bore their ministrations in silence, though he could feel her annoyance, a wave of heat that washed past his mind. Having opened the link to find her, he could now feel her emotions as easily as he breathed. Touching her thoughts was only a matter of reaching out…But he had no intention of playing with that sort of fire. He'd shared such a link with Andrea. Once was more than enough.

"Severe bruising around the hip and torso area, but otherwise, you seem okay," The ambulance officer said. "You might want to go to the hospital as a precautionary measure—"

"No, I'm fine, really." She flashed Gabriel an I-told-you-so look. "I'll just go home and rest."

"Good idea." The two officers packed up their bags and walked back to the ambulance.

Gabriel called a cab and then held out his hand. She hesitated only briefly before accepting his assistance. She was still wobbly on her feet, no matter how fit she claimed to be.

The cab came within minutes. He helped her inside, climbed in beside her and punched her address into the onboard computer. Despite his earlier thoughts to the contrary, she asked no further questions. Maybe she'd finally given up.

It took half an hour to reach her apartment. Several SIU gray fords were parked out front, but the police vehicles had gone. No lights shone in any of the windows above or below her apartment—perhaps the neighbors were getting used to being woken by bomb blasts in the middle of the night.

They made their way up the stairs. Sam showed little

emotion as she stepped through the shattered doorway to her apartment.

He watched her limp to the bedroom, and then he moved across the living room to the window. Yet again she'd escaped a bomb blast by diving out into the night. He stopped and stared at the pavement below. At the very least, she should have broken a limb in a fall like that. But her bruising had come from the car, not the fall.

It would be interesting to see what O'Hearn came up with.

He turned from the window as two SIU men, bags in hand, filed out of the bedroom.

"Anything to be found, Burton?"

The big man shook his head. "Bomb was incendiary, as you can see by the flame damage. Meant to kill rather than cause structural damage. We picked out a few fragments and we'll see where they lead."

"Send me a report as soon as you can."

The big man nodded. Gabriel got out his viaphone and ordered a pickup on Dr. Jane Francis. Then he walked into the bedroom. Sam stood in the middle of the room, staring at the mess of soggy boxes almost blindly.

"Sometimes I wish I could step back in time," she said, voice a little distant, and etched with pain. "Just go back to a time when my partner was my best friend, and I was just a plain old orphan, not some kind of freak."

Her pain ran through him, a living thing he could almost taste and touch. He ached to reach out, to hold her. *Remember Andrea*, he told himself sternly. *Don't get involved too deeply.*

"We all wish for things that cannot be," he said, voice sharp. "Sometimes we just have to accept fate and get on with it."

She snorted softly. "Like you're getting on with it, Assistant Director?"

He frowned. "What do you mean?"

She didn't answer, simply shook her head and picked her way toward the window. "What do you want me to do about Francis?"

"She'll be charged with attempted murder. I've ordered her to be picked up. You'll have to write up the report as soon as you can."

She nodded. "Do you want a written report on my meeting with the general as well?"

"Yes. But you can give me the basics now, if you like."

One thing was for certain—he wasn't sending her to watch over Jeanette Harris. She'd been through enough for one night.

She crossed her arms. To anyone else she might have looked calm. Casual, even. But her anger washed through his soul and burned him with guilt.

"Nine of the seventeen children placed into Greenwood's care have Emma listed as their birth mother. She, and more than likely her sister, was a hybrid shifter-changer."

"I'd already guessed we were dealing with a hybrid."

"Did you also know that the purpose of Generation Eighteen was to design psychically-endowed hybrids for the military to use as weapons?"

So Hopeworth was playing in the genetic minefield. Maybe the kites *were* one of their creations. "Anything else?"

She was silent for several heartbeats, staring out the window. "I think there'll be trouble with the general in the future."

Her voice was almost subdued. He frowned. "What do you mean?"

"Why did the general agree to meet with us?"

"You requested information."

"Information you found out without the general's help. He told me nothing, really. But he thought I was one of the rejects trying to get information on where I came from."

His confusion deepened. "Why would he think that? You're too old, for a start."

"He said it was my hair color. Apparently, it's something of a signature in their projects."

That would certainly explain the birth certificate with eight names on it. But the general seemed to know the exact location of all his rejects. Why wouldn't he know if she was one of them?

"If you're one their rejects, you have nothing to worry about." Hopeworth had showed no interest in the Generation Eighteen rejects.

"But what if I'm not a reject? What if I'm something else entirely?"

"From what I can see, you're either a reject or in Hopeworth. What else is there?"

"I don't know." Her voice was so soft he barely caught it. "But I've a feeling I'm going to find out."

She rubbed her arms. He clenched his fists and fought the urge to walk across and comfort her.

"I've got to go," he said abruptly. "I want you to do a search through our records. See if there have been any official requests for information on our Generation Eighteen rejects."

She looked around at him, one pale eyebrow raised. "You think the killer might be a cop or agent?"

"There's a good chance. The only way she could have found these seventeen people so quickly is through official access. No alarms were raised, so the records weren't hacked into."

"And if I find anything?"

"Contact me or Stephan. Under no circumstances are you to go after her yourself."

"Edging me out again, huh?" She shook her head slightly. "I never took you for a coward, Gabriel. I guess I was wrong."

Anger rose, swift and hard, and her eyes widened. Maybe she wasn't as unaware of the link as he'd thought.

"Better me being a coward than you being dead." He hesitated and ran a hand through his hair. "Damn it, just do what you're told. I can't deal with this now."

"And you won't deal with it later," she murmured.

He smiled grimly. She knew him too well. "My viaphone is on. Contact me if you find anything."

"I've already said I would."

He stared at her for several seconds longer, taking in her slender form, the almost defiant way she stood. Like hell she'd contact him when she found anything.

But short of tying her to a chair to keep her safe, there was nothing he could do. "Make sure you lock the door when I leave," he said, then turned and walked from the room.

***

Sam scrubbed a hand across her eyes and wondered where the hell her brains were. Antagonizing Gabriel would only make him more determined to get rid of her. *If* that was possible.

He appeared on the street below and climbed quickly into a SIU car. She wondered where he was going, as it was pretty obvious he had no intention of going back to SIU. For half a second, she thought about following him, but she knew that would only get her into deeper shit. And she was in enough of that now.

She sighed softly and turned away from the window. Though her bones ached with tiredness, she knew sleep would elude her. Not that she could sleep here anyway. What the fire hadn't destroyed, the water had. The insurance company was going to love her making another claim so soon.

She walked through to the living room and locked the front door. The firebomb's damage had been confined mainly to the bedroom. Parts of the living room had been scorched, but it was more water damage out here. The books she'd salvaged after the first bombing had borne the brunt of the second. It was doubtful she'd save anything this time.

Her portable com-unit hadn't survived the blast, but that no longer mattered. She'd downloaded the information she'd collected from Jack's computer onto disks she carried in her handbag. A backup copy was stored at the bank.

She walked into the bathroom. After taking a quick shower, she filled a large overnight bag full of clothes, collected her toiletries and the few jewelry items she had, then left.

And she had no intentions of coming back, unless it was to clear out the rubbish and hand over the keys to the new owner.

Half an hour later she walked into her office.

"Computer on," she said, dropping her bags on the floor beside her desk.

Izzy's image flicked to life. "Morning, sweetness."

"Iz, I want you to run a check on the seventeen Greenwood adoptees. See if anyone besides myself and A.D. Stern has requested information on them."

"Might take a little while."

"Time is something I have plenty of." She leaned back in her chair and rubbed her eyes. The first thing she'd better do was find a new place to stay. Somewhere secluded, perhaps. At least if she was bombed again, there'd be no neighbor's to disturb.

"Could you also dig up an accommodation guide for the Melbourne metro area?"

"On screen, sweetie."

She spent an hour scanning through the list and arranging appointments, and then she grabbed a coffee and several painkillers in an attempt to ward off the growing aches in her stomach and head. No one had ever told her having periods was so damn painful. But then, her education in that regard had come from computerized health books, not from a mom who could impart *real* facts.

Izzy reappeared on the com-screen. "Search results in. There's only been one other request for information, I'm afraid."

One was all they needed. "Who?"

The purple boa twirled for several moments. "One Michael

Sanders, State Police."

"Michael? Not Michelle?"

"Yep."

The killer was female, that much was certain. Still, that didn't mean this Michael wasn't an accomplice. He was certainly worth talking to.

Not that *she'd* be talking to anyone. "Iz, send the information to A.D. Stern's viaphone, and CC it to Director Byrne. Mark it urgent."

"Consider it done, sweetie."

"Thanks."

She leaned back in her chair and propped her feet on the desk. Her eyes ached beyond belief, and everything else seemed to thump. It was nearly eight in the morning. Time, perhaps, to catch a nap. Certainly she was in no danger of being caught. Gabriel was the only one who seemed to know the location of her broom closet.

"Iz, turn off the lights and lock the door, will you? And screen calls. I don't want to be disturbed unless it's urgent."

The room went dark. She closed her eyes.

And dreamed.

She stood in the middle of an empty room. Whiteness surrounded her, so bright it made her eyes water. Though the room was empty, she was not alone.

He was here.

Though she couldn't see the hirsute stranger, his presence filled the room, a powerful, unseen shadow that circled slowly around her.

"Why have you called me?" she said.

"It is you who have done the calling, Samantha. I merely answer."

"Then show yourself."

He smiled, a sensation that ran like fire through her mind. "When you are ready to see me, you will."

"More riddles."

"No. A truth you are not ready to accept."

It made no sense. Nothing this man said made any sense.

"Tell me your problem, Samantha. Is it the kites?"

"No." She hesitated. "Did you send the kite after the five scientists?"

His smile rippled through her like shadowed sunshine. "No. And you will regret saving them."

"Why?"

"Because of their past. They deserve no future for what they have done. Their death is long overdue."

"It all ties in with the mysterious Penumbra project, doesn't it? You're the one who originally tried to destroy it." She hesitated again. "It's my duty to protect Haynes and Cooper, you know."

He said nothing for a long moment, but his thoughts continued to circle. She could almost see them, a blaze of unhappiness as bright as the sun.

"Though I rejoice their deaths, as I said, I am not the one killing the scientists."

"Who then?"

"Hopeworth has realized that their reconditioning is not as strong with some as they thought. You are not the only one Allars has talked to."

So Hopeworth was killing the scientists? Why, then, did they send those cars out to collect Allars and the others? "If our murderer has talked to him, why wouldn't she have killed him? Especially since Haynes and his mates were on the project that Emma was involved in?"

"Sometimes it is better to leave foe alive."

"Like you've left Gabriel alive?"

The fierce sunshine of his unseen smile rippled through her again. "Stern plays an important part in our future. As much as I want to destroy him, I can't."

Our future? Her and this stranger had some sort of future together? Now that was a scary thought.

"These questions are not the reason you called me here, Samantha. What really troubles you?"

"I'm selling my apartment." Why she came out with that, she wasn't entirely sure. It was a guess, maybe. This stranger seemed to know an awful lot about a past she couldn't remember. Maybe he'd also know an awful lot about the apartment she'd inherited.

His essence stopped moving. A slither of surprise ran round her. "That is your choice, of course, but can I ask why?"

She tilted her head and contemplated the shadow that was Joe Black. "People seem to like bombing it. You gave it to me, didn't you?"

"Perhaps."

"Why?"

"Because I could."

Annoyance spun around them. Hers, not his. "Why can't you just drop the riddles and give me a direct answer?"

"Why are you so afraid to seek the answers?"

She frowned. "What do you mean?"

"I gave you a clue, Samantha. A key that will unlock some answers and solve at least one riddle. You have not yet sought the lock."

"The pin," she said, remembering it.

"The pin. Seek its image and you will find your murderer. You will also find the first stepping stone to your past."

"If you know so damn much, why don't you tell me?"

"Because you will never believe. Some things we must find for ourselves."

His presence faded. With it went the bright room. She woke with a start. She rubbed a hand across her eyes and glanced at the clock. Eight forty-five. She hadn't even been asleep an hour. Sighing softly, she reached down to her bag and searched around until she found the pin. It was an abstract man and woman, standing side by side, one dark, one light. A gift from her hirsute friend when he'd saved her life about three months ago.

She leaned forward. "Iz, scan this for me." She held the pin up to the electronic eye on the upper corner of the com-screen.

Izzy reappeared, boa whirling lightly. "Scanning, sweetness." A blue light ran the length of the pin.

"Run a search on the image. I want the name and address of every company who uses it."

"Will do."

"Thanks. Can you get me personal file for Michael Sanders?"

The file appeared on screen almost instantly. She raised her eyebrows. "That was fast, Iz."

The pink fuzz ball reappeared, somehow managing to look mighty pleased with himself. "Put in a request for the file when you asked for the search results to be sent to A.D. Stern. Just in case."

Sometimes, the artificial intelligence they'd installed in these things was scary. "Good thinking, Iz."

"Thanks, sweetie."

Michael Sanders was a baby-faced man with a slender build and thinning brown hair. It was only when you looked at his eyes that you realized he was not as young as he first appeared.

Those eyes, a brilliant, unfathomable green, were the eyes of a man who'd seen, and done, too much to be merely twenty-five years old.

He had a clean slate, both as a police officer and in his private life. Good arrest record, lived alone, no wife. His parents were killed when he was a baby, but there was no mention on file about who had raised him after that. Relatives, presumably, though there was no next of kin listed.

So why didn't something feel right?

"Iz, don't suppose you could dig up whatever info and photos we have on Sanders' parents?"

"Looking for needles again, are we?"

"Could be." She frowned and stared at his photo. Those eyes just didn't belong in that face. "And dig up anything you can find on the accident that killed them."

"I may have to search through insurance reports. Might take a while."

"I've got the time Izzy, believe me." Whether the next reject did was another matter entirely.

"Found driver license photos. Not the best quality, I'm afraid."

"Enhance and display."

"Can do."

Two photos appeared on screen. Michael Sanders looked absolutely nothing like his parents. Nor did he have any siblings she could compare him with—he was an only child.

"Display Sanders birth certificate, Iz."

"On screen."

Bingo. Michael Sanders was adopted. His birth mother and father were one William and Barbara Ryan. "Iz, see what you can dig up on these two." She pointed to the two names.

The boa began to whirl. "I'm starting to stress here, darlin'."

She grinned. "You'll live."

"Three companies found using a design similar to that logo I scanned."

"Display."

The names appeared on screen. There was a textile manufacturer and a plastic surgeon, neither of which was what she was after. But the third name probably was, as it was an adoption agency.

What were the odds that *that* adoption agency was the one Michael Sanders was adopted from? Whoever this Joe Black really was, he seemed mighty aware of just what was going on. But did that make him a friend or an enemy?

She didn't know. But she had a suspicion that he was really neither, that the connection between them was deeper, more mysterious—and more dangerous—than anything like mere friendship.

"Information found on adoptive parents, Frank and Margaret Sanders."

"Hit me with it, babe."

"Frank Sanders was born in Sydney in 1955 and worked with the Metropolitan Fire Brigade. Margaret Sanders, nee Jones, was born in Melbourne in 1956 and worked as a waitress while attending night school. She became a doctor and worked at the Royal Women's Hospital. The two married in 1990, after Frank Sanders transferred to Melbourne. They adopted a child, a five year old girl named Rose Pierce, in 1995."

She stared at the screen, wondering if she'd heard right. Rose Pierce? The elusive sister of Emma Pierce? Why, then, was Michael Sanders listed as their son? "Anything else?"

"They were killed in an automobile accident in 2020."

Which was the year Michael Sanders was born. She frowned. "They adopted only the one child?"

"According to the records, yes."

She rubbed a hand across her eyes. This didn't make sense. If they only adopted Rose, why then did the records list squeaky-clean Michael as their son?

"We got anything on Rose Sanders, then?"

"Searching."

At least they now knew the reason why the initial search for Rose Pierce had come up blank, though the adoption *should* have come up.

Unless, of course, someone had deliberately buried the information. It was only due to her search on Sanders' parents that she'd even discovered Rose Pierce.

"What agency was Rose adopted from, Iz?"

"Goes by the name of Silhouettes."

A chill ran down her spine. That was the same adoption agency who used the pin's logo. Joe Black had pointed her to Rose, *not* Michael. He obviously knew a *hell* of a lot more than he was letting on. "Get me a warrant, Iz. I want to go through their files."

"Warrant on the way, sweetie. No current information on

Rose Sanders available."

She frowned. "What do you mean?"

"Driver's license lapsed in 2040. No record of utility payments since then. No credit transactions recorded. No usage of Medicare card."

"No death certificate?"

"None issued or recorded."

Interesting. Rose dropped out of site about the same time as Sanders graduated from the police academy. How the two were connected, she wasn't sure. But they *were* connected, she was sure of that.

"Warrant approved, sweetness."

"Good. Grab the adoption records and do a scan for Rose and Michael Sanders."

"Can do." The boa twirled for several minutes. "Record for Rose Pierce onscreen."

She looked through the documents. There was nothing out of the ordinary. Rose was placed into Silhouettes care when she was twelve months old, after being in the hospital for several months. A search for relatives had come up with no one. Rose stayed at the state run home until adopted by the Sanders family. "Print me a copy of the ID photo, will you?"

"Printing. No records available for Michael Sanders."

For some reason, she wasn't entirely surprised. She glanced back to Rose's file. The officer in charge of the adoption was one Mary Elliot. She frowned—that name was familiar, though she wasn't entirely sure why.

"Found a police report for the Sanders' accident, sweetie."

"Read it out loud, Iz. My headache's back."

"If you work yourself as hard as you work me, I'm not surprised."

She grinned. "Just read the report, Iz."

"The Sanders' car was run off the Great Ocean Road and plowed into a tree at high speed, killing both instantly. Several witnesses' report seeing a red four-wheel drive hit the rear of the Sanders car just before the accident. The four-wheel drive was later recovered in Warrnambool."

"Stolen?"

"Yes. There were no prints beyond the owners within the car."

"Did the witnesses ID the driver?"

"Description was deemed too vague. A big man with red-gold hair was all that the witnesses' were able to provide."

A cold sensation crept over her skin. Red gold hair—the signature of Hopeworth's children. Maybe the military *had* discovered Rose's existence, and rather than jeopardize their precious project, they'd tried to destroy Rose and her parents.

So who had looked after Michael? Rose? "Did you find anything on Michael Sanders birth parents?"

"Not a dot, sweetie."

"There has to be something on record."

"Sorry, sweetness. There's no record of a William and Barbara Ryan having a son named Michael born in 2020."

"But how is that possible? Background checks are a part of joining. With such a discrepancy in his records, he should never have been cleared to join."

The boa twirled. "I'm not the recruiting officer. Don't ask me."

She rubbed her chin. "Did anything untoward happen around the time of Sanders' supposed birth date?"

Izzy tapped a knobby foot for several seconds. "Headlines on screen, sweetie."

After flicking through several pages, she found her answer. A fire had swept through the hospital in which Michaels was supposedly born. Though no one had been killed, most of the records and computing systems had been destroyed."

She leaned back in her chair. If she was a gambler, she'd put money on the fact that the fire had been deliberately lit. It was just a little too convenient.

"Iz, search through Emma Pierce's file. See if there's any mention of when she retired from the military."

The bony foot tapped again. "March 2040."

Basically the same time as Michael Sanders appearance. Coincidence? Probably not.

"Does Mary Elliot still work for Silhouettes?"

"Retired five years ago. Currently resides at the Greensborough home for the aged."

If she was in a home, then the odds of her remembering anything of note were not good. Still, it was worth a chance. She grabbed her handbag and placed the photo of a young Rose Pierce inside. "Book me a car, Iz. If anyone's looking for me, I'll be with Mary Elliot."

Twelve

Gabriel glanced at the clock for the umpteenth time. He hated stakeout duty. Hated sitting alone in a car watching a dark apartment. Especially when there was a murderer at large who could easily slip through their carefully laid net.

Jeanette Harris had been spirited away to safety. In her place was an SIU agent, a multishifter who'd assumed Jeanette's form. The apartment itself was wired—no one would get in or out without raising an alarm.

Yet he had a vague suspicion it wouldn't be enough.

He scratched the back of his neck and looked around. A paperboy pedaled slowly down the street, flinging papers haphazardly at each house. Sometimes they landed near the front door, but more often than not, they burrowed deep into bushes. The kid gave him a cheerful grin as he passed, and the next paper soared over the front fence and splattered against a window. The faint sound of curses could be heard. The kid chortled as he pedaled away.

Gabriel smiled and glanced back at the apartment building across the road. Nothing had moved. The black dog still sat guard near Jeanette's front door, and the sparrow hawk was lost amongst the shadows within the branches of the gum. Two more SIU agents, in human guise, watched out back.

If the murderer was a cop, she'd know of the precautions taken both here and with the remaining adoptees. If she had any sense, she'd back away and bide her time.

But something told him that wouldn't happen. The increasing urgency and violence in each of the murders pointed to a killer running out of time.

His viaphone beeped twice into the silence. He flicked the answer button. "Stern here."

Stephan appeared on screen. "Did you read the file from Sam?"

He pressed a button and saw the second call was from her. "It's just arrived."

"Apparently the only request for information on the adoptees, outside yours and her's, came from one Michael Sanders."

Sanders. The State Police officer with the strange eyes. "You've requested he come in for an interview?"

"Yes, but he's off duty and not home. I've got a team watching his apartment."

"Good." He glanced at the rear view mirror and frowned. The paperboy had disappeared. Odd, given that this was a cul-de-sac, and the only way out of the street was the way he came in. "Call you back, Stephan. I've got to check something."

He hung up and climbed out of the car. For a moment, he stood still, listening to the sounds of the morning. The wind was chilly and thick with the scent of rain. The flow of traffic from the nearby Western freeway was a steady hum, as was the usual morning noises as people woke and readied for work. The only thing missing was the trill of birds waking to greet the dawn.

Given the early hour, they shouldn't be silent. And usually, the only reason they did fall quiet was if there was a predator near—or something that looked like a bird but wasn't.

He reached again for his viaphone. "Brigg's, Francis, keep alert. Something's happening."

"Will do."

He pocketed the viaphone and headed down the court. Two houses from the end, he found the kid's bicycle, thrown under a large tree, papers scattered everywhere.

The house, a two-story, slab-style building, showed no sign of life. The windows were dark, and he couldn't hear any movement. Frown deepening, he walked down the driveway and around to the rear of the house. Again, nothing.

He scratched the back of his neck irritably, and returned to the street. Jeanette Harris' apartment block looked undisturbed and silent. He shifted shape and rose skyward.

To his hawk senses, the wind was a rich plethora of smells and sound. Toast burned two houses down, mingling with the rich aroma of coffee and the almost too powerful scent of rotten meat from the overflowing rubbish bins in the house just below. A mouse ducked for cover as he flew over some bushes, the creature's shrill shriek music to his ears. Beyond that, the startled cry of a budgie from a nearby tree.

Budgies—wild budgies didn't actually live in suburbia. He circled towards it.

Blue feathers exploded from the tree as the budgie rose skyward, wings pumping frantically. He circled. If this budgie was the shapeshifter they were after, then its sudden flight didn't make sense. All it had to do was sit quietly in the tree and he probably wouldn't even have seen it. His hawk sight was keen, but he wasn't capable of seeing past the thick, dark canopy of the treetop.

He watched the budgie's flight for several more seconds, and then he slowly winged after it. Every sense he had suggested this bird was their shifter. Just as everything suggested this sudden retreat was a setup that smelled worse than Stephan's gym shoes in summer.

Still, he had little option but to follow. He'd tried once before to catch a felon in his claws and had almost killed the man. Hawk claws were meant to rake and kill, not gently capture. Of course, killing might be considered justifiable in this case, but he wanted answers as well as her death. He needed to know why she was killing people like Miranda—people who had done nothing more than survive the odds to be born.

They winged their way along the Western Freeway and across to the industrialized suburb of Altona before the budgie finally began to descend.

He circled, watching the small blue bird arrow through a broken side window of what looked like an abandoned factory.

The smell of a trap was so strong he could practically walk on it. He drifted down, watching the factory, trying to see if there was anyone else about. Two cars were parked around the back of the building, which meant the budgie could have a friend waiting below. He circled down, shifting shape as he neared the ground.

The hood of the gray Ford was warm to the touch and had been driven very recently. The other car was cold, suggesting it had been here for a while.

The wind tugged at several loose sheets of metal along the factory's roof and whistled through the many gaps in the walls. The building had been abandoned for some time. Why, then, were the murderous budgie and her friend here?

He pressed the locater switch on his viaphone, and then he drew his gun and slowly approached the door. The handle turned somewhat stiffly, and the door opened with the slightest of creaks. He moved inside quickly, dropping to one knee to present less of a target, and quickly scanned the darkness. The windows that weren't broken were caked with dirt and cobwebs, and the few beams of light that managed to filter through them did little to break the blackness. He could barely see more than a few feet ahead.

He rolled his shoulders slightly, trying to ease the tension in them. Once his eyes had fully adjusted to the darkness, he moved along the wall. There were several large shapes across the other side—offices, by the look of them. There was also what looked like a set of stairs, leading down into a deeper pit of darkness.

He'd find the budgie there, instinct suggested. But he'd also find the trap.

He checked the two offices, but they held nothing but a scattering of broken furniture and years of dust. If there was anything in this old warehouse to find, it was definitely on the floor below. He stopped in the doorway of the second office, studying the stairway to his left.

He *should* call for backup, but in this thick silence, his voice would carry all too easy. He could text, of course, but he'd never really mastered any sort of speed with text, and it would take him longer than he suspected he had. They had to know he was here—if he didn't make a move and appeared to be waiting for help, they'd surely leave. He couldn't cover all exits, couldn't stop two of them, and while he could fly fast, it was doubtful he'd be able to out fly a car intent on losing any pursuit. Meaning they might lose their only opportunity to get close to their murderer. He had no idea what game she was playing right now, but he had a feeling it was one he had to continue to the end.

He edged down the stairs. The darkness wrapped around him, so blanket thick that he could barely see the steps. The wind didn't extend this far, and the still air smelled old.

When he reached the bottom step, he stopped. Though he could hear no sound, awareness washed over him. Someone stood close.

He swung, sweeping with a booted foot. His kick sliced through the thick darkness but connected with nothing more than air.

A malevolent chuckle ran around him. He moved right, keeping his back to the wall and his gun set on stun and ready to fire.

Sound whispered across the silence. Footsteps, moving through the darkness. The back of his neck began to itch again. The air stirred and he dove away, catching a brief glimpse of a knife as it sliced through where he'd stood only seconds before. He hit the ground, rolled back to his feet, and fired.

The pulsating light of the laser briefly illuminated a bloated, red-veined face, but the stranger moved far too fast, and the shot missed. Footsteps slithered away.

He backed to the wall. Breath stirred the silence, its rhythm rapid, as if full of terror. Or excitement.

Another footstep scraped across the silence, this time only yards away. He dropped to a crouch and crept forward. The harsh breathing continued, each intake of air a whisper of pain. This wasn't the budgie, but her friend with the bloated face.

He rose and swung his fist. It connected with a wall of flesh that felt as solid as a brick wall. A stomach, not a chin. The man had to be huge.

There was a grunt of pain and then air stirred. He ducked. The knife sliced passed his chest, the tip of steel nicking one of his shirt buttons. Obviously, they were trying to hurt rather than kill him.

He stepped back and fired the laser. In the brief flare of light he saw a bulbous nose, mismatched eyes and ragged, flapping lips. All on a figure over eight feet tall. The man looked like a cross between a giant and an ogre.

The shots hit the stranger's shoulder. The big man grunted and stumbled away, right arm flapping uselessly. Gabriel sighted the laser on the sound of his footsteps and fired again.

The man hit the ground with a thump and didn't move. He listened to the silence for several seconds, wondering where the hell the budgie was, and then he moved cautiously forward. A human form loomed out of the darkness. The stranger was a mountain, even lying down. Gabriel nudged him with a boot. He didn't move.

This close, he could see the rise and fall of the stranger's chest, giant bellows that struggled to work. Gabriel frowned. It almost seemed as if the weight of his flesh pressing down on his lungs was almost too much to move. He might die if he remained in that position for very long.

Air stirred, warning him of movement behind him. He ducked, but not fast enough. Something smashed into the side of his head and the lights went out.

***

Sam dug out her ID and showed it to the nurse manning the reception desk. "I need to see Mary Elliott."

The nurse frowned. "Mind if I ask why? Mary's not in the best condition, nowadays."

She put her ID away. "What's wrong with her?"

"Short term memory loss, stroke." The nurse hesitated. "She's still regaining speech and mobility."

Damn! Why was it that every lead they seemed to get was damaged in some way? "I need to see her, if it's possible, as we think she might be able to help us with a case. If she begins showing any signs of stress, I'll leave."

"Make sure you do. I don't want her upset." The nurse pressed a button on her desk. Seconds later, another nurse appeared. "Lisa, take Agent Ryan to see Mary, please."

Sam nodded her thanks to the receptionist and followed the second nurse down the corridor. The rooms were all locked. Apparently, they were taking no chances on an inmate walking free.

The second nurse stopped at a door about halfway down. "Mary, like most of the patients in this wing, tends to live in the past. They have no concept of current time or events—if we let them wander at will, they'd become dazed and confused."

And it was a hell of a lot easier on the staff if they weren't free to roam, Sam thought grimly. "Thanks," she said, as the nurse opened the door.

The woman nodded. "Just buzz when you want out."

"Will do."

The door closed behind her. The room wasn't the glorified prison cell she thought it would be. Huge windows lined one wall, overlooking a garden that was a mass of flowers and trees. The remaining walls were a buttercup yellow and lined with brightly colored prints. There wasn't much furniture, but what there was added to the cheerful feel of the room.

A thin, gray-haired woman sat statue still on the sofa, apparently mesmerized by the children's show on the television. Sam walked over and sat beside her. There was no reaction from the older woman.

"Mary?" she said softly.

The woman turned around. For one second, there was little life in her blue eyes, then she blinked, and the right side of her face lit up in a smile.

"Josephine!" Her words were slightly slurred, but not beyond understanding. "As I live and breathe, fancy seeing you after all these years."

What were the odds of getting mistaken for someone else twice in as many days? She dug out her ID and showed it to Mary.

Confusion ran across the old woman's face. "You're not Josephine?" Her gaze darted from the ID to Sam's face.

"No. My name is Samantha. I'm a police officer."

"You look like young Josephine did."

Maybe she did—and if she was a product of Hopeworth, then it was very likely that there were others out there who resembled her. Right now, it wasn't a point worth arguing. "Mary, do you remember working at the Silhouettes Adoption agency?"

A smile tugged the right corner of her mouth. "Yes. I worked there for many years. Lovely place. Lots of bonny babes to look after."

"Do you remember a child named Rose Pierce?"

"Rose Pierce," the old woman mumbled, face locked in a frown. "The name does seem familiar."

She dug the photo out of her handbag and handed it across.

The old woman studied it for a few minutes before a smile touched her lips. "Rosie Pierce," she murmured, gently touching the child's image with one gnarled finger. "Now, there was a strange one."

"Strange how?"

"We could never settle her as a babe. She kept screaming and reaching out for something—though we never did figure out what. Not until later, that is. And, of course, no one wants to adopt a child that forever cries."

"She was in the hospital for many months, wasn't she?"

"Yes. We got her from the hospital, once it had been confirmed her parents were dead and there was no living relative to look after her."

"Why wasn't she sent to the same adoption agency as her sister?"

The old woman frowned again. "We didn't know about the sister—not until later. And by then, it was far too late. The sister had been adopted and her new parent's weren't interested in a second child."

"How did the separation affect Rose?" She'd heard tales of twins sharing emotions, thoughts, and even pain, no matter how many miles stood between them. Was it possible that Rose, even at such a young age, had such a connection with her sister?

It might explain the growing anger with each of the murder victims. Perhaps everything that had been done to Emma over the years had reverberated through Rose, right up until the moment Emma had actually been released from Hopeworth, and Rose had finally discovered the truth about her sister's pain.

"She was such a dear little thing, but so, so serious. As soon as she could talk, she wanted to know where her sister was. We couldn't settle her, no matter what we tried."

"Wasn't she only twelve months old when she came to Silhouettes?"

"Yes, but the bond of the twin is sometimes very strong." Mary hesitated, blue eyes sharp. It was hard to imagine this woman being anything but in full control of her memories. "But you should know that, Josephine. You're a twin, are you not?"

"My name is Sam. I showed you my ID, remember?"

"Did you?" Confusion flitted across the good half of her face. She rubbed her forehead wearily. "Sometimes my memory is not so good."

"You're doing just fine, Mary." She patted the old woman's hand gently. Her skin felt like rough paper. "Tell me about Rose's adoption by the Sanders."

Mary sighed. "They were such a serious couple. Not the sort our little Rosie really needed. She was too serious herself— she needed to laugh, needed someone who would bring her out of her shell."

"Did you advise against them adopting Rose?"

"Yes." She sighed again. "But Mrs. Sanders fell in love with her. In the end, that was the important thing. Little Rose needed lots of love."

She raised an eyebrow. "Why? Was she traumatized by the separation from her twin?"

"In a sense, yes. But she was having serious identity problems by the time she hit three."

Identity problems at three years old? Most kids could barely speak at that age, let alone have concerns about who or what they were. "What caused Rose to have these problems?"

"She was a shifter," Mary said, and patted Sam's hand.

Obviously, *being* a shifter should have explained it all. She cleared her throat. "Would being a shifter traumatize her to such a degree?"

"Oh yes. Most shifters have identity problems when they find their alternate shape at such a young age. In Rose's case, it was compounded by the fact that she could take any form."

"So she was a multishifter?" Just like her sister.

"Yes. But also a female to male shifter."

She stared at the old woman, wondering if she'd heard right. Female to male? "That's not possible."

"I didn't think so, but there it was, happening to little Rosie right in front of me."

"But...how?"

The old woman shrugged. "There are some people in this world who claim to be born in the wrong bodies—males trapped in female forms, and vice-versa. Maybe that's what happened to Rose—only she *could* do something about it."

"Her male form—did he have a name?"

Mary considered the question for several seconds. "Michael. I think she called him Michael."

Michael Sanders, she thought grimly. Their young cop with the old eyes. Gabriel would want this information straight away.

She stood. "Thanks for all your help, Mary."

"You're welcome, Josephine." She hesitated, tilting her head to one side. "How's that brother of yours?"

"Mary, I don't have a brother," she said gently.

Confusion clouded the old woman's face. "Yes, you do. Joshua. Sprightly lad with a mass of red hair."

A chill ran down her spine. Joshua. The boy she'd dreamt about nearly every night. She licked suddenly dry lips. "Mary, I think you're confusing me with someone else. My name is Samantha, not Josephine."

"So you've changed it again. I can't keep up with you two." She sighed softly. "I wish them damn doctors would give you all names instead of numbers. Hell of a lot easier on the rest of us."

The chill increased. Hadn't Joe Black mentioned something about only being a number and never having a real name? She sank slowly back to the sofa. "Mary, when did you know Josephine and Joshua?"

"Years and years ago. I was in the military before I retired and became a nurse at Silhouettes, you know."

"And Joshua and Josephine—they were twins?"

The old woman smiled, her eyes distant, lost in the years. "And the liveliest of all my charges. I guess that's why you managed to survive at all."

She rubbed her arms. "Survive? Then many didn't?"

"Oh no. So many bonny babes were lost." She hesitated, sniffing back a tear. "That's why I left, you know. I couldn't stand to see all the dead children."

"And Hopeworth let you leave?" From what she'd learned about the place, she'd have thought no one would get let loose until they were well past their use-by date.

"They had no choice. The project was destroyed." Her gaze met Sam's, blue eyes shining with tears. "Until you walked into the room, I thought both you and Joshua were dead."

Allars had mentioned that the Penumbra Project had been destroyed by fire. Coincidence? Somehow, she doubted it. Joe Black had sent her to Silhouettes, with the warning she would find the first stepping stone to her past. Silhouettes had led her to Mary. Was the old woman that stone? Or was she so lost in the past that she was confusing reality with fantasy?

"What was the name of the project you worked in, Mary?"

"I...I can't remember." She rubbed her forehead with gnarled fingers. Tears ran silently down her weather worn cheeks. "It hurts if I try to remember."

Behind them, the door opened. A nurse stepped into the room. "Enough questions, agent Ryan. Mary's heart rate just leapt alarmingly. We can't afford to let you stay any longer."

She silently cursed, then rose. "I'll come back another time."

Mary caught her hand, squeezing it gently. "Do please come back, Josephine. I don't get very many visitors nowadays." She hesitated and frowned, looking around the room in sudden confusion. "This isn't my home. Why am I here?"

The nurse motioned Sam to the door, and then she squatted down in front of the old woman, gently taking hold of her hand.

"Mary, you were sick, dear. You came here to get better, remember?"

The door swung shut on the nurse's soft words. Sam stood in the corridor and took a deep breath. It was hard to decide whether she'd found a clue to her past or simply more confusion.

She glanced at her watch. It was close to ten o'clock. She needed to get something to eat, and she needed to call Gabriel. She reached for her viaphone, but at that moment, pain hit her head, hammering into her brain. She gasped, felt her shoulder hit the wall, then slid to the floor, holding her head and fighting the wave of nausea and darkness washing through her body.

Footsteps came running. Hands touched her shoulders. "Agent Ryan, are you all right?"

As quickly as it had come, the pain left, leaving her only with a vague sense that something was wrong. She took several deep breaths and nodded. "Yeah. Sorry about that. The sudden movement must have set off my headache again."

The reception nurse frowned. "If the headaches are as bad as that, you need to go see a doctor."

"I am." She struggled to her feet. If these damn headaches were an indication of what she had to look forward to every month, why the hell did she ever wish to fully develop as a woman? It was certainly a case of watch what you wish for, because you might damn well get it.

"Maybe you'd better sit down for a while," the nurse suggested, touching Sam's arm in concern.

She shrugged the touch away. "I'm fine, really. I just haven't had breakfast yet, and I do have an appointment with a doctor at eleven." She glanced at her watch. It was nine-thirty now. Time enough to get something to eat before she headed into the city.

"Maybe you'd better not drive until you do eat. Just in case that headache comes back."

She nodded. "I'll walk down to the shops first. Thanks for your help."

The woman shrugged. "No problem."

Sam headed out to the main street, and she quickly dialed Gabriel's number. No answer. She frowned. Last time there was no answer, something had been wrong.

Something was wrong this time, too.

She studied the long line of shops in front of her and headed for Subway. Then she dialed SIU.

"Christine, put me through to Director Byrne please."

"One moment, please." Christine reappeared in half that time. "Director Byrne is currently in a meeting and cannot be disturbed."

She swore under her breath. "Could you leave a message with his secretary? Let him know Rose Pierce is Michael Sanders, SPO."

"Message forwarded."

"Thanks."

She shoved the viaphone back in her bag, stepped into Subway and ordered herself a roll and coffee.

By the time she finished both, it was time to head into the city.

Doctor O'Hearn's office was situated near the Spencer Street end of Bourke Street. Located on the thirteenth floor, it overlooked the old rail yards and the newly refurbished Telstra

Stadium. It was the sort of view that cost millions, though she couldn't see why. She'd prefer a view over parkland any day.

She was ushered in to the doctor's office almost immediately. O'Hearn was studying several reports on her desk, but she glanced up as Sam settled into the well-padded visitor's chair.

"Samantha. How are you today?" She leaned back in her chair, a smile crinkling the corners of her gray eyes.

O'Hearn was what she called the mother type—full figured and kindly looking. But there was a hawk like sharpness in her eyes that suggested this was a woman who missed little.

"Fine, thanks. I finally figured out what was causing those headaches, though."

The doctor smiled. "Yes. Your hormone level did indicate you were about to menstruate, which must have been somewhat surprising, given what you'd been told."

That was an understatement if she'd ever heard one. "Have you any idea why this should suddenly happen now?"

O'Hearn picked up one of the files and studied it for a few seconds. "Well, we did find some interesting anomalies in your test results."

No surprise there, given what Finley had already discovered. "Such as?"

The doctor considered her, gray eyes calculating. "What do you know about genetic coding?"

"Absolutely nothing."

She smiled again. "Then I shall attempt to explain this simply. Each race has a set genetic code, though, of course, there are various definitions available within each code. Humans have one base pattern, shapeshifters another, and so on. But with you, we have found that your basic genetic coding has been spliced with the partial coding of at least two other races."

"Shapechanger would be one," she said, thinking back to what Francis had said about sensing others of her kind.

O'Hearn nodded. "And also shifter. But there's at least one other partial code we've not yet identified."

She raised an eyebrow. "If I have the coding of these races, why am I not able to shift or change?"

"That I don't know. Nor do I know how this has happened, other than suggesting it is not natural."

She rubbed her arms. While the news was far from surprising, it was a confirmation that she didn't really want.

Hopeworth was looking more and more a parental possibility. Bang went her dreams of finding kin.

"Would having the mixed coding explain the development delay?"

"To some extent, yes. Both shifters and changers do not fully mature until they hit thirty or forty human years. It is nature's way of compensating for their extended life span."

She rubbed her forehead. "Then why was I told at fifteen that I would never develop? Surely they would have picked up the shifter/changer coding as easily as you did."

"My tests are a little more intense than your average physician's, and I have spent a good part of my life focusing on the health and welfare of nonhuman races." A hint of pride crept through the doctor's warm voice. "I'm sure the physicians who examined you were good, but I'm a damn sight better."

And modest besides. "So you're saying they wouldn't have been able to pick up the genetic abnormalities?"

"Why would they look is more the question. You're listed as human on your birth certificate. They'd have no reason to search beyond that, really."

Especially not for an orphan at a time when medical expenditure of any kind was being closely watched by the government. "What about these other sensations I seem to be getting? Being able to sense the presence of other races, being able to pick up my partner's emotions and, sometimes, even thoughts."

O'Hearn interlaced her fingers. "Most psychic abilities don't start to fully develop until the onset of puberty."

She sighed. "I was tested for psychic ability when I entered the State Police. I came up with a big fat zero."

"And yet you told me that in recent tests done at the SIU, you came in neutral."

"Yeah. So?"

"Those tests were designed by Gabriel. Designed specifically to indicate whether or not a person has psychic ability. You either have, or have not. You don't come in neutral."

"But I did."

"Yes. And that would indicate a talent strong enough to evade both the psi nullified environment of the SIU, and the tests themselves."

"This is too weird." In the space of a few days, she'd gone from being an orphaned nobody to a multi-raced fertile woman with growing psychic talents and maybe even a brother.

"It certainly is a puzzle," O'Hearn agreed. "But one I think we can eventually solve."

She took another deep breath. No doubt the solving would involve more damn tests. "What do you want to do?"

"First, I want your permission to request the test results from the SIU. I think they would complement my research. Who's the physician in charge there?"

"A man called Finley."

"Finley?" The doc raised a gray eyebrow. "He's one of the best in his field. Didn't realize he was working for the SIU now."

"He's been wanting to do more tests himself. So far, I've refused."

"Why?"

She shrugged. "Obstinacy, perhaps. Or maybe even fear of discovering the truth."

"Both of which are understandable. Sometimes it is better not to know."

She smiled grimly. "There are things happening to me that I need to understand. I can't sit on my hands any more. Do what it takes to find out what the hell is going on in my body."

"Good girl." She leaned forward and picked up the second folder. "I'll book some more tests and let you know the times. I'll also contact Gabriel and request the SIU test results." She hesitated, frowning slightly. "It might also be worthwhile if I work with Finley on some of these tests. He's more familiar with gene manipulation than I am."

"The SIU will probably have to approve it, but it's okay by me. Though Finley's not due back from leave until the eighteenth."

"We'll get around that." She shuffled the two folders together. "I'll get onto this straight away."

She stood. "I'll wait for your phone call, then."

O'Hearn nodded. "Don't worry, dear. You'll have your answers within a week or two."

A minute from now was not soon enough. Still, she'd waited nearly thirty years for some answers. Two weeks more wasn't going to kill her.

A chill ran over her skin. She couldn't escape the sudden notion that she was wrong.

Very wrong.

Thirteen

Sam spent several fruitless hours apartment hunting, then gave up and went back to SIU headquarters.

The estate agent had given her a vague idea of what her apartment would fetch, and while it was a sizeable sum, to buy anything close to the city was going to cost her almost double that. She'd have to go further afield—which meant, in turn, either buying a car or putting up with the overcrowded transport system for a good hour each day. The twenty minutes she suffered now was more than enough.

She dumped her bag on the floor beside her desk and flopped back in her chair. For tonight, at least, she'd have to find a hotel.

"Computer on."

Izzy appeared. "You have a call, sweetness. General Frank Lloyd."

"Fuck." She rubbed her eyes. The last thing she wanted, either now or anytime in the immediate future, was to speak to the general. She couldn't shake the image of a crocodile toying with its prey—that prey being her.

"Put him onscreen, Iz."

The general's powerful features appeared. A chill ran over her skin. This man would play some part in her future, and none of it would be good.

She rubbed her arms. "What can I do for you, general?"

"The question is more, what can *I* do for *you*."

His smile made her skin crawl. "General, it's been a long day. Just get to the point."

He raised a bushy eyebrow. "Given your questions regarding the Generation Eighteen project, I thought you would be interested to know that we've discovered the identity of the man who hacked into our system."

And he'd only just discovered this name? Somehow, she doubted it. "It's not Michael Sanders, I suppose?"

The general frowned. "No. Orrin Whittiker."

He seemed to place an odd emphasis on the man's name. Was she supposed to know the man? "Who is?"

"A reject from a different project."

"Jesus, general, how many rejects do you have wandering around the streets?"

"At last count, one hundred and forty-five. There could be one or two more I don't know about, though."

One hundred and forty-five rejected children. How many successes must they have had? How many deaths? If what Mary said was true, then the latter number, at least, was very high.

"Do you keep track of all your rejects?"

"Oh yes. We can't afford not to."

Then Hopeworth had known about the murders. Had known, but had done nothing. "Do you intend to pick up this Orrin Whittiker?"

"We thought you might choose to. He might be able to assist in your inquiries. Once you have questioned him, we'd appreciate you handing him over to us."

That was not up to her. "What project was Orrin rejected from?"

"I cannot tell you that."

"General, I need to know what to expect when I go after this man."

The general hesitated, his eyes going curiously blank. There was no doubt that he was telepathic—and right now, he was obviously contacting higher authorities.

"Orrin," he continued, barely skipping a beat. "Would be of an unusual height and girth. He would also be extremely strong."

"What sort of unusual height are we looking at?"

"He'd be over eight foot tall, and at least half that wide."

She blinked. She'd be trying to arrest a man almost double her height. Like, that was going to happen. "What the hell were you trying to achieve with Orrin's lot? Man mountains?"

The general's almost cynical smile suggested she wasn't that far off the mark. "We have his address, if you're interested."

"Yeah, I'm interested." It was a shame she'd never be able to charge the general and his military cohorts with obstruction of justice. They'd had this information from the beginning of the murders, of that she had no doubt. Yet they'd sat on it. Had simply watched while people like Gabriel's sister had brutally died.

It was just as well that she wasn't standing face to face with the general. She'd be tempted to punch him.

"Orrin lives in the Government housing estate in Melton. Twenty-eight Erin Street, to be precise."

She frowned. From memory, Emma Pierce had lived on

that same street. "Thanks for the help, general."

He nodded and disappeared. Izzy reappeared onscreen. "Need anything, sweetie?"

"Yeah, request me a gun and a car."

"Feel like shooting someone, do we?" Izzy's foot tapped several times. "Stun or dual?"

She hesitated. If this man was as big as the general had suggested, she wasn't going to get caught having only a stun gun to defend herself with. "Dual, just to be safe."

"Request being processed."

"See if you can get Gabriel Stern for me, will you?" She leaned back in her chair, watching the boa twirl.

"No answer, sweetie."

She frowned. This wasn't like Gabriel. Not when he'd said he'd leave the phone on. "Try Director Byrne, then."

Stephan's face appeared on screen. "Agent Ryan," he greeted, voice neutral yet somehow sharp. "What can I do for you?"

"I've just been in contact with General Frank Lloyd. He discovered the name of the man who hacked into their system and recovered the information on the Generation Eighteen rejects."

"Do you need assistance in picking him up?"

"If what the general said about his size is true, then yes, I will."

"I'll assign you teams seven and twelve immediately."

"Thanks." She hesitated briefly. "Sir, have you heard from A.D. Stern? I've been trying to get ahold of him for several hours now."

"No. I haven't." Stephan rubbed his chin. "He was on watch detail at Jeanette Harris' place, but he went to investigate something else and hasn't been seen since."

And Stephan was worried, though his face, like his voice, showed absolutely no emotion.

"Have you talked to the remaining teams? No idea what he might have seen?"

"Yes, I did, and no, they haven't. The two agents at the front of the building reported he climbed out of his car about five minutes after a paperboy had gone past, and that he walked up the street into a house. He was seen flying away in his hawk form."

"No location indicator after that?"

"We investigated his last known location, with no result." He hesitated, leaning back in his chair. "Don't suppose you've felt anything?"

She hesitated. How much should she tell Stephan? In many ways, she didn't really trust him, simply because her desires and needs were of no consequence to him. The only thing he cared about was the Federation, the SIU and his wife. And in that order. "Not exactly, sir."

Something in his eyes suggested he didn't believe her. "If he hasn't reported in by this evening, I'll be in contact."

Her frown deepened. *That* sounded almost like a threat. "Yes sir."

Stephan signed off. She leaned over to collect her bag from beside the desk. Time to go collect a man mountain.

***

Awareness returned slowly. At first, Gabriel felt nothing beyond the pounding ache in his head. Gradually, though, he became conscious of something sharp under his side, digging into his ribs. Became aware that his shoulders burned, as if stretched back too long and too hard. He tried to shift into a more comfortable position, but couldn't, mainly because he was trussed up tighter than a roast for Sunday's dinner.

He opened his eyes. The room in which he lay was enclosed in darkness. There were no windows, no chance of light getting in or him getting out. The air was still, and it tasted almost foul.

As his eyes adjusted to the darkness, he found the door. Heavy set and metal, it looked like something you'd find on a commercial refrigerator. He looked around his prison again. Saw the rails above him, hung with empty hooks. He was in a meat cold storage locker. No wonder the air held a mix of death and fouled meat.

He shifted his legs. The object under his ribs dug deep, biting into his flesh. He swore and jackknifed away. Glass, not stone or rubble, as he'd presumed. Probably the remnants of some drunk's cheap wine bottle. Judging by the amount of glass surrounding him, the drunk had spent a fair amount of time here. Obviously, the building in which the meat locker was housed had been abandoned long enough for street people to consider it a refuge.

Unless they were in the same building that he'd followed Rose into, the chance of immediate rescue was next to zero.

But the glass itself might provide a means to escape, if he

could just free enough fingers to grab a piece. He shifted his shoulders and arms, trying to work some slack into the ropes. After a good ten minutes, he had to rest. Whoever had tied him had had done a damn fine job. He could barely breathe, let alone move.

The sharp tattoo of footsteps came from beyond the confines of his prison, and then the metal door screeched open. Brown leather boots appeared. He looked up and found himself staring into Emma Pierce's face. The sister, he thought. The elusive Rose Pierce.

"Good to see you're finally awake, Assistant Director." She stopped a good three feet away and stared at him with an expression that wavered between contempt and caution.

"What are you doing, Rose? None of this will bring Emma back. Especially not killing innocent adoptees."

Her smile was cold. "Especially when one of them was your sister, huh?"

Anger flashed through him, but it was useless, given the circumstances. He could no more attack her than he could fly right now. "What's the point of all this? We know who you are. We know who your next victims will be. You're insane if you think we're going to let you get anywhere near them."

She began to pace. Her walk was long and powerful, almost masculine. "I only realized how close you were when I cycled up the street and saw you all there. Up until then, I had thought the trail untraceable."

Which was pretty much the downfall of most criminals, he thought. They never thought they could be caught. "Taking me as a hostage will get you no closer to your victims. The SIU doesn't bargain."

Her smile was a slash of contempt. "I know that. I have no intention of going down that road, anyway."

"Then what do you intend?"

"You'll see soon enough." She hesitated, studying him almost too intently. "What, no other questions?"

She wanted him to talk, though he wasn't entirely sure why. He could see no harm in obliging though, especially if it gave him some answers. "Why are you killing these people? If you hold a grudge, it should be against Hopeworth, not the innocent by-products of their experiments."

"I have no grudge against the adoptees. I'm only carrying out my sister's final wish."

"Emma wanted her children dead?"

Bitterness ran across her face. "These aren't *her* children. They were never conceived by her, never grew to life in her womb. They're an aberration of nature, something that should not exist. So they die, as Emma wished."

"How did Emma find out about the adoptees in the first place?" He was pretty confident Hopeworth wouldn't have told her.

"A chance encounter with a reject from another project gave us the clue, though I reckon Em might have had her suspicions anyway. We formed a pact with the reject—we helped him, and he helped us."

"Then why cut out the wombs in the women, or the penis and scrotum in the men?"

For a moment, Rose didn't answer. She paced the floor behind him, long aggravated strides. "Do you know what it is like to be a twin? To share your twin's every thought, every desire, and every anguish?"

His smile was grim. He should, but he didn't. Perhaps he would regret it one day, but for now, he was happy to continue blocking Stephan.

"I spent half my life physically locked away from my sister," Rose continued softly. "It didn't matter, because even as a child, all I had to do was reach out, and she was there, in my mind, ready to comfort or talk."

So, even as babes, the two had known about each other. "What kept you apart as you got older? Hopeworth?"

Rose came back within sight. Her face darkened. "The bastards sucked her dry, and then they spat out the husk. They didn't care what happened to her once they'd finished with her. I was the one who had to pick up the pieces. I was the one who had to see and feel her agony as the cancers *their* treatments and explorations had left her with ate away her body." She hesitated and clenched her fists. "I was the one who had to watch her die and feel her relief as death sucked her soul away."

And the experience had obviously left her more than a little off-center. "Why didn't you bury her, Rose? Why not offer her the dignity in death that she couldn't get in life?"

"Because once the soul has gone, the body is only a lifeless shell. It doesn't matter what happens to it."

Rose and Emma where born shifters, and yet, they obviously had none of the beliefs that were ingrained into most shifter families. Maybe it was because they'd been adopted at such a young age and raised by humans. But even humans buried their dead.

He shifted slightly, trying to ease the ache in his side where the glass had cut. His fingers brushed against something sharp. More glass. If he could grab it, he might just be able to cut the ropes and escape. All he had to do was keep her talking and her attention elsewhere.

"It is a belief among my people that if the body is not properly interred, the soul cannot go on and be reborn."

Rose raised an eyebrow. "And sticking them six feet under is supposed to aid this rebirth?"

He smiled grimly. "Sticking them six feet under is nothing but a waste of good planting soil."

"Well, at least we agree on something." She turned away and continued her pacing. "Let's go back to your earlier question. Why do I cut up these innocents, as you call them, so badly?"

He raised an eyebrow. He'd asked that question a good five minutes ago. Had she just decided to answer, or was she simply trying to keep him talking?

"Emma wanted them dead, I'm sure," he said. "But you wanted them to suffer. To suffer as much as your sister had suffered."

She stopped, and regarded him in surprise. "Very good, Assistant Director. And yes, I wanted them to know what Emma had suffered to give them life. I wanted them to die suffering, just like her."

She turned away and resumed her pacing. He caught the shard of glass between his fingers and began to saw at the rope.

"You must understand something about Hopeworth—it never lets people go. Not completely. Everything Emma did, everything she said, Hopeworth heard. Even though she was useless to them, they couldn't let her go completely. It was the same with the adoptees, though not for the same reasons."

"You can't be sure of any of that." Blood was slick on his wrists—he seemed to be cutting himself more than the damn rope.

"Yes I can." Her sudden smile was bitter. "Emma was microchipped, you know. Hopeworth wanted to be certain of her location at all times. The adoptees didn't need it, however. They were bugged psychically."

Several strands of rope gave away, giving him a little more

movement. Blood rushed to his fingertips, tingling painfully. He ignored it and kept on cutting.

"How can you bug someone psychically without them knowing?"

"The same way a thief can pick your pocket without you knowing. It just takes knowledge and timing."

If this were true, then Hopeworth might know a damn sight more about the Federation than anyone in the Federation wanted. Miranda had been privy to more than a few secrets.

"So Hopeworth has stealth-trained telepaths?" Which was harder to do than most people realized. The human population seemed to think telepaths could just read thoughts anywhere, anytime. In reality, it was nowhere near that simple. If it were, telepaths would be on a fast track to insanity. Besides, even the most psychic-dead human could usually tell when he was being read—it was like walking into your house and realizing you'd been burgled. It was something you could just sense.

"My, you're not just a pretty face, are you?" Her voice held a sarcastic edge. "Of course Hopeworth has stealth trained telepaths. They've been breeding talents and God knows what else for close to fifty years."

He met her gaze. In the green depths of her eyes, intelligence mixed with madness. A deadly combination. "How do you know all this?"

"My reject friend told me. He'd been doing a little investigating himself, trying to figure out where, and what, he'd come from. He's stolen an amazing amount of information from the military with them being none the wiser."

If they believed that, they were fools. He had a suspicion very little escaped Hopeworth's attention. "Your reject friend wouldn't happen to be that misshapen giant I felled, would it?"

"And he's more than a little pissed off over that, you know. I had to promise to let him kill you after I'd finished with you, just to calm him down."

He snorted softly. "I'm sure you intend to kill me anyway."

"Oh yes. But at least I would have been quick about it. Old Orrin savors the suffering. It feeds some need in his soul."

Which was as good a reason as any to be well and truly out of here by then. Another strand of the thick rope snapped loose. Time. He just needed more time.

"Sounds to me as if you should be attacking Hopeworth more than the innocent by-products of their experiments."

She gave him a cold smile. "We intend to, once I fulfill Emma's dying wish."

The woman was definitely mad if she thought she could go up against the might of Hopeworth and win. "Just what do you intend to do with me in the meantime?"

"You will help us more than you can know." Rose regarded him steadily for a moment. "Shall I show you how?"

Amusement mingled with the madness, and his gut clenched. Whatever it was, it wasn't good.

Her body began to shift, to mold itself into a new form until what stood before him was his own image. Rose wasn't just a shifter. She was what they'd long thought impossible—a cross-gender hybrid.

"So what do you think, Assistant Director?"

Her voice was his. That's why she hadn't minded answering his questions. She'd wanted to hear how he talked, the inflections in his voice, the way he used words.

"I think you're mad." Mad enough to get away with it. He sawed desperately on the last few strands of rope. He had to stop her here, now, or the adoptees would die. The agents watching them wouldn't question his sudden appearance or his need to check each adoptee personally. They were all too used to his eccentric ways.

She smiled. "I don't intend to hold the disguise long. Just long enough to get to the rest of the adoptees and kill them."

"You'll never find them."

"Your computer doesn't have their location? I very much doubt it."

It did. And as good as her disguise was, she'd probably get past the voice and eye scans. If he got out of this alive, he'd have to talk to Finley about finding another way to secure vital information.

She glanced at her watch, which, like her now too short clothes, hadn't changed. "Time runs away from me, unfortunately. As much as I enjoyed our little chat, I now have to go. Be good, Assistant Director. I'll be back in a few hours."

She turned and walked to the door. The last of the rope strands fell from his wrist. He jerked upright as Rose opened the door. He threw the rope to one side, and lunged for the door.

It slammed shut in his face. He punched the metal in frustration. Her laughter ran around him, fading as she walked away.

***

Sam climbed out of her car and studied the house opposite. A red brick, single story house with a metal picket fence and well-tended garden, it looked no different from its immediate neighbors.

Only it was. Evil resided inside.

She rubbed her arms and then reached back into the car to collect her coat. The viaphone buzzed against her side. She slipped on the coat and answered the phone.

"We're in position, agent Ryan."

"Give me five minutes, Briggs, and then move in around the back." She glanced down the road, studying the gray Ford parked several houses down. She pointed toward the side of the house and saw an answering nod from inside the car. Taking a deep breath, she walked across the road and opened the front gate.

The front curtains moved. Evil had been watching.

She climbed the front steps and pressed the doorbell. When there was no response after several minutes, she banged her fist against the door. "SIU. We know you're in there, Mr. Whittiker. Please come out."

King and Francis climbed over the front fence and edged down the side of the house. She fisted the door again. "I have a warrant for you arrest, Mr. Whittiker. Please, come out, or I'll be forced to break in."

Again, no response. She drew her weapon, took aim at the lock and fired. The door smashed back against the wall. The head of the armory hadn't been kidding when he'd said it would stop an elephant. The damn thing hadn't even been set to full.

She edged into the shadows lurking in the hall. There was a door to her immediate left and another further along the hall to the right.

Evil waited near the right door.

"Stop playing games, Orrin, and come out. We just want to question you." She ducked into the left-hand doorway.

Footsteps moved away. He was trying to circle around her. She turned and studied the room. Heavy drapes shrouded the window, keeping the room locked in night-like darkness. And yet she could see as clearly as if it were day. A vidscreen dominated the far wall. In the center of the room were several old chairs, separated by a coffee table. To the left of these, another doorway.

It was to that door evil headed.

She walked across the room and stood in the obscurity of the far corner. After several minutes, she heard a whisper of breath. He was close, so close.

She waited. The air stirred again. Orrin appeared, mouse quiet as he ducked through the doorway and padded forward. For a moment, she could only stare. His damn fists were bigger than her entire head. He was beyond *huge.*

She widened her stance, and aimed her gun. "SIU, Orrin. Put your hands on your head and do not move. I'll shoot if you do."

He hesitated. Fear and anger sizzled through the darkness, slamming into her brain. She reeled back into the wall, trying to keep her balance through the sudden dizziness, unsure what was happening but aware the giant was somehow responsible.

Orrin dove for the window. Though tears blurred her vision, she pulled the trigger. Blue-white light sizzled through the darkness and struck the giant's thigh. Orrin yelped, but he somehow managed to climb to his feet and keep on running. She grabbed her viaphone.

"Orrin's on the street, running west."

The dizziness cleared as she ran out of the house. She leapt the front fence and pounded down the street after Orrin. But she was taking three steps to his one and losing ground fast. She'd have to bring him down.

"Orrin, stop, or I'll shoot."

He put his head down, arms pumping as he tried to run faster. She fired a warning shot over his head. It did no good.

She aimed at his legs and fired. The shot took him in the thigh again, and this time it bought him down. The ground shook as he hit. She stopped several feet away. He lurched towards her, trying to grab her feet. She danced away, the laser primed and ready to fire again.

King, Francis, and Briggs joined her. Even then, it took all four of them to handcuff him and get him into the back of the van.

She slammed the door shut and wiped the sweat from her forehead. "Take him back to headquarters and get his leg seen to, Briggs. I'll meet you there."

The older woman nodded. Sam watched the van drive away, and then she got out her viaphone and called Gabriel. Still no answer. Uneasiness stirred anew. Something was very, very wrong. She scratched her head, turned and walked back to her car.

For now, there was nothing she could do. If Stephan didn't know where Gabriel was, what hope did she have of finding him?

She headed back to headquarters. After dumping her handbag in her office, she made her way down to the holding cells. Briggs and Francis were waiting in the corridor.

"How is he?"

Briggs shrugged. "He's loud, he's as ugly as sin, and the rudest bastard I've ever met."

She smiled. "I meant his wound."

"To be perfectly honest, I hope it festers and causes his leg to drop off." She turned her face to the side. A bruise darkened her skin, stretching from just below her eye down to her chin. "I'm lucky to escape with just bruising. He knocked King through the front doors. Cut him up pretty badly."

Shit. She glanced at Francis. "You okay?"

The big man smiled. "Yeah. By the time he got to me, security had swarmed. They sedated him and brought him straight down here."

The cell door slid open and the doc stepped out. "The wound is fine. His temper is not, however. I've given him another dose of sedatives and ordered him chained. Under no circumstances are you to undo those chains. Not if you value your life."

"Any prospect of him breaking free?"

The doc hesitated. "Under normal circumstances, I'd say no. But that man is not normal."

Wasn't that the truth. She glanced at Briggs. "You two keep close watch. If he does happen to achieve the impossible, flood the room with the stun lasers."

Briggs frowned. "We'll hit you."

"Better the lasers than man mountain's hands." She headed into the cell.

Orrin glared at her. He had the sort of face only a mother could love. One eye seemed to ride higher than the other, his nose was bulbous and lumpy, reminding her somewhat of cauliflower, and his lips were ragged, flapping loosely whenever he moved. His bald dome shone in the artificial light. A few strands of hair clung just behind his ears, and these, a bright red-gold in color, stuck out like chicken feathers, thick and bristly.

Briggs was right. This was one ugly son-of-a-bitch. She walked around him and checked the restraints. So far, they showed no stress, though Orrin was constantly flexing the muscles along his shoulders and arms, trying to work free.

She walked back to the front and stopped, hands behind her back. "What can you tell me about Rose Pierce?"

He hawked and spat. The yellow mass landed near her left boot. She didn't move. "We know she's responsible for the murder of five people. What we're not sure of is your involvement in those murders."

He made no response, simply continued to glare. His eyes were a muddy brown and full of anger, full of hate. She'd seen that sort of hate before. It wasn't aimed at her in particular, it was just a hate of anyone in a position of power. Government, police, and in particular, the military.

And that's the angle she needed to attack from.

"We got your details from a General Frank Lloyd. Seems they've been watching you for quite some time."

He jerked slightly. "They don't know nothin' about me. You're lying."

His lips were like jelly, and they continued to wobble after he'd finished speaking. It was a God-awful sight. No wonder Orrin was a mass of anger—he'd probably grown up the butt of many jokes.

"On the contrary. It was the military who gave us your name and address. They know you've been breaking into their system. They know it was you who stole the Generation Eighteen records. They've requested we hand you over to them once we've finished."

"You do that, and I'm dead."

She raised an eyebrow. "You think I care?"

Orrin regarded her balefully. "Why are you doing this? You're one of us. You should understand."

She crossed her arms. "One of what, Orrin?"

"A reject. A castoff."

"And that's what you are? A military castoff?"

He nodded. "You think nature is this cruel? This face is man-made. And the bastards deserve to die."

On that, she had to agree. "Then why attack other rejects? Why not attack the military themselves?"

"I needed help. That was the price."

"Whose price, Orrin?"

He opened his mouth, then shut it and continued to glare at her.

She tried a slightly different tact. "You know Orrin, if you don't cooperate, we'll have nothing to hold you with. I'm afraid we'll simply have to hand you over to Hopeworth."

He scowled. His bottom lip dropped, almost touching the end of his chin. It was not a pretty sight. "You can't do that. You know they'll kill me."

"And why would they want to kill you Orrin? You just said you were a reject."

"A reject who knows too much about their projects. They've wanted to get their hands on me for some time."

He was obviously paranoid, if not psychotic. "Orrin, Hopeworth have known all along where to find you. They could have picked you up at any time."

"Not true." But he licked his lips and regarded her just a little fearfully.

"Very true, I'm afraid. Hopeworth bugs its rejects, you see." She stepped forward, and pressed two fingers against his side. "Feel that lump? It's a microchip capable of sending voice and movement."

Orrin growled. He lunged forward, teeth bared. She jumped back out of reach. The chains creaked as Orrin's full weight fell against them. They held, but she wondered for how long.

"You lie," he hissed, flexing his massive shoulders again. "They would have picked me up if they had known."

She shrugged. "Maybe you rate yourself a higher threat than what they actually think you are."

"I know things."

"So do I." She started pacing, more to settle her rising nerves than anything else. "I know for a fact Hopeworth has been monitoring both the rejects and the retired scientists. I know for a fact that they've been aware of your involvement in the murders for quite some time. I know that each of the victims evolved from eggs taken from Emma Pierce. I know Rose Pierce is responsible for those deaths. I also know Rose Pierce and Michael Sanders are one and the same person."

"You know nothin'."

She stopped and quirked an eyebrow. "I know that the military want to get their hands on you. I know that you don't want to go. But unless you start cooperating, to Hopeworth you *will* go."

He snarled, his arm muscles tensing as he flexed his shoulders. She watched warily, certain the chains wouldn't hold out much longer.

"You help me, I'll help you," he said, after a few minutes.

She resumed her pacing. "Is that the sort of deal Rose offered?"

"Maybe."

"In what way do you think you can help me?"

"Rose has insurance. One of your own."

Alarm slivered through her. That's why no one could get hold of Gabriel. Rose had him.

"The SIU does not bargain for the life of its operatives."

"No? Then he dies." Orrin shrugged, but the gleam in his eyes was malicious.

She stepped closer. "If you know what is good for you, you'll tell us where he is, right now. The SIU is not bound by the same rules as the police. We play a whole lot rougher, believe me."

Orrin snorted. "Like, I'm really afraid."

"Well, that's a damn shame." She glanced to the mirrored wall on her right. "Briggs, get a break team in here immediately, please."

"Will do." The metallic edge the speakers gave Briggs's voice could not disguise her enthusiasm.

The big man frowned. "What's a break team?"

She crossed her arms. "What does it sound like, Orrin? You had one chance to play fair, and you declined. Now we get nasty."

He lunged against the chains again, teeth snapping. His canines were sharp, she noted. Almost as sharp as a vampires. "You won't get nothin' from me."

"We'll see." She glanced at the wall again. "Buzz me if he changes his mind and decides to talk, or when the break team finishes."

"Will do," Briggs repeated.

Sam walked from the room. Out in the corridor, she stopped and took a deep breath. Tension oozed from every muscle. There was something about the big man that made her skin crawl. And it was more than just the sense of evil. It was if he were something that should not exist—something obscene, like the kites.

She glanced at her watch and decided to get a coffee. The

coffee machines in the building produced a black substance that tasted little better than dishwater, but right now, she didn't feel like walking down the street to get something better. She wanted to be on hand when the break team started in on Orrin.

She headed up to the foyer. Being a public area, the machines there tended to offer better quality dishwater.

Only everyone else in the building had to have the same thought, because by the time she got down there, the damn machine was out of coffee. She thumped it in frustration and then punched the button for hot chocolate. Better than tea, she supposed. She was watching it pour when Gabriel walked through security and headed for the elevators.

Orrin had been lying. Odd that she hadn't detected it. She grabbed her chocolate, almost burning her fingers as the hot liquid splashed up over the sides of the plastic cup, and hurried after her partner.

"Gabriel, wait!"

He continued walking, but he looked over his shoulder. There was no recognition, no emotion, in his eyes when his gaze met hers.

Heat crawled over her skin, whispering secretes to her mind. She stopped abruptly. Hot chocolate splashed over her hand again, breaking wetly across the pristine tiles near her feet.

This wasn't Gabriel.

This was a shapeshifter, taking his form.

Fourteen

Sam dropped the chocolate in the nearby bin and drew her gun. "A.D. Stern, please stop right now."

The shifter looked over his shoulder. Surprise flitted through the familiar hazel eyes, and then he dove into the nearest elevator.

She cursed and ran for the doors. They shut a whisper too soon. She punched the call button and watched the floor indicator. The shifter was heading to the lower levels—probably to Gabriel's office.

A second elevator appeared. She punched the floor number and paced the confines of the elevator as it began its descent.

Why would a shifter come in here imitating Gabriel? What would Gabriel have that would be important enough for someone to take such a risk? Truth was, she didn't know. At no time in the last month had he brought her into his confidence— the only case she'd really been involved with was the rejects.

She stopped. It wasn't just *any* shifter. It was *Rose*. Here to get the location list of the remaining rejects. The woman had to be stark raving mad to take such a risk.

And yet, she'd made it past security without a hassle. Might even have gotten past *her*, had it not been for her weird ability to pick out certain races.

The elevator stopped. She squeezed through the doors before they'd fully opened, and ran into the foyer. The shifter was halfway down the hall, heading for Gabriel's office.

"A.D. Stern, please stop right there."

The shifter turned and fired. She dove to her left. Laser fire sizzled down her right leg, and she yelped. The smell of burning material mingled with stench of crisped flesh. *Her* flesh. The bitch had the laser set on full.

Ignoring the deep-set throbbing in her leg, she rolled to her feet and squeezed off several shots. The shifter ducked into the nearby hall, firing as she moved. The shots hit the wall inches above Sam's head.

Sam scrambled forward as a strident alarm shattered the silence. Footsteps pounded towards them. The shifter appeared, gun aimed. Sam dove to one side. A blue-white beam sizzled half an inch from her stomach, striking the wall behind her. Metal fragments zinged into the air, mini bullets that sliced past her hands and face.

She rose on one knee and fired again. Again the shot missed the fleeing shifter. She cursed. Security appeared from the hall to her left, weapons raised.

"That's not A.D. Stern," she said, pointing to the fleeing shifter. "Take her out immediately."

"Agent Ryan, please put down the weapon."

"For Christ's sake, didn't you hear what I said? That is *not* A.D. Stern. Stop him immediately."

Footsteps echoed in the silence. The shifter, running away. And the morons in security uniforms were letting her go. She swore and rose.

"Put down your weapon," the security officer repeated, "or I'll be forced to shoot."

There was no understanding in the security officer's dour features. No realization of the evil he was letting loose. All he saw was an agent firing at a superior officer. She had no doubt he'd shoot if she fired her gun again.

She dove for the hall anyway. As she hit the ground, she sighted on the fleeing form, and fired. The shifter jerked, her squawk decidedly unmanly as she stumbled into the wall. Then laser fire burned into Sam's body and she knew no more.

***

Gabriel paced the confines of his prison for the umpteenth time. There had to be some way out of this box. Had to be. He couldn't let Rose get into the system and find the new addresses for the adoptees. She had to be stopped.

He had no doubt that she would get into his office. The SIU, for all its security, hadn't really considered the problem of multishifters taking the form of their operatives. His only real hope lay with Sam and her odd ability to sense the evil in people.

Only he'd pissed her off so severely lately that she was likely to avoid him anyway. Especially given his lack of reaction to her none-too-subtle seduction attempt.

He punched the wall in frustration. It buckled under the force of his blow. Hope stirred, and he leaned forward for a closer look. Several of the rivets were missing in the strips holding the metal sheeting in place. Daylight gleamed through the small gaps.

This section of the refrigerator must have been built on top of existing walls—walls that had once been plasterboard. Over the years of abandonment, the plaster must have disintegrated, leaving only the insulation and the metal sheeting of the refrigerator itself.

This was his escape. He stepped back a pace, then booted the wall. The pinpricks of daylight became brighter. He kicked it again. A fist sized gap appeared along the left-hand side.

But as he raised his leg for a third try, pain hit him, flashing fire down his leg. He grunted and dropped to his knees, clutching his thigh and trying to regain his breath.

Fire hit again, this time his shoulder and side. Agony seared his brain, burned through his body. Then it was gone, leaving him shuddering and gasping for breath for far too long.

Sam had been hit. How or why he didn't know, but she was hurt, and badly. He had to get out of this damn prison.

He climbed slowly to his feet. The wall gave away after half a dozen more kicks, peeling back like dented butter. The room beyond was small and dust laden. The two small windows to his right were barred, though the glass had long gone. Not even his hawk form would get through the bars.

He climbed through the wall and walked to the door. It was locked. He stepped back and kicked it. The lock broke after the fourth boot, and the door slammed open. The hallway beyond lay wrapped in dusk. Light filtered in from the strip of glass high above, and dust, stirred by the door opening, danced lazily in the sunbeams.

He couldn't hear any movement, but the sudden prickling sensation along the back of his neck suggested he was no longer alone.

Rose was back. He had to move.

He ran to the end of the hall and cautiously opened the door. It led into the factory proper—a huge space filled with little more than dust. A roller door dominated the wall to his left. Beside it was a second door. From where he stood, it was impossible to tell whether it was locked or not.

His footsteps echoed in the cavernous space. Though he could hear no other sound, the sensation that Rose drew close burned. Keeping near the walls, hoping to be less obvious in the dust-laden shadows, he made way around to the door.

The handle turned when he gripped it. He opened the door and looked out. The room beyond was a loading bay. A second roller door at the far end stood open. Beyond it, he could see thunderous skies.

He rubbed the back of his neck. Though he couldn't see her, Rose was close. Watching. Waiting. It didn't matter. He had to take the risk. Had to try to escape, while he still could.

He shifted shape and flew toward the open roller door. Movement caught the corner of his eye. Rose stepped out of the shadows, weapon raised.

He pumped his wings, flying as hard and as fast as he could. He felt rather than saw the retort of the laser, felt the heat of the shot burn toward him. He flicked his wings, soaring up and sideways.

The shot sizzled past him, gouging a bullet-sized hole in the metal wall. He arrowed through the door and into the freedom of the storm-clad skies. Footsteps raced behind him, and then a second shot burned through the air.

Again, he dove away, this time to his left. He wasn't fast enough. The shot tore through his wing, exploding through flesh and bone as easily as it had the metal wall. Agony fired through his brain. Then he was tumbling, careening out of control, back to the earth and Rose's waiting arms.

***

Footsteps echoed through Sam's brain, the rhythm of barely restrained anger. It was a beat accompanied by a muted throbbing in her shoulder and leg. Waking was not something she wanted to do—not if the throbbing was any indication of the pain that waited on the return to full consciousness.

But she had little choice. Someone was shaking her good shoulder, demanding she wake.

She forced one reluctant eye open. A woman's face swam into view. It was a strong face, a pretty face. A face that would take no shit.

Oddly enough, it reminded her of Gabriel.

Why, she had no idea. The woman's hair was dark brown and curly, her eyes almost catlike and mint green in color. But it was in her eyes that she could see the kinship, if nowhere else. Her gaze was at once sympathetic, demanding, and hostile—a look she'd seen all too often in the warm hazel depths of Gabriel's eyes.

"Who are you?" she asked.

The woman raised a dark eyebrow. "A direct, lucid question when you should be screaming in agony. Interesting."

"Would screaming in agony get me an answer any quicker?" Truth was, she probably would be screaming in agony if she didn't have the damn feeling it wouldn't matter one jot—not to this woman, and not to the man who paced so angrily beyond her line of sight.

"Probably not." A smile that was impossibly white flashed briefly. "My name is Jessie McMahon."

No wonder she could see a similarity to Gabriel—the woman was his damn sister. No doubt the angry pacer was Stephan. "Where am I?"

"At SIU headquarters, in holding cell number nine."

Which was probably the most secure area in the whole of the SIU. Even if she screamed her lungs out, no one would be the wiser. The room had more shields than parliament, and was generally reserved for the most dangerous criminals.

What a laugh, when all *she'd* done was try to stop an enemy. They were the ones who should be locked up, since they were the ones who'd undoubtedly let the enemy go.

"Why aren't I in the damn medical center?" Her voice came out cracked, harsh. She swallowed, but it didn't ease the burning dryness in her throat, though a dry throat was the least of her problems. She stunk of burned flesh, and her whole body ached—even if in a lackluster way. But once the numbness from the laser burns wore off, she'd be screaming in agony.

Jessie's smile was cold. "Because, my dear, you tried to shoot my brother. You're lucky it was security firing at you and not anyone else."

Like Stephan, she surmised. Anger washed over her, a wave of heat that momentarily echoed in Jessie's cat eyes.

"God, have you two any idea what you've done?"

Jessie grabbed her hand, her grip like steel, her skin like ice against the heat of Sam's flesh. "We stopped you from killing my brother."

She laughed harshly. She couldn't help it. These people supposedly dealt with the supernatural all the time, yet they were willing to believe the obvious without questioning.

"I bet you haven't even bothered looking at the tape, have you? You dragged me down here and just can't wait to beat the so called truth out of me." She tilted her head back a little, but she still couldn't see the man who paced behind her. "Well, the truth is, I've had enough of you people. I fucking quit."

"You can quit after you've told me why you shot at Gabriel." Stephan's voice was unemotional, yet it sent a chill down her spine all the same.

"You're incredible." She tried to wrench her hand free of Jessie's, but couldn't—because her arms were strapped down, as were her feet. "Go view the tape and see if you can't guess the goddamn answer yourself."

"We've both seen vid-footage. And all we're actually sure of right now is that Gabriel has left the building and can't be contacted, and that you shot at him. Security shot you when you ignored their order to lower your weapon"

"And did you bother rewinding far enough to see him shooting at me first? Did you hear me tell security it wasn't A.D. Stern, but a shifter? Did you bother going far enough along the tape to hear the girly scream he emitted when I actually hit him?"

Stephan finally came into her line of sight. Though his face was emotionless, his blue eyes were stormy with anger. "How do you know it was a shifter? He passed all security checks."

"Meaning you didn't view the tapes properly." She snorted softly and shook her head. "I would have thought that you, of all people, would not have let emotion cloud your judgment."

"Just answer the damn question."

"The shifter who took Finley's form in the labs a month ago passed all security checks, too. But that fact didn't make him the real Finley."

Jessie regarded her intently. "Why do you think it was a shifter and not Gabriel?"

She frowned. "I don't know. It's just something I sometimes sense."

"Gabriel did mention this ability, remember?" Stephan shared a brief glance with his sister, and then his gaze returned to Sam. "Why didn't you alert security first?"

Because *that* would have been the smart thing to do. She blew out a breath. "I didn't stop to think. She was heading for Gabriel's office, probably to get the relocation list of the adoptees."

Stephan's gaze narrowed slightly. "You keep saying she. Why?"

"Because the shifter in question is Rose Pierce, also known as Michael Sanders, State Police Officer." She hesitated and watched the realization dawn in their eyes. "Yeah, your sister's killer. And you just let her walk away in your rush to get me to the torture room."

"We are not torturing you," Stephan growled.

"Then what do you call not offering someone with severe laser burns medical help? A picnic in the damn park?"

"Security, get medical help in here right away."

She smiled grimly. One point won for the innocent victim.

"How can this woman be a cross-gender multishifter?" Jessie glanced at her brother. "That's not possible, is it?"

Stephan frowned. "It's extremely rare."

"Rare doesn't mean nonexistent," Sam muttered. The fire in her leg and shoulder was beginning to fade against the deeper burning in her left side. If medical help didn't get here soon, she *would* be screaming.

Stephan met her gaze again. "You're certain it wasn't Gabriel?"

"Yes. And if your security people had done their job properly, you would have had Rose confined, not walking free. You might even know where Gabriel is right now, rather than continuing this aimless conversation with me."

His brief smile was grim. "Ah, but see, you're going to help us find Gabriel."

She blinked. "I think you just lost me."

Stephan resumed his pacing. "Jessie is not only both an empath and clairvoyant, but she also teaches the use of psychic abilities. She's going to help you find Gabriel."

"You've still lost me."

"You and Gabriel have formed a connection—a bond, if you like. He has used the link at least once to find you. You are about to return the favor."

She shook her head. "I don't—"

Stephan took four strides and leaned down, his face inches from hers. Anger radiated from every pore. She met his stormy gaze and swallowed. There was no compassion in this man's eyes, no humanity. The only thing he cared about was his family, and she had no doubt he would kill *anyone* who threatened his family's safety in *any* way.

"You will do this." His voice was soft, without inflection. He didn't need it. His eyes held enough violence to spark a war. "You will find my brother, whatever the personal cost. You owe him your life, and you *will* return the favor."

"Stephan," Jessie warned softly, touching his arm.

He swung away and resumed his pacing. There was a savageness in every action, a raw brutality that had not been evident before now. Was this the real Stephan, or was it merely a by-product of his worry for Gabriel?

She suspected the answer lie somewhere in-between the

two.

Jessie touched her hand again. Sam met her cat-green gaze.

"I showed Gabriel how to use the link. That's how he found you at that demolition site."

"Then thank you for saving my life. But that doesn't mean I can return the favor."

"Yes, it does. The link would not have formed if one or the other did not have the capacity."

"But I don't have the capacity. Ask him." She pointed her chin toward the pacing Stephan. Even that small movement sent ripples of pain down her body. Her stomach turned, threatening to rise. She swallowed heavily. "He's seen the test results. I came in negative."

"You came in neutral," Stephan corrected. "Not the same thing."

"I've never attempted anything like that. I wouldn't even know where to start."

"As Stephan said, that's why I'm here." Jessie's gaze was shrewd, calculating. "Are you willing to try?"

She had a choice? "What do you want me to do?"

"Close your eyes." Jessie's soft voice took on an almost hypnotic quality. "Concentrate on the darkness and the sound of my voice. Take deep, slow breaths."

She closed her eyes and took a deep breath. Pain ripped through her, as sharp as knife. She swore vehemently. "Get me some damn pain killers or I'm out of here."

As threats went, it was pretty lame, not only because she was strapped down, but because her leg was as numb as her arm and any sort of quick movement would be nigh on impossible anyway.

"No." Stephan said, voice abrupt, harsh. "Pain killers will dilute your ability to concentrate."

She glared at him. She was really beginning to dislike the man. Yet, it was easy to see why he, rather than Gabriel, ran both the SIU and the Federation. "So does pain, buddy, believe me."

Jessie squeezed Sam's fingers lightly. "This won't take long, as long as you concentrate. Then we can let the medical help in."

Meaning they were going to keep her in confinement until they'd thoroughly checked her story? *Bastards.* And that fact, if nothing else, hardened her resolve. She'd meant what she'd said before—she'd had enough of these people. She wanted out, wanted to go back to the State Police. At least there she'd be treated a little more fairly—even if she had shot her partner.

"Let's get on with it, then." She closed her eyes and tried to ignore the throbbing aches in her body.

"Bring Gabriel's image to you mind. Concentrate on it."

She frowned and did as Jessie asked. Gabriel's image swam through her mind, its focus blurred, distant.

"Concentrate," Jessie whispered. "Imagine your mind as a hand, capable of reaching out and touching him."

Sweat trickled into her closed eyes, stinging. She tried to ignore it. Gabriel's image went in and out of focus, as if viewed with some ill-adjusted lens.

"Reach for the image, Samantha. Reach out and touch him."

"I can't," she whispered. There was some sort of barrier between them, preventing her from reaching across. A fence of her making, not his.

"Focus on the image, Samantha. Focus until you can feel his presence within every fiber of your being. Then let your mind touch his."

She concentrated on the blurred image, willing it to become clear. Sweat trickled through her hair, along the side of her face. Abruptly, the image became focused, and she was there, sharing his mind, his thoughts. His eyes.

The ground sped underneath them. They arrowed toward a doorway, heart pumping as fast as their wings. Behind them, the air shuddered with sound. Heat sizzled. They soared upwards. The shot hit the wall, spraying metal through the air. They flew through the doorway and into the open skies. Freedom, if they could get clear fast enough. Another shot. Again, they dodged. But this time the shot hit, exploding through wing and muscle and bone.

Agony surged through every fiber and tore her mind from his. She screamed, then darkness hit and she lapsed into unconsciousness.

When awareness returned, it was again to the sensation of someone shaking her shoulder.

It should have hurt but it didn't. She frowned. Gabriel had been shot, not her. He was alive, that much she knew. For how much longer was anyone's guess—and there wasn't one damn thing she'd seen that could help them in any way.

"Samantha, open your eyes and look at me," Jessie

demanded, her voice cracked with worry.

She opened her eyes and said, "He was shot while trying to escape. That's all I know, all I saw." All she felt.

"Fuck." Stephan thrust a hand through his hair. "There has to have been something you saw that can help us find him."

"He was in a warehouse of some kind. It was abandoned."

"Which leaves us with probably a thousand choices citywide," Jessie commented, her expression worried as she glanced up at Stephan. "How much man power can you muster?"

"Not nearly enough, quickly enough," Stephan muttered, and resumed his pacing. "Even if we pull in Federation operatives, it'll still take hours."

In which time, Gabriel could have bled to death if he didn't get medical help. The phone rang in the brief silence.

Stephan grabbed the receiver almost savagely. "Byrne here."

He listened quietly for several minutes and then said. "Get all available teams down there immediately, but don't move until I join them."

He hung up and swung round, his expression an odd mixture of anger and surprise. "Why didn't you tell me you'd ordered a break team on Whittiker?"

"When did I have the chance? I was shot and dragged down here for questioning. I don't believe I was given much of a chance to say anything." She hesitated, more to keep her growing tide of anger in check than anything else. Stephan was not someone she wanted to get on his bad side. "Why? Have they got an address out of him?"

"Yes. A warehouse in Altona." He pressed a button on the side of the phone. "Security, cancel the medics and take agent Ryan straight down to medical. I want a twenty-four hour guard placed on her."

"Gee, nice to know I'm trusted."

Stephan barely glanced at her as he walked towards the door. "Until I check out your story thoroughly, you will remain under guard."

And if they didn't find Gabriel at the warehouse address Orrin had given them, she was in big trouble. That much was obvious.

The door opened. Three gray-clad security officers strode in.

"Barnes, I want full identity tests taken on anyone entering the building."

Barnes, a big man with craggy features, frowned. "That'll cause a bit of hostility, sir."

"I don't care. Just do it."

Barnes nodded and stepped aside as two medical officers came in, guiding a gurney between them.

"I'll let you know what happens," Jessie said to Sam, then rose and stepped away as the two doctors approached.

One shoved a needle none too gently into her arm. Thankfully, it was her numb arm, she thought wryly. After a few seconds, the throbbing aches that assailed her body began to ease and her eyes grew heavy.

The doctors picked her up and placed her onto the gurney. The last thing she saw was Stephan handing Jessie a laser rifle as he walked from the room.

***

She dreamt again of the white room. This time Joe's shadow was less indistinct, more man-shaped than merely a blot of darkness.

"You call to me again. Why?" His voice held just a hint of annoyance.

She shrugged. "It's not as if I do this consciously. It just happens."

"Nothing just happens, Samantha. You reach out because you wish to talk. But your timing right now is not the best."

"Why? What does a street bum have to do that is so important?"

His amusement ran round her. "Who said I was a street bum?"

"That's the image you present to the world, isn't it?"

"It is. But I am not what I appear. You'd best remember that."

The soft warning sent a chill down her spine. She knew nothing about this man, who, conversely, seemed to know so much about her. She didn't even know if she could trust him. And yet, he'd saved her life, had given her somewhere to live when she most needed it, and had come to this room when she called—even if she wasn't aware that she *had* called.

His sigh was a breeze that stirred past her hair. "What troubles you?"

"I did a search on the pin. It led me to Mary Elliott."

"Did it now?" There was no surprise in his voice. He'd obviously known all along where it would lead.

"She kept confusing me with a woman named Josephine. Kept insisting I had a brother named Joshua."

"And do you?"

His shadow swirled slowly around her. Though he appeared relaxed, she could almost taste his tension.

"I have dreamed about Joshua, but I don't know who he is." She studied the shadowed form in front of her for a second. "Just as I don't know who you are. You might be Joshua, for all I know."

"I might. I might not."

"And the answer will be found in here," she retorted, lightly touching her chest, just above her heart. "When I am ready to find it."

She sensed more than saw his smile. "Took the words right out of my mouth."

"What a surprise." She stared at the ceiling for several seconds. Though the bright light was harsh, it did not hurt her eyes or make them water. "Am I a product of Hopeworth?"

His essence stilled. "I have said before that I cannot provide you with answers. You must seek them yourself."

"Cannot or will not?"

"Will not."

She nodded. He knew more than he would ever tell, that much was obvious. "I met with a General Frank Lloyd yesterday."

"I know."

"How do you know?"

His smile swirled around her. "As I said before, I know more than you know."

She didn't bother raging against his obtuse answer, simply because it wouldn't get her anywhere. "I have a feeling the general and I will meet again."

Joe's shadow began to move. Agitation stirred the still air. "Be wary of the General. He sees more than most men."

"That's because he's not exactly a man, is he?"

Joe hesitated. "No, he is not. He *is* a product of Hopeworth, born and bred to do the bidding of the military. He is not someone you want anything to do with."

She rubbed her arms. On that, at least, they agreed. "I may not have any choice in the matter."

Concern churned around her. "You had a premonition?"

"Maybe."

"Then get the hell away from here. Leave the state, if that's what it takes."

"I can't. At least not until I know my partner is safe."

"Your partner? The man who has been trying to get rid of you?" He made no attempt to disguise the derision in his voice.

"Yeah, that one." She shrugged. "He saved my life. Now his life is in danger."

"Then find him and get far away from the general."

"Finding him is the problem. His sister seems to think we have formed some sort of mind bond, but when I tried to find him through it, all I got were his emotions and pain."

Joe didn't answer immediately, though his essence continued to swirl around her. "Your talents are only now truly developing, and as yet, no one can be really sure which way that development will head. One thing is obvious, though. It will not be standard."

She raised her eyebrows. "Another riddle?"

"No. A simple truth." He hesitated. "Maybe this linking with Stern, at least on your side, is one more emotional than thought. Perhaps your ability is empathic rather than telepathic."

"And yet, here I am, talking to you."

Again she felt his smile. "This is very different. This is something neither of us can really stop or control."

"Why not?"

"The answers will—"

"Yeah," she retorted. "I know the rest of the rhyme, so don't bother."

"If you wish to find your partner, leave tonight and go to where he was last seen."

She frowned. "Why tonight?"

"It storms."

"Yeah? So?"

Impatience ran around her. "Just go, and you will see. For now, I must go."

His essence and the white room, fled. She woke suddenly. Rain pelted against the window to the right of her bed. Lightning cut across the night, and the power of it stirred the air, filling her soul. She breathed deeply. Every pore seemed to tingle with the storm's energy.

From beyond the doorway came the sound of footsteps, a tattoo that was both angry and impatient. Jessie appeared. Water dripped from her burgundy coat, splashing across the tiles as she walked over to Sam's bed.

"What happened?" Inane question when all she had to do was look into Jessie's eyes and see the answer. They hadn't found Gabriel.

"We found his viaphone, but nothing else. There was no clue as to where they might have gone."

She rubbed her forehead. Joe had told her to go to the warehouse. Though she had no idea why, she wasn't about to doubt him. Not when Gabriel's life might be at risk.

"Where's Director Byrne?"

"Interviewing Whittiker again."

She almost felt sorry for Orrin. Almost. "You have to take me to that warehouse."

Jessie frowned. "Samantha, you're in no condition—"

"Yeah, right," she snapped back. "Like you were so concerned about my condition down in the holding cell."

Jessie had the grace to look uncomfortable.

"Do you want to save your brother or not?" she continued.

"Of course I do. But you can't even walk."

"That was hours ago. I'm better now." Even if she wasn't, she had no intention of mentioning it. She owed Gabriel—though certainly not any of his damn relations—and she intended to repay that debt. Then she'd be free to leave and get back to a normal life, with normal people.

But could anything ever be normal for her, when her discovery of self was only just beginning? Deep down, she suspected not.

Indecision rolled across Jessie's face. "Stephan's ordered that you be kept here. That under no circumstances are you to be allowed to leave."

Obviously he had plans to cross-examine her again if Orrin failed to deliver. "I think I may be able to find Gabriel, but I need to get out of here now. I can't wait for Stephan."

"I'm not SIU, and I can't countermand Stephan's orders."

"Then call him. Tell him if he wants to find his goddamn brother, he has to trust me, and he has to release me."

"I don't think he'll listen."

"Try."

Jessie nodded and walked from the room. Sam stripped the covers away and swung her legs over the edge of the bed.

Her right leg, from thigh to knee, was a scarred, red mess. But at least it was a healing, scared red mess. Though the skin pinched slightly when she moved, it didn't seem to restrict her. Nor did it hurt. She rotated her shoulder. Again, though there was a definite tightness in the skin, she could move it without pain. How was this possible after only hours of being shot? She didn't know, and right now, she didn't really care.

All that mattered was getting to Gabriel before time ran out.

She padded across to get her clothes, the tiles cold under her feet. She dressed quickly, and then went back to bed—just in case one of the med-staff walked in before the clearance came through for her to be up and about.

But come through it did.

Ten minutes later she walked out of the building and into the power of the rain swept night.

Fifteen

Gabriel woke to the sound of pacing—short, vicious steps that spoke of anger and frustration more eloquently than any words.

He lay on the floor of an office of some kind. The star-shaped base of a chair sat less than a foot away from his head. Beyond that, he could see the sturdy metal legs of a desk. The carpet underneath him rubbed almost harshly against his skin, and it was a practical gray color. It was the sort of hard-wearing carpet they used in State-owned buildings and in housing developments.

That he was no longer in the warehouse was obvious. He shifted fractionally, trying to see the rest of the room. Bad move. Pain shot through his body, a red wave of heat that not only left him gasping for air but soaked in sweat.

The tattoo beat of violence hesitated and then headed his way. Boots appeared before him, wavering in and out of focus. He squeezed his eyes shut, trying to shake the sweat from his eyes, and then opened them again. The boots were still there. Black and practical. The kind worn by the state police force.

He looked up. Even that slight movement forced new rivulets of sweat to run down his forehead.

Rose stared down at him, her eyes as dark as the night-dark window at her back. "Good to see you're finally awake, Assistant Director."

Despite the cheerfulness of her tone, the fury in her eyes suggested all had not gone well.

"Wish I could say the same."

Her smile was thin, bitter. "Arm hurt a little, does it?"

She nudged it with the tip of her boot. Pain tore through his body, and he grit his teeth against the scream that tore at his throat. He glared at her through the drips of sweat. "Bitch."

"Yes, aren't I?" She laughed and turned away. "You didn't tell me about your partner, Assistant Director."

Something cold ran through him. Rose had shot Sam. "You didn't ask."

"True." Rose leaned against the front of the desk, contemplating him silently for a few minutes. "What is she? A shifter sensitive to others of her kind?"

"Something like that." It was obvious from the annoyance

etched into Rose's features that Sam *had* managed to stop her. And had been shot for her efforts. He hoped she wasn't too badly injured

"It's unfortunate, you know, as it calls for an extreme change of plan."

And he was supposed to be sorry about that? Anything that sidetracked this woman's mad schemes *had* to be a good thing. "Try my shape again. You never know. You might get through a second time."

"I am not a fool, Assistant Director. Please don't treat me like one."

There was no point in replying. He carefully ran his fingers up his broken arm till he found the laser wound. The cut felt clean, but his arm was definitely broken. Which was no real problem, because his shapechanger bones healed extraordinarily fast. He just had to set the bones straight, and the healing would begin. He could also feel an ominous damp patch under his right shoulder, but he had no idea where that blood was coming from.

"You stated before that the SIU does not bargain for its operatives," she said. "You'd better hope that you're wrong, because it's your only chance to live."

"Then there's no chance at all." Nursing his shattered limb with his right arm, he rolled fully onto his back. To say it hurt would be an understatement, but he needed to see where he was. The room was small, and the only exit points were the window behind the desk and the two doors, one opposite to where he lay, and the other close to his left. He could hear no sound beyond this room. Hopefully, it meant it was just him and Rose here.

"I want Director Byrne's silent number," she continued.

He gave it to her. If she thought to get around the automatic tracing by using Stephan's silent number, then she was very wrong.

He waited almost impatiently for her to grab the phone. All he needed was for her attention to be diverted for a second or two, and he was up and out the door. His arm might be shattered, but he still had two good legs. And the desperation to survive was a mighty fine pain killer.

Rose picked up the laser near the phone and pointed it in his direction. "Move and you die."

She set the phone to speaker and dialed the number he'd

given her. After several rings, Stephan's familiar voice came on-line.

"Byrne here."

"Director Byrne. How nice to finally speak to you."

There was a brief silence. Though the trace was automatic, he knew Stephan was now ordering a second trace to start, this time involving the satellites to track the exact location.

"Who is this?"

Rose glanced at her watch. As a cop, she'd know the call would be traced, but he doubted if she knew it could be tracked via satellite as well. That capability was a well-kept secret.

"I think you know who this is, Director. Shall we cut to the chase?"

"What do you want, Rose?"

"You know what I want. I have something to offer in exchange."

"You must know we do not make exchanges for the lives of our operatives. We can't afford to."

"Then you condemn him to death."

The silence seemed to stretch forever. Gabriel nursed his arm and wished, for the first time in his life, he knew what was going on in his brother's mind. They both knew the rules—they both knew the risks of being caught in a situation like this. Both knew that, in the end, there no real choice.

But had it been *him* on the other end of the phone, he would have found some way to give them another choice.

"Let me speak to him," Stephan said eventually. "I want to know if he's still alive."

"Oh, he's alive. Bleeding, sweating, and silently cursing me, but he's definitely alive." She motioned toward the phone with the gun. "Speak to the man, Assistant Director."

"Here, sir," he said.

"Situation?"

Rose clicked the safety off the gun. A soft whine filled the room as the laser powered to full.

He took heed of the warning. "As she said."

"Enough," Rose cut in. "I want an answer, Director, and I want it fast."

"Look, I haven't the power for a decision like this. I need to go higher."

Rose glanced at her watch again. "You have precisely two hours. Then he dies."

"Just make sure he lives until you get my damn—"

Rose hit the receiver, cutting him off. "Four seconds until the trace was complete. That will really piss him off, don't you think?"

Maybe. Maybe not. It depended on how fast the satellites got into action.

Rose reset the laser. "I'm afraid there's a lot more to do, the least of which is ensuring you don't bleed to death within the next couple of hours. Can't have my insurance policy expiring before its proper time now, can I?"

The woman was certifiably crazy. He replied, "It's not something I want, I can assure you of that."

She gave him a thin smile. "No doubt," she said, and squeezed the trigger.

Gabriel swore and rolled away from the beam. His injured arm hit the floor, and agony exploded. Then the second burst of laser fire hit, sweeping him into unconsciousness.

**

Sam studied the warehouse through the mustang's rain-washed window. Even with the headlights on high beam, the building was little more than a hunched shadow in the stormy night.

"I can't see what coming out here is going to achieve," Jessie said, leaning on the steering wheel to peer through the windshield. "We went over everything already. There's nothing here to find."

"Maybe." She had to try, at the very least. "You'd better wait here. No sense in the two of us getting wet."

Jessie's gaze was dubious. "You're sure you're okay?"

"Yeah." She opened the car door. The wind snatched it from her hands, flinging it fully open. She winced. "Sorry about that."

Jessie shrugged. "There's a flashlight in the glove compartment. Grab that."

She did, even though she didn't really need it. With all the lightning, the night was almost as bright as day. She climbed out and slammed the door shut. The wind tore at her hair, blowing it in all directions. The rain sheeted down, sluicing off her coat and soaking into her boots. Yet in the wildness, there was power. She could feel it, running across her skin, crackling across her fingertips. She breathed deeply, drawing that energy inside, feeling it surge through every pore, every fiber, although she wasn't entirely sure how this would help her find Gabriel.

She walked toward the warehouse. The wind howled through the shattered windows lining the front of the building, an eerie sound that had goose bumps fleeing across her skin. Mixed with this moaning was the high pitched scream of metal as the wind tore at the roofing. It sounded like the dead being tortured.

Shoving her hands in her coat pockets, and half-wishing she'd brought some gloves, she made her way down the side of the building. It briefly protected her from the full force of the wind, though the night was still bitterly cold. Thunder peeled in the distance. She began counting the seconds, but she had barely gotten to three before jagged lighting split the night sky. The center of the storm was only a few miles away. Whether this would make any difference to what might happen, she wasn't sure.

She reached the back and came out of the protection of the building. The wind slapped against her, forcing her to stagger several steps before she regained her footing. Lighting tore through the sky again. In the residue brightness, she saw the ramp and loading bay. This is it. This was where Gabriel had gotten shot.

She walked forward slowly, not toward the loading bay, but away from it. He'd been flying when he'd been hit, striving upwards to escape the loading bay. He wouldn't have come down close to it.

Overhead, thunder rumbled again. The power of the storm echoed through her, a force that filled her, completed her, in way she couldn't even begin to understand or hope to explain. When she clenched her hands, sparks danced across her knuckles, a visible sign of the energy coursing through her being.

It scared her. Terrified her. But if this power helped her find Gabriel, then she'd use it and worry about the consequences later.

She splashed through puddles, following the rain-slick pavement toward the rear of the property. Hopefully, there she'd find a clue that Stephan and Jessie had missed.

The fence line came into view. The double gates leading out of the property were padlocked. She turned left and walked along the perimeter, following instinct and hoping it wasn't leading her astray.

Again, the sky rumbled. In the following flash of lightning, she saw something flapping wildly in the wind torn darkness. A piece of material, caught in the fence.

She splashed quickly through the mud. The material was dark gray and felt like silk. The sort of material Gabriel favored in his jackets. She tore the strip free and rubbed it between her fingers. He must have snagged his jacket against the fence as he fell. Hopefully, his jacket was the only casualty.

Thunder reverberated. Its power shuddered through her, and energy, as bright as the lightning itself, sparked again between her fingertips, this time dancing over the small strip of material.

Power hit her with the force of a hammer. She grunted and dropped to her knees, splashing mud into her face. She ignored it and clenched the material tight, struggling to breathe under the weight of the energy running around her, through her.

Images struck—jagged pieces of information that knifed through her mind. A suburb full of red brick houses. A street name. A factory perched between two supermarkets. A "For Sale" sign out front, bearing the number fifty-two. Gabriel, pale and unconscious, stretched out on a gray carpet.

The power faded, leaving her trembling and gasping for breath. She shuddered and swiped the muddy water dripping from her nose. What the hell was that? And how had Joe known it would happen? Jesus, she had to find out just who he was and how he knew so much.

But right now that was not her main priority. She struggled upright, the material still clenched in her hand. But with most of the night's power having left her system, it was little more than a sodden strip. Even so, it was proof that he'd been here, proof that she'd found what they could not. A clue. A possible hope.

As she made her way back to the car, she dug her viaphone from her pocket and quickly dialed the SIU.

"Christine? Patch me through to Director Byrne."

Stephan came on-line. In the background she could hear strident alarms. "What do you want now, Agent Ryan?"

For the first time since she'd met him, Stephan actually looked, and sounded, stressed. "I know where he is, sir. I'm heading there now."

"The address?"

She gave it to him. "I wouldn't call in too many reinforcements, though. Might inflame the situation."

"The situation is already inflamed. She gave us two hours," he hesitated, glancing down. "Forty-five minutes ago. And

Whittiker has escaped."

That was not a good development. "Escaped? How?"

"We don't know, and we can't find him."

"He'll be heading to the factory to meet up with Rose and help fulfill his end of the bargain.

"Maybe. I'll meet you there, Agent Ryan." He hesitated again, blue eyes sharp with anger. "Under no circumstances are you to move in until we get there, understand?"

"Yes, sir." Whether she actually obeyed was another matter.

Stephan grunted and signed off. She put the viaphone away and climbed into the car.

"I'm going to drown your seats, I'm afraid."

Jessie waved a hand. "Forget it. Did you find anything?"

"Certainly did." She grinned and punched the address into the onboard computer. "Let's go rescue your brother."

***

Jessie halted the Mustang in the supermarket parking lot two doors down from the factory. Sam shivered. Even though the car's heating was on full, she still felt as cold as a snowflake in a storm. At least she'd discovered one thing tonight—this damn coat wasn't exactly waterproof. At least not when the rain was more like a torrent than a gentle shower. Her sweater was sodden underneath.

She peered through the waterfall running down the windshield, trying to see the factory. A solitary light glimmered in front of the building, but against the force of the storm, it did little more than illuminate the small patch of ground directly beneath it.

She glanced at her watch. It had taken them half an hour to get here. That gave them forty-five minutes before Rose's deadline ended. If Stephan didn't get here soon…

Headlights glimmered through the rain. The car cruised past the factory, not slowing until it reached the parking lot entrance. It turned in and came to a halt beside them.

She climbed out of the Mustang. The wind cut through her sodden coat, as sharp as a knife. She shivered again and shoved her hands in her pockets. Not that it helped much.

Jessie stopped beside her. "Bitch of night," she said, as she wrapped a rubber band round her hair.

Stephan climbed out of the gray Ford. "Might play to our advantage," he said. "With the force of the wind, it's doubtful Rose will hear any noise we might make."

"Orrin will." Sam didn't know why she was so certain of this. "Did you bring any backup, sir?"

Stephan nodded. "Briggs, King and Francis. They're making their way around to the back of the building."

"Let me go in and scout the situation. If Orrin's there, we'll have to get rid of him first."

"Definitely not—"

"With all due respect, sir, we haven't the time to stand here and argue. Orrin will hear you—he won't hear me." Not with the storm and the night as her ally. She held out her hand. "Give me an ear phone and just trust me."

"I don't care to risk my brother's life—"

"Stephan," Jessie interrupted softly. "It's Gabriel's only chance."

He glanced at his sister and then handed Sam the ear phone. "I want a running commentary, and I want you to call us in the minute there's a problem. Understand?"

She tucked the small device into her ear and nodded. "I'm not stupid enough to tackle Orrin alone, believe me."

"Good." He reached into his pocket and withdrew a Holcroft laser. "Take this with you."

The laser clung to her palm like a second skin, and she felt safer. "Thanks."

She turned and walked toward the factory. The wind tore at the gums lining the fence line. Leaves and twigs littered the footpath, becoming miniature boats as they were caught in the rush of water streaming toward the gutters. At least the tree canopies protected her from the worst of the rain. She climbed the waist high fence at the front of the building and stopped, letting her gaze roam across the dark factory.

Thunder rumbled across the night. Power surged, dancing through her soul. Energy again leapt across her fingertips, warming the chill from her flesh.

But through the power came the sensation of evil. Orrin was inside the factory, keeping watch near the back. The softer bite of evil that was Rose's presence came from near the front of the building. Obviously, her best bet was to enter from somewhere near the middle

She headed right. Most places had at least one fire exit, and there was more of a chance of such an exit coming out to a large, gated driveway than the rubbish-strewn strip of fence line to the left.

Once she reached the meshed gate, she shoved the laser in her pocket, grabbed the links and began to climb. Her coat caught on one of the top rungs, tearing as she swung over. Water dripped past the sodden neck of her sweater, chilling her already cold flesh. She cursed softly.

"Problem, Agent Ryan?" Stephan's voice breezed through the ear phone, cold and efficient.

"No, sir," she answered, keeping her voice low so that Orrin didn't hear. "Just tore my friggin' coat."

"We'll buy you a new one. You near the factory entrance yet?"

"Approaching side door now, sir."

She splashed through the puddles and up the stairs. The side door was padlocked. She picked up the lock, studying it in frustration. Just great. She didn't have her pick with her, and if she shot her way in, it might alert those inside.

She studied the long building. In the brief flash of lightning, she saw windows high up. Too high for her. Unlike Gabriel, she hadn't the option of flight—nor were there any trees close enough to use as a ladder.

Her gaze returned to the lock. Thunder rumbled, and once again, the force of the storm surged through her body. The energy tingling across her fingers became a bright, blue-white flame that danced across the lock, encasing it in fire.

In a heartbeat, it was little more than dust in her hand.

The flame muted again, but it didn't completely disappear. She stared at the blackened scraps in her hand. What sort of psychic ability was *that*?

She didn't know, and right now, she didn't care. Not if it helped free Gabriel.

She raised her hand, letting the wind scatter the lock's remains. Then she carefully opened the door. The passageway beyond was dark, and narrow. Not the sort of place she really wanted to get caught in. There was absolutely no fighting room.

But she had little choice. Orrin still stood guard near the back. Rose was near the front. Gabriel was probably somewhere between the two.

"Entering the factory now," she said, closing the door carefully behind her.

"See if you can find Gabriel and get him out of there. We'll take care of the rest."

That was just fine by her. She'd never had a death wish,

and Orrin was not someone she ever wanted to confront.

She eased forward, her fingers wrapped so tightly around the laser her knuckles practically glowed. The air smelled stale, old, and a steady, moaning creak filled the silence. The wind tearing at loose roofing.

The passage curved around to the right and opened onto a set of stairs. She stopped, listening. The awareness of evil stirred through her. Orrin still stood guard near the back of the building. Rose was on the move, though. The sense of her flowed across the darkness, moving steadily closer. Had Rose heard the door open? Did she suspect something was wrong?

Sam had no idea. Nor was there any use worrying about it. She had to get off these stairs and out of Rose's way before she appeared. Right now, it was better she avoid being seen—at least until she'd found Gabriel and knew he was safe.

And once she knew that, she was more than willing to back away and let Stephan vent his anger. Would Orrin and Rose survive that? She very much doubted it.

She edged quietly down the steps, stopping again at the bottom. Thunder vibrated through the air. The following flash of lightning briefly illuminated a vast, empty space. She looked up. Skylights were regularly spaced along the roofline. She'd have to watch that she wasn't caught in the open during the next flash. It'd be just her luck that Rose would be walking by at that precise moment.

Once on the factory floor, she headed left, keeping in the deeper shadows under the stairs. Sound stirred the silence—the scuff of a heel against concrete. She squatted in a corner, waiting.

The sense of wrongness flooded the night, making it difficult to breathe. From the hallway to her right, a woman appeared. Rose, obviously, as she was the image of her dead sister.

"Orrin?" the woman said. Though it was barely a whisper, Sam heard her clearly. Perhaps it was the night and the power of the storm. Perhaps it was just the emptiness of the factory allowing her voice to carry so clearly. "I'm heading up to check the side door," the woman continued. "If you don't hear from me, presume the worst. Kill Stern and get the hell out of here."

Damn. Once Rose walked up those stairs and discovered the unlocked door, she'd know *someone* was here. She had to find Gabriel and get him out of here. Fast.

Rose drew close. Sam's skin crawled. The stink of the other woman's evil was almost suffocating. She didn't move, barely dared to breathe. Rose grabbed the banister and hesitated, her gaze sweeping the shadows in which Sam hid. Sam's breath caught, and she tensed.

After a moment, Rose moved on, her footsteps fading away as she disappeared down the hallway above. She had, at best, a few minutes left to find Gabriel.

She ran across the factory floor, heading for the rear of the building and Orrin. Gabriel had to be near the giant somewhere.

She came to a door and opened it cautiously. Another hallway. She stepped inside, stopped, and reached into her pocket for the strip of material. Sparks leapt across her fingertips, firefly bright in the darkness.

Gabriel was two doors down, to her left. She padded forward. The door wasn't locked, nor did it appear alarmed. An ominous sign, because it meant they were sure Gabriel couldn't escape.

She quickly stepped inside and closed the door. It was the office she'd seen briefly in her visions—small, and cramped, with wall to wall cheap gray carpet. Gabriel lay near the desk, not moving but breathing.

She waited, listening to the silence as she studied the room. There had to be something here, something that would warn them if Gabriel woke up. Surely they wouldn't be foolish enough to think the ropes that bound him would hold him.

Or maybe they were that foolish. Maybe Rose was delusional *and* overconfident.

She knelt by Gabriel's side. His skin was pale, and clammy, his breathing rapid. Shock, she thought. He shouldn't be moved, but she had no choice. She pressed the earphone. "Found him."

"Alive?" Stephan's voice was tightly controlled. He'd feared the worst.

"Yes. Unconscious, though."

"We're moving in."

And Orrin was moving out. The giant had sensed her, though she had no idea how. But then, if she could sense him, why wouldn't he be able to sense her, especially if they were both products of Hopeworth?

One thing was obvious, though. She couldn't stay here. To do so would risk Gabriel's life. Rose wouldn't kill her insurance policy unless she had no other choice. Sam would have to do the one thing she'd been trying to avoid—confront Orrin.

"Orrin's on the move. I'm going to try and lead him away

from Gabriel. Have Briggs and the others wait near the back entrance."

"Be careful."

A totally unnecessary warning. She rose, and then she hesitated. She couldn't leave Gabriel here, unprotected. Rose obviously wasn't sane. Why *wouldn't* she come back here and kill Gabriel, just for the she hell of it?

She quickly undid the ropes binding his arms and legs, but she left them looped, so that he still looked bound to the casual glance.

Then she touched his cheek, pinching it gently. "Gabriel, wake up."

He groaned, eyelids fluttering. She pinched harder. Right now, there was no time for niceties. Not when Orrin was drawing close.

"Gabriel, wake up, goddamn it."

He did. Pain burned bright in the hazel depths of his eyes. His gaze was unfocused, and he blinked several times, struggling to stay awake and regain some semblance of alertness.

She couldn't wait for that.

"Here, take this." She shoved the laser into his hand. "Protect yourself. The ropes are undone. I'm going to lead Orrin away from this room. Stephan's on his way. Leave if you can."

He blinked owlishly. She wondered if he'd heard anything she'd said. Sweat dripped into his eyes, and the stink of burned flesh was heavy in the air. His shattered arm was obviously bad. So, too, was the cut he'd sustained on the fence, if the wide circle of blood near his shoulder was anything to go by.

Still, if he hadn't bled to death by now, he probably wasn't in danger of doing so within the next five minutes.

His eyes started to close again. She touched his cheek gently. "Gabriel, stay awake. Stay alert. Orrin's on his way. Wait till he has checked this room, then get up and run."

If you can. He showed no sign of real understanding. She bit her lip, rose and walked across to the internal door. It led into another office. She slipped inside.

Outside the factory, lightning flashed, something she heard and felt rather than saw. Energy crawled across her skin. Stephan was closing in. So was Orrin. His lumbering steps reverberated through her brain, as sharp as the evil that stung the stale air.

This room also had two doors. She took the left, simply because Orrin approached the other. It led into another corridor.

She turned right. The back door had to be down here, somewhere. If she could find it and open it, Briggs, King and Francis might be able to help her take out Orrin before Rose woke up to the fact that something was wrong.

She came to another door and opened it to find another set of stairs, this one leading down into a wide dark room. A roller door dominated the wall opposite. A smaller door was beside it, padlocked and bolted from the inside rather than the outside. Briggs had no chance of getting in without blasting her way in and telling the world of her presence in the process.

In the hallway behind her, a door opened. It wasn't so much the sound she heard as the stale air stirring. Orrin hunted.

She descended the stairs and ran to the outer door. The sparks dancing across her fingertips leapt to the padlock the minute she picked it up. Within seconds, it was dust.

If she'd had the time to be frightened about this new ability, she would have been. But right now, Gabriel's safety mattered more than anything else, including her fear.

She pulled open the bottom deadbolt and reached for the top lock. But it was too high, and she couldn't get anywhere near it. Cursing, she swung round, looking for something to stand on.

And saw the door near the top of the stairs open.

Sixteen

Scent stirred him. Sam's scent. Vanilla and cinnamon, such a warm and enticing mix. Like her. He opened his eyes, blinking several times before his vision swam into focus.

He was still in the office, still on the floor. His arm was numb. That numbness didn't extend to his back—it felt as if every muscle was being torn apart. Even the mere act of blinking made his gut churn uneasily.

Sam wasn't in the room. But she had been, otherwise he wouldn't have smelled her.

Or was it merely wishful thinking?

No, he could feel her closeness, as surely as he could his heart. And she'd left him a laser. It clung like a limpet to his palm.

Where had she gone? And why?

Rose, he thought. She was hunting down Rose. He had to find them—help if he could.

He rolled onto his back, and a dozen fresh aches assaulted his body. Sweat beaded on his forehead and dripped down the side of his face. For an instant, darkness loomed. He would have welcomed the fall back to unconsciousness except for the sudden realization that if Sam was here, she would need his help. She couldn't cope with the likes of Rose by herself.

He grabbed the edge of the desk with his good hand and, gritting his teeth, slowly, carefully, eased himself upright. His legs wouldn't take his weight and buckled beneath him. His knees hit the floor, his back scraping against the desk as he fell sideways. A scream tore up his throat, but it came out as little more than a sharp hiss.

When the room stopped spinning, he tried again. This time he made it. He wiped the sweat from his eyes, then staggered across to the door, where he stood, trembling like a newborn just learning to walk.

The door opened into a corridor. Two doors to choose from— the right one closer. He didn't have much strength left, and he didn't know how much longer he could keep going. Headed right.

The door led into a deeper darkness, and he had the feeling of a vast emptiness. There were no sounds beyond the creak of loose roofing. He stepped out. Overhead, lightning flashed, briefly illuminating the room. He was in a factory of some kind. There were stairs directly in front of him, leading up.

He staggered across the emptiness and grabbed the banister—had to, because otherwise he would have fallen. His heart felt like it was ready to tear out of his chest, and the darkness whirled around him. He took several deep breaths and slowly, carefully began to climb.

Footsteps whispered across the night. He stopped, listening. They were coming to the top of the stairs and heading directly toward him. It wasn't Sam. He would have known if it were. Probably Rose.

He held his ground, simply because he had no other choice. He couldn't move with any sort of speed, and Rose would hear him if he tried. Better to remain where he was and hope for the element of surprise.

He clenched his fingers around the laser and waited. The steps drew close, a tattooed beat of violence that ricocheted across the night.

Rose appeared on the top step. She began to descend and then stopped abruptly. There was a click and light flooded across his face, momentarily blinding him.

"Well, well. Here I am expecting an intruder, and I find you instead. How did you escape the ropes?"

"Double jointed."

He squinted, trying to see her silhouette against the brightness of the flashlight. He dared not use the laser until he was certain of her position. Surprise would only give him one shot, so it had better be a good one.

"Why don't you just turn around and head down the stairs? Can't have my insurance policy running around injuring himself. Orrin wouldn't be pleased."

"You're fuckin' mad, you know that?" Which probably wasn't the sanest thing to say, given the situation.

"Why, thank you. That's the nicest thing you've said all day. Now move."

He pressed the safety off the laser. "And go meekly to my death? I don't think so."

"Assistant Director, don't be a fool. I have a gun, and I'm not opposed to shooting a hole the size of a football field in your knee. Dragging you across the floor would be a pain, though, so I really prefer not to."

From the hallway behind her came a second whisper of

sound. A door creaking open. Her gaze hardened. "It appears we have a visitor after all, which leaves me with little choice. Can't have you wandering around unattended now, can I?"

He raised the laser and aimed for the flashlight. The bright beam went out. Rose yelped and then swore. He threw himself sideways. His back hit the banister and agony exploded. Laser fire bit through the night, burning into the step he'd just vacated. Another burst of laser fire lit the darkness, its source the hallway beyond Rose.

There was a thud, and then Rose's body fell past him, landing with a sickening crack at the base of the stairs.

He looked up. Stephan, still in his Byrne disguise, appeared out of the darkness, a laser held by his side.

"And the lesson to be learned tonight is never attack my bother without first looking over your shoulder for me." He squatted next to Gabriel, eyes grim despite his half smile. "The bitch didn't deserve to die so quickly, of course. How you feeling?"

"Like shit. Help me up."

"I don't think that's a—"

"Damn it, Stephan, don't argue. Sam needs help."

"Then let me and Jessie handle it."

"The way you let the SIU handle this? This is not a responsibility the director should be handling."

"I'm not here in my capacity as the director."

"I realize that. Help me up."

Stephan gripped his arm and steadied him as he rose. Pain tore across his back. For a minute, it felt as if someone was shoving red-hot pokers into his backbone, clear through to his gut. He hissed and blinked the sweat out of his eyes.

"Brother, you're useless to everyone like this. Let us handle it."

"Would you, if it were Lyssa?"

Stephan regarded him steadily. "Lyssa's my wife. We're talking about your partner—a woman you're trying to get rid of."

A woman who was dead, if he didn't get moving. "Yeah. So just shut up and help me down the stairs."

***

Orrin stepped onto the landing. Sam couldn't see him—the night hid him as surely as it had hidden her earlier. But she could feel him, feel the stink of his evil.

"I knew you were one of us." His voice jarred the night, edgy and somehow out of tune with the power that flowed through the darkness.

She backed away from the door. If she could get to the deeper shadows, maybe he'd lose her...

"I can see you, you know. See you as clear as day. It's one of the advantages of our gift."

"What gift is that, Orrin?" If he could see her, why couldn't she see him? Why could she only sense him?

"The gift of darkness. The ability to ghost, to become one with the night."

No mention of the power within the storm. No mention of the firefly dance of energy that could shatter locks as easily as she breathed.

Perhaps Orrin thought to keep it a surprise. Perhaps he didn't even know about it. There was no way of knowing if her apparent ability to disappear into shadows was, in any way, linked to his. They might not even be talking about the same type of ability.

But Orrin had come from Hopeworth. The more she delved into her past, the more obvious it was that the military base was her birthplace. The gifts Orrin spoke of were a cousin to her own, of that she was sure.

The giant walked down the stairs. She backed away, her gaze sweeping the large room, searching desperately for some sort of weapon. It was no use running. Orrin was twice her height, and would catch her in no time.

How close were Briggs and the others? Or Stephan? She still had the earphone on—maybe she should just shout for help. But that would warn Orrin and Rose that the others were out there, and if Orrin's behavior was anything to go by, that was something they weren't aware of yet. For Gabriel's sake, she had to play this solo.

Besides, there was no guarantee that even with the help of Briggs and the others, they'd be able to take the giant out. Not when he had the night as his ally. To be able to shoot someone, you had to be able to see them.

Orrin reached the bottom step and stopped. Though she couldn't see his smile, she could feel it.

"Nowhere to run here, little girl. Just one big room with only the two exits."

Her back hit the wall. She edged along to the right. "You can't cover both of them at the same time, Orrin."

"I don't need to. I move too fast, faster even than you."

"You can't know that." Though she had a suspicion that he could. After all, if it was possible for her to taste evil, why couldn't it be possible for him to know instinctively what she could and couldn't do?

But if that were the case, why wasn't he saying anything about the power of the storm?

Her foot hit something. Metal scraped harshly across the concrete. Orrin laughed.

"You think that little metal pick is going to hurt me?"

Shoved deep in some unlikely orifice, yes, it probably would. She quickly picked it up. Orrin's so-called pick was a good three feet long and as heavy as sin. Should make a rather nice dent, even in a head as thick as Orrin's. *If* she dared get that close.

He stepped toward her. Heat crawled over her skin, whispering secrets. Orrin was a true creature of the night, but one who could walk through the day without fear. He was Dhampire, the offspring of a human and vampire, created in the lab rather than during those few vital hours after rebirth, when the newly risen vampire still held life in his loins.

And he drank blood, not through necessity, but for enjoyment.

She hefted the metal rod, holding it in front of her like a staff. Why hadn't she sensed Orrin's true nature earlier? Was it because the daylight hid his vampire half, or was it more a case of these new abilities coming into focus because of the storm's power?

"Why not simply turn yourself in, Orrin? At the moment, you're guilty of little more than being an accessory. A few years, max, in prison. Piss easy for a man like you."

"And Hopeworth? You think I don't know they'll swoop in and get me?"

"You have a real fixation on the military, haven't you?" She balanced lightly on her toes, ready to run, given the slightest hint of movement from Orrin.

"You're one of us. You should know what it's like, being poked and prodded and examined endlessly. I won't go back to it. Can't."

She frowned. He seemed to have awfully clear memories of something that happened when he was a babe. "That was a long time ago, Orrin."

"Twenty years," he agreed. "I was four when they dumped me. But I remember. And I will have revenge."

Not if she could help it. Not that she wanted to protect Hopeworth—far from it. Everything she'd learned over the past few days had only convinced her they deserved everything Orrin had planned, and a whole lot more.

No. The problem was Orrin himself. His desire to kill was so strong she could almost taste it. He planned to play with her, planned to drink her blood until he drained her dry. Then he planned to do the same to Gabriel.

To stop him, she'd have to kill him. If she could.

He rushed at her, a gale force she felt rather than saw. She danced away and swung the bar with all her might. It connected against flesh with a sickening crack. The force of the blow shuddered up her arm and momentarily numbed her fingers.

He laughed. *Laughed.* He was as mad as Rose.

She backed away, gripping the bar hard, her gaze locked on his evil stain.

"You're good, little girl. Not many can match me for speed."

Gabriel could. No doubt Stephan could as well. She hoped like hell he was listening in—no, make that running to the rescue. It had been nothing short of madness to ever think she could play this game with Orrin. The giant was too fast, too strong.

"As you said, we have something in common. Give it up, Orrin, while you still can."

"You're all talk, little girl. And if you're waiting for those others to come to the rescue, I have to tell you, five is not enough."

Fear slivered through her. "What are you talking about?"

He chortled. "Those five heartbeats that draw close. I sensed them ages ago, though I have to admit, I didn't feel you until you were really close."

Why? That was the question that needed to be answered—but she wasn't going to risk asking Orrin. The less the giant knew about her—or rather, her appalling lack of knowledge about her past and her skills—the better. "If you know they're there, you must know that you're never going to escape."

"They don't hold enough fire power to stop me."

"One laser set to full is enough to stop you, Orrin."

"But I am of the night. They can't see me. Only you can."

A point she'd mulled over not so long ago. "This is the SIU we're talking about here, Orrin. You think they don't have weapons to bring down rat-bait like you?"

He snarled, a sound that crawled across her skin, sending shivers up her spine. It was a malignant, angry noise.

"Then I'll just have to use you as a shield before I kill you."

"Not something I'm planning to let happen, I can tell you."

"Who said anythin' about choice?"

He rushed her again. Air surged from her left—a fist, looking for a target. She ducked and then swung the bar. Felt it caught in some gigantic vice before it was ripped from her hand.

She turned and ran. He didn't follow. Playing with his prey, enjoying the hunt, she thought.

She stopped at the far end of the room, her breath short gasps that tore at her throat. Fear, more than exertion.

He flung the bar to one side. It hit the wall hard enough to leave a dent and clattered to the floor. Halfway between herself and Orrin.

"Come get your toothpick, girlie."

Said the spider to the fly. "No, thanks. I'm comfortable right where I am."

He sighed. "You really aren't playing the game right, you know."

She flexed her fingers, trying to ease the tension knotting her limbs. Energy tingled across her fingertips, firefly bright in the darkness. Maybe she really didn't need the bar. Maybe she had a weapon primed and ready to go.

If only she could figure out how to use it without getting too close to Orrin.

"Fire won't hurt me, if that's what you're planning with that lighter."

He'd seen the brief dance of flames across her fingers, obviously. Overhead, thunder rumbled. The storm was close, so close. She could feel the vibrations of it shuddering through her soul.

Orrin swept toward her again. She ducked away, but this time he was ready for it. His fist connected against her chin and sent her flying. She hit the concrete with a grunt, the air leaving her lungs in a whoosh. For a moment, stars fizzed across her vision.

Then she felt the wind of Orrin's approach. She scrambled upright and staggered away. He stopped.

"I haven't had a good fight in ages," he said, almost wistfully. "Perhaps I shall kill you fast at the end, just to show my appreciation."

"Gee, thanks." She gingerly touched her chin. Blood dripped from a cut a good two inches long. Orrin must be wearing a ring of some kind.

"You're welcome, little girl."

Obviously he'd missed the sarcasm in her voice. Thunder rumbled across the night again. Every nerve ending seemed to respond to the call of the storm. Power tingled through her body, a wildness that burned at her fingertips, aching for release.

She clenched her hands, and watched the stain that was Orrin. Again the air stirred. This time she didn't move, simply stood watching and waiting. His evil rolled over her, a black wave of darkness that made her shudder in revulsion. His steps drew close.

At the last possible moment, she ducked. The wind of his punch stirred her hair. She reached up and grabbed his arm. Fire leapt from fingers, jagged pieces of lightning that raced up his arm and across his body.

She could see him, she realized. See the sudden flash of terror in his eyes.

He screamed. His arm was wrenched from her grip, and his body was flung across the room. The lightning died, and weakness washed through her. Her legs collapsed from beneath her, and suddenly, she was kneeling on cold concrete, gasping for breath, her whole body trembling with exhaustion. Whatever the power was, it had limitations—physical limitations. The force was a hell of a lot stronger than she ever could be.

Orrin hit the concrete with a splat that shuddered through the foundations. He groaned for several minutes, the smell of burned flesh heavy in the air.

She took a deep, shuddering breath and pushed upright. Now was the time to run for the stairs, to try to escape. She staggered forward. Orrin rose. For a moment, he simply stood and watched her. His arm hung by his side, blackened and withered looking. His eyes were dark, glazed, and certainly no longer human. The vampire half of his soul had risen fully to the surface.

There would be no mercy for her now. Nothing but death, long and lingering, if she didn't get the hell out of here.

The darkness cloaked him once more, and with a primeval scream of fury, he ran at her. She'd never make the stairs. As the realization hit, she swung away, running for the back door. Energy still tingled at her fingertips, a muted echo of the force she'd unleashed on Orrin. Perhaps it would be enough to shatter the top lock and open the door. She had to get help. She couldn't survive Orrin without it.

She leapt for the door, slapped a palm high up, fingers barely brushing the lock despite her leap. Fire danced across the bolt. There was a brief retort, like gunfire, and then the bolt was ash falling across her face.

Orrin closed in. She didn't have time to get the door open. She leaped and hit the ground, thrust an arm against the wall to steady herself, and then ran. Away from Orrin. Away from the door.

He gave chase. His steps echoed in her ears, drawing closer with every beat of her heart. Fear surged, as did the fire. It pulsated through her body, burned at her fingertips. But to use it, she'd have to stop. Have to let him get close enough to touch her. And that could be fatal.

She neared the stairs again. Thought briefly about climbing them. But he'd catch her at the door, and there was no room to fight on the landing itself. Nor could she afford to block the entrance, just in case Stephan or the others came to the rescue.

She ran past the steps, headed once again for the far side of the room. The thump of Orrin's footsteps drew closer, until it was almost all she could hear.

Wind stirred, a cyclonic force reaching out to grab her. She ducked to the right, felt his fingers tear down her arm, and headed back across the room, knowing she had little time left.

He caught her hair and wrenched her backward. She yelped and fought for balance, but he was far too strong and threw her backwards. She hit the floor with another yelp, and then he was on her, his weight crushing her chest and stomach, his fingers around her neck, squeezing hard.

Desperation burned. Her arms were pinned by his knees. She couldn't move. Struggled to breathe. Light danced before her eyes, star-bright light that wavered in and out of focus.

She *had* to free her arms. The fire that burned through her soul was her only chance to live. She began to struggle, bucking her body, trying to shift his bulk enough to free her arm. One would do. One would kill.

He laughed. The sound crawled across her skin, leaving behind the stain of his evil.

"Fight, my pretty. Fight, while I watch you die."

She tried to reply but couldn't. Her breath was little more than short, sharp gasps. The dancing lights were getting brighter, and the darkness of unconsciousness threatened. She didn't have much time left.

The door at the top of the stairs opened. Footsteps whispered across the silence. Two sets—two men.

"Sam?"

Gabriel's voice. Etched with pain, but strong. Relief swam through her. At least he would live.

"Sam, are you here?"

Of course she was here. Couldn't he see her? Couldn't he see Orrin? See that the fucker had her close to death?

She blinked. No, he couldn't. Orrin was cloaked in darkness. Perhaps she was too.

She struggled harder, bucking her body, trying to dislodge the giant's weight or loosen his fingers. Orrin made no noise, and no acknowledgment of the two men on the landing. Either the blood lust had made him oblivious to his surroundings, or he just didn't care.

"Sam, I can't see you, but I know you're here somewhere. Where's Orrin?"

Right here, she tried to scream, but it came out little more than a weak gasp. Her lungs burned with the need for air. His fingers were digging deeper and deeper into her flesh. He'd soon crush her larynx. Then he'd drain her, while her goddamn partner stood by and saw nothing but darkness.

The blue-white beam of a laser fire bit through the night, striking the concrete very close to them. Orrin jerked in surprise. She bucked and managed to get one arm free from the weight of his knee.

Overhead, thunder rumbled. Lightening flashed, not only across the night, but right through her soul. Fire scorched through every nerve ending, aching for release.

Another laser beam bit through the darkness, close enough to touch. Orrin swore under his breath. Just for an instant, his fingers relaxed. She sucked in a great gulp of air.

"Gabriel, here," she screamed, then slapped her hand against Orrin's thigh.

Power surged, a lightning flash that poured from her fingers to him. He jerked, mouth open in shock, as electric fingers of light swam across his body.

The storm-held power wrenched his weight from her, shattering his cover of darkness as it flung him across the room.

The laser light flashed again. Two beams, a deeper blue this time. Orrin landed near the base of the stairs, a gaping black hole where his face had once been.

He was dead. Thank the Gods, he was dead.

Relief stirred, but she didn't. It was all she could do just to gulp in great gasps of air. Her throat burned, as if his fingers were still around it, digging deep. But she'd survived. With the power of the storm, and a little help from Gabriel, she'd done the impossible.

Survived Orrin.

Footsteps drew close. Gabriel appeared, his movements stiff and slow, like those an old man. His face was white, etched with pain. His hair was matted, black with sweat, and stiff with blood.

He knelt beside her, and then he reached out to touch her bruised cheek. "I've seen you look healthier."

"And here I was thinking you'd never looked better." Her voice came out little more than a harsh whisper. It didn't matter. She knew he'd understand her, even if no words came out.

He raised an eyebrow in surprise. "Oh yeah?"

"Yeah," she said. "You're alive."

A smile twitched his lips. "How did you find me?"

"With those psychic abilities I don't have."

His smile grew. With one finger, he gently traced the line of her cheek to her chin, his touch like fire against her skin. Awareness surged between them, and just for a moment, she saw the desire in his eyes. The longing. Then his gaze hardened, and the warmth disappeared, right along with his touch.

Anger fired through her. She was sick of playing these games, sick of being shoved into a shoebox and being told to stay. Sick of his words and actions saying one thing, yet his *reactions* saying another. He didn't want her as a partner, and, truth be told, probably wouldn't have her as anything else.

Let him win the war, if that's what he really wanted.

It was time she started taking control of her life. Part of that start was not only finding her past, but creating a future as well. If Gabriel wanted no part of that future, then fine. It was time she accepted the fact and just moved on.

"Stephan's calling an ambulance for us both," he said, voice all cool efficiency. "And organizing a cleanup team."

"Rose?" Her voice was still scratchy, but it was filled with barely controlled annoyance.

"Dead. Stephan shot her."

"Good." She rolled sideways and carefully climbed to her feet. The effort left her head swimming, and for several seconds, she rested her hands on her knees and gasped for breath.

"What the hell are you doing?"

He reached out, perhaps to steady her, perhaps to stop her. She jerked away from his touch and saw the flicker of surprise on his face. "I've told you before, I don't like hospitals. I'm going home." Or, at least, to the motel she'd booked into for the night.

He frowned. "You should get checked out first. Besides, what have you got to go home to?"

Nothing—the same as ever. And that was just something else she'd have to change. Placing her trust, and her need for friendship, in the hands her partners had been nothing short of stupidity. And in the end, it had only led to grief. All her life she'd been longing for friends, for family. Maybe she couldn't do anything about the second desire, but she could certainly get off her ass and do something about the first. Life was there to be explored—and it was about time she started doing just that.

It was a pity she hadn't realized that before Jack had come along to wreck her life. Though in many ways, he had perhaps saved her. She was no longer content to drift. She wanted, needed, something more out of life. "What does it matter to you what I have and haven't got to go home to?"

His gaze briefly searched hers, and then he shrugged and said, "It's your life."

"That it is," she muttered, and turned away.

She could feel his gaze on her back, curious, and, perhaps, a little angry.

"Sam," he called softly after a few seconds.

She hesitated, and half turned around. "What?"

"Thanks."

In the hazel depths of his eyes, she saw the warmth, the longing, he would never admit and never unleash. In many ways, Gabriel Stern was just as imprisoned by his memories of the past as she was by her lack of them.

And there was nothing she could do or say to free him. The choice was his, and it had been made long ago.

"Forget about it," she said, and walked away.

Printed in the United States
46306LVS00002B/409-429

9 781893 896499